DAUGHTER OF THE DRAGON

To Mary M.,

Thanks for not killing me after reading the epilogue of Highland Wolf

And all the hard work you put into making my books extra special

(Yes, I can hear you screaming from here).

Highland Wolf

Daughter of the Dragon

Shadow Wolf

A Touch of Magic

Heart of the Wolf

THE BLACKSTONE MOUNTAIN SERIES

The Blackstone Dragon Heir

The Blackstone Bad Dragon

The Blackstone Bear

The Blackstone Wolf

The Blackstone Lion

The Blackstone She-Wolf

The Blackstone She-Bear

The Blackstone She-Dragon

DAUGHTER OF THE DRAGON

TRUE MATES GENERATIONS BOOK 6

ALICIA MONTGOMERY

CHAPTER ONE

Desiree Desmond Creed, Deedee to her friends, placed her hands on her hips. *I never thought I'd be in a mess like this, but here I am.*

And how did she end up here? Well, as it did with most stories, this one started with a boy.

Er, man, really.

But she had known Cross Alexander Jonasson since they were children. Indeed, their mothers were best friends, and they were born months apart. They grew up together. Playmates. Neighbors. Best friends, along with his sister, Astrid. Heck, they even experienced their first shift into their Lycan forms the same summer.

And when she was of that age when girls started to notice boys, she noticed *Cross.*

How handsome he was.

How tall he was—which was rare especially after her unfortunate six-inch growth spurt at fourteen.

And how nice he was to her. He knew everything about her, and she knew everything about him.

At least, she thought she did.

So, after years of unrequited pining, she had hoped to make it ... well, requited.

But as it turned out, it wasn't.

In a fit of passion—or perhaps, the thought of the end of the world coming—she confessed her feelings to him. Which turned out to be unequivocally *un*requited.

"I'm sorry, Dee. I love you, but only as a friend."

And so, with her heart trampled, she did the only logical thing: run away halfway across the world.

Which is how she ended up lost in the desert, somewhere in between the border of Afghanistan and Pakistan, in the midst of an impending sandstorm.

Her inner she-wolf huffed. Nope, it definitely did not like sand. It had taken great exception to being stuck out in the desert for nearly six months. Her wolf hated the dry, hot weather, instead, it longed for fertile brown earth and lush greenery.

Her inner animal didn't understand anything about its human counterpart. Didn't know what it was like to rise up in a field dominated by men. It didn't care that Deedee was a highly sought-after archeologist. And most of all, it didn't comprehend why one male could cause her so much distress that when the offer came to lead her own team on a year-long dig across the Middle East, West and South Asia, she grabbed the chance if only to put some distance between herself and the man who broke her heart.

However, she had to admit Cross wasn't the reason she ended up in this *exact* predicament. No, that honor went to Charles Hanford—Dr. Charles Hanford, PhD—professor emeritus from Cambridge University and all-around creep.

White-haired, distinguished, and a superstar in the archeology world, one would have thought a man with two doctorates would have better things to do than chasing after a woman half his age. Before he retired, she'd met Dr. Hanford at several industry conferences. Female colleagues had warned her about him—Handsy Hanford, he'd been nicknamed.

She thought it couldn't be true. But a year ago, during the second night of the European Archeological Institute's yearly conference in Rome, Dr. Hanford had cornered her during the after party at one of the suites, trying to get her alone. When she feigned jet lag and said she wanted to go to bed, he had insisted on walking her back to her room. And when he tried to get, well, *handsy*, she could barely control her inner she-wolf from coming out and ripping him to ribbons. She somehow managed to break free of his grasp and close the door behind her, locking the deadbolt just in time.

That was the last she'd seen of him. Or so she thought. When the dean of the archeology department of New York University—where she'd worked as a professor and been given the generous grant to study the migration patterns on the people of Mesopotamia—came to visit, he brought an "old friend" along—Dr. Charles Hanford, PhD.

Her she-wolf growled. It hated Dr. Hanford as much as it hated the desert. Hated the offending, cloying cologne he wore, the way he licked his lips, and how his eyes never went above Deedee's chin. And of course, it hated that he had dared touch Deedee without invitation. Her inner animal was a protective thing, after all.

Sometimes when she couldn't sleep at night, she'd take a walk outside their camp in an attempt to tire herself out.

Tonight, after everyone had retired, Deedee found herself tossing and turning, and it was nearly midnight when she decided to get dressed and go for a late stroll.

However, she'd only walked for about ten minutes when she heard that voice that made her cringe.

"Deedee?" came Hanford's voice. "Where are you?"

Son of a seabiscuit! She had been pretty sure no one saw her leave the camp. Picking up her steps, she marched ahead into the desert, guided only by moonlight, not caring where she was heading.

All of a sudden, her inner wolf alerted her to danger. The hairs on the back of her neck stood on end, and even in the darkness of night she could see it up ahead—a sandstorm, swirling around like a living wall.

"Deedee! Oh, Deedee. I thought that was you I saw walking out of the camp."

Fudge nuggets, the man was persistent. But seeing as she had a choice of facing the sandstorm or Hanford, she decided he was the lesser evil.

"Dr. Hanford." She spun around. "What are you doing out here so late?"

With her enhanced vision, she could see the look of glee on his face. "Deedee. There you are."

Oh, how she hated the sound of her nickname on his lips. Despite the many times she'd subtly insisted he call her Professor Creed, he ignored her.

"Yes, here I am."

His tongue darted out, and as usual, his eyes went straight to her generous bustline. Her immediate instinct was to cover them with her arms, but she wouldn't give him the satisfaction. Unfortunately, along with her growth spurt came a growth of another kind, and needless to say, the cruel nickname of "Double Dees" followed her all throughout middle school.

Hanford took two long strides to come up to her until they were nearly nose to nose. "Deedee, my dear, I wanted to have a word with you. Seeing as you were up and about I thought I'd take this opportunity to speak with you in private."

"It's rather late, couldn't it wait until morning?"

He shook his head.

"Is it about my research?" she feigned. "Dean Thayers has all my notes if you'd like—"

"No, no, my dear." Ugh, his breath still smelled like the baked beans they had for dinner. "It's about ... Madrid."

"Oh?" Her heartbeat quickened, and her wolf was chomping at the bit at the reminder of that night. She reined it in, since despite her personal feelings on the matter, there was just so much to lose. Her job, her grant, her standing in the archeological community. After all, who would everyone believe—a distinguished professor with decades of experience, or a nobody and a woman to boot. It just wasn't worth it. Besides, she didn't report him or say anything to anyone, so hopefully, he wasn't going to press his luck. "What about Madrid?"

Something in his expression changed, and his mouth drew up into a grin. "I'm guessing you must have been *really* tired that night." His fingers traced up her arm. "But maybe you're not too tired tonight."

She really was tired. Tired of his stares, and innuendos, and of *him*. Maybe she'd let her she-wolf out tonight. "Yes, I was. And it's been a long day." She wrapped her hand around his wrist and pulled it away. "So, Dr. Hanford, I'd really appreciate it if you would leave me so I can unwind."

There was a brief moment of shock on his face, but it was quickly replaced by a smile. "Unwind? Why didn't you say so? We can *unwind* together."

Pure shock made her freeze as his arms came around her, pulling her body against his. "Oh, Deedee, you don't know how long I've been waiting for this," he breathed against her mouth.

Before he could mash his lips to hers, she turned away, his slimy lips and tongue landing on her cheek. "Dr. Hanford! No!" Her she-wolf growled, fangs bared, but she kept a tight rein on it. Pushing him away with all her might, she sent him to the ground. However, the force made her stagger back. Her heel tripped over something on the ground, and she found herself landing on her back.

"Deedee," Hanford sneered. "No one says no to me. Not if they still want a career in the academe."

He leapt on top of her, his arm raised. In a split second, she saw something large in his hand—a rock maybe—and then pain shot through her head.

There was a loud sound in her ear—like howling, but with the pain rocketing in her brain, she wasn't sure if that was real or not.

She looked up and saw a faint, winged shadow in the distance, up in the sky.

Was that—?

A shadow blocked her vision. It was Hanford leaning over her, a manic grin on his face. "See what happens when sluts like you say no to me?"

He must have hit her hard, because she could still feel the

wound on her head bleeding. Though her Lycan healing abilities helped her recover quicker than humans, it wasn't lightning fast. And while she didn't feel like passing out, those beans she had for dinner were threatening to make a second appearance. With a deep breath, she attempted to get to her feet.

Two hands pushed her down. "How are you still moving?" Hanford's legs locked around her knees, his body pinning her under the soft sand. "Let's see you say no now."

She struggled against him, and the second blow to the side of her head came much faster this time, and another round of pain made her vision spin and stomach violently churn.

"You—what the hell?"

It was hard to keep her eyes open, but maybe that was a good thing. Wind whipped around them, a cloud of sand swirled around.

"Where did this ...? Who the hell are you—ow!"

She saw his body lifting away from her and heard the roar of the sandstorm as it engulfed her. But somehow, she felt her body lift off the ground. A pair of arms were under her knees and back, and her legs flailed. Fatigue and the pain from injury pressed down on her like a heavy rock, and she allowed the darkness she'd been fighting to claim her.

CHAPTER TWO

THE HUMUNGOUS BEAST'S WINGS SPREAD WIDE AS IT flew, shadowing most of the city below. Such a sight would have brought fear into the hearts of anyone, but in Zhobghadi, The Great One's form overhead brought comfort to its citizens, knowing their guardian was watching over them.

The long, spiked head stretched and opened its great maw to let out a deafening roar. Leathery wings snapped in the wind as it swooped low, turning gracefully before heading back in the direction of the capital city, toward the largest structure in the entire country—a massive palace made of dark brown brick and decorated with gold. Near the topmost tower was a colossal balcony, big enough for the great beast to land on. However, it was not scaly, talon-tipped feet the size of elephants that landed on the tile, but completely human ones.

"How was your flight, Your Highness?"

Prince Karim Idris Salamuddin took the offered robe and wrapped it around his naked, heated body. "Tiring," he grunted, then shook his head. *A prince of Zhobghadi would never say that.* He could almost hear his father's voice chastising him. A prince should always act confident, commanding, and never show any sign of weakness.

However, he was talking to Arvin, his older cousin and most trusted Vizier, and possibly the closest thing he had to a friend growing up, so perhaps some informality between them was permitted.

"I don't know how your father did it, at seventy-five years of age." Arvin shook his head. "He was doing it up until—"

When his cousin stopped, Karim continued. "Until last year." Before his untimely death. "I don't know either, but you know the old man was stubborn as a camel."

It is important work, his father had said. *It is my duty as their king and the bearer of The Great One to reassure them that our enemies will never defeat or capture us.*

It had been a millennium since any threat had come close to taking over Zhobghadi. Still, tradition was tradition. Since the first time the sandstorms came, every year the king calls upon the beast residing in his body to protect the city, flying overhead from midnight until dawn to scout for enemies. It was the will of the gods, of course. For they were the ones that sent the *Easifat*—the sandstorms—to form a magical protection over the city as well as blessing the royal family line with The Great One.

Karim guffawed. Blessed. *Right.*

Of course, no enemies had ever come back since that first time, a thousand years ago. And as civilizations rose and fell, no other nation enslaved Zhobghadi, so perhaps it was only right to keep up tradition as thanks to the gods.

But it was a bloody exhausting tradition. And today was

only the first day of many. How he wished he was back in Scotland with his friend. Duncan MacDougal had welcomed him, despite the unexpected visit and his own troubles. Karim had to chuckle to himself thinking of Julianna Anderson and what a merry chase she'd be leading his erstwhile playboy friend. He wished them both well, as he had a feeling that Julianna was definitely Duncan's match.

"You did well," Arvin noted as he gestured for them to head inside. They passed through the large, arched doorway leading into the living area of Karim's suite of rooms. "Your father would be proud."

Karim snorted as he walked over to the side table and poured himself a glass of water from a brass pitcher. "I'm sure he would have some criticisms. Perhaps my flight path was not efficient. Or I hadn't changed fast enough. Or I took too long." He took a long swig of the cool liquid. Of course, no one was harder on Karim than himself, even though it had been less than a year since his beast was unlocked and he assumed The Great One's full form. Despite the fact that he had shared his body with an animal his entire life, the transformation could only be completed once the previous bearer passed away. It was an unwieldy body, and he sometimes still struggled to control it.

"And is that why you haven't taken the throne? Because you think he would have criticisms?"

The glass was still on his lips, but he stopped swallowing and slowly put the glass down. "Only you would say such things to me."

Arvin grinned at him. "Of course. I've known you since you were in diapers." He crossed his arms over his chest and narrowed his dark eyes on Karim. "Well? You didn't answer my question."

"It's complicated."

"It's not." He gestured toward the door. "The throne lies empty, and you are the crown prince. Therefore, it's only logical that you take your rightful place as king. It's not right, during this holiest time of the year that you are the bearer of The Great One and—"

As if on cue, the beast—The Great One, as the people of Zhobghadi called it—roared inside him. Heat burned under his skin, and he knew his own eyes were glowing silver, the same color as his beast's scales.

"And I can do my duties during the Easifat without being king. There's no need for me to wear the crown."

"There is every need." Arvin stepped back. "But it's not my business. I am only one of your subjects, after all."

Karim threaded his fingers through his hair. "You know you are more than that. Otherwise, neither Father or I would not have appointed you to your position." As Vizier, Arvin ran the day-to-day operations in the palace, similar to a Chief of Staff. When the old Vizier had retired ten years ago, it was Karim who suggested Arvin for the position, and King Nassir had agreed. His cousin had been Vizier ever since.

"And I'm grateful for the honor." Arvin nodded his head in a small bow. "You only have a few hours to sleep before your first meeting."

"I'll be fine. An hour's all I need." Indeed, that was one of the perks of sharing his body with the creature. Even in human form, he could draw strength and stamina from the beast if needed, and he could recover from fatigue and injury quicker than any ordinary human. "But I am eager to clean up."

"How about some food? I can have Ramin bring you something."

"I'll be fine. But ..." he glanced around, "where is the boy, anyway?"

"He's hardly a boy at seventeen years old," Arvin said. "Hmm ... he's usually around here, waiting for you. I've never seen a more loyal valet. But I suppose you inspire that in him. He idolizes you."

Karim let out a grunt. "I should have never let my father convince me to take him on."

"And what would you have done?" Arvin asked. "Toss him out on the street?"

"Ramin is a ward of the royal family," Karim pointed out. "He could have done anything with his life once he finished his schooling here, like studied abroad, or opened a business."

"Yet he chose to stay and shadow you as your valet. You know he's only waiting until he's old enough to join the military. When he's not serving you, he spends his time training and building his body. He's nearly as large as you at that age. You know he's going to apply to be part of The *Almoravid*," Arvin said, mentioning the elite guard who protected the royal family of Zhobghadi.

"It is not a glamorous life."

"Would you blame him though?" Arvin asked. "He only wants to repay you. You saved him from—"

"Bah." Karim waved his hand in a dismissive manner. "I'm tired. I'm sure the boy will turn up when I awaken." He didn't bother to say goodbye to Arvin but marched into his rooms without a backward glance. It was his privilege, after all, as crown prince.

Heading straight to the opulent bath area, he decided against a long soak in the huge tub and opted for a quick shower instead. After finishing his business, he leaned against the marble and gold sink, looking up at his reflection in the mirror. Weary cerulean blue eyes looked back at him. Eyes that he got from his mother.

Not liking where his thoughts were going, he turned away and headed back to his bedroom. It was dark, and a shadow fell over the enormous bed. Numerous soft pillows formed lumps under the silk sheets, but the bed was big enough that he found an empty spot where he was able to lay down and stretch out. In seconds, his eyes shut, and he fell into a dreamless sleep.

But it wasn't dreamless. No, he definitely did dream. And what a delicious dream it was—that of curling up against a soft, warm body. Of the scent of something sweet, like the rich desserts he loved as a child, but with a touch of burned sugar. And plush flesh pressed up against his hardening cock. It had been too long since he'd had a woman, which was probably why the dream was so vivid.

His dream woman turned, sighing softly. Again, it seemed so real that he could feel the warmth of her breath. Wanting more, he moved his head a fraction of an inch forward, until his lips met velvety ones.

A spark of electricity nearly made him pull back, but The Great One awoke in him.

More. Mine. Ours.

The voice was alien in his head, but at the same time, *not*. He'd had the creature—a dragon, his mother had called it—

inside him since he could remember, but he'd never heard it speak.

Claim.

Strange, but that's when he realized it wasn't a dream.

Still, he could not stop himself. He was like a man dying of thirst in the desert who found an oasis. He kissed—no, devoured—those lips like they were his salvation. And they responded back in kind. Or their owner did. Feminine hands crept up his bare chest, fingers gripped his shoulders as his tongue snaked out and parted her lips to taste more of her sweetness.

A few women had snuck into his bed before, and usually, he threw out anyone uninvited. But he just couldn't bring himself to stop. Moving his body over hers, he pinned her to the mattress. She didn't protest his weight; in fact, she moaned into his mouth and spread her legs to accommodate him. There was only fabric between them, which was probably her clothes as he was naked. His cock strained against her, and she gasped.

"What—I—no!"

He blinked, the words making him freeze. Limbs disentangled from him, and he saw a figure quickly crawl away to the edge of the bed, just as he surged off the mattress and slammed his palm on the light switch.

"Who the heck are you?" she shouted in English.

Karim didn't know if he was going to laugh or shout. "Who am *I*? I should be asking you that, seeing as you are in my bed."

"Your ... bed?"

With the room filled with light, he was finally able to see the dream—or rather, *not*-dream woman. Light brown hair tumbled down her shoulders like ribbons of rich toffee. Tanned skin that he knew was soft to the touch. Pouty pink lips that were still swollen from his kisses. But what made him momentarily forget who he was were those eyes—a green so light they were almost yellow.

"Yes, *my* bed." He managed to scrounge up every bit of authority he could muster. "Who are you? And what are you doing here?"

"I'm—" Her mouth opened wide. Even under her tan he could see her flush, and those pale eyes turned away from him. "Um, would you mind putting on some ... pants or something?"

He glanced down, only realizing that he was naked as the day he was born, not to mention, his erection was practically jutting out like the tower of Babel. Quickly, he grabbed the first thing he could—a pillow—and planted it over his hips. "Now, tell me who you are, and how you came here."

"I ..." She shook her head. "I'm Professor Desiree Desmond Creed, from New York University."

An American?

"My archeological team and I were on a site just forty miles outside the Pakistan border. I was going for a walk and then ..." A gasp escaped her mouth, and she ran her fingers through her hair. After checking her fingers, she let out a sigh of relief. "I was hit in the head by ... I mean, I was injured and then the sandstorm came before I passed out."

Injured? The Great One roared in displeasure.

Opening his mouth, he took a deep breath. When he focused his sense of smell and taste and ignored her delicious sweet scent, he realized that it was there, tinging the air. The scent of dried blood. *Someone had hurt her!* He wasn't sure if the growl that was rattling in his chest was from The Great One or *him*.

"Then I woke up ... here?" She glanced around. "Where am I again?"

"You're in Zhobghadi," he said.

"Zhobghadi?" She cocked her head at him. "But how?"

"You don't remember how you got here?"

"No ... I mean." Her eyes shut tight. "Maybe ... I felt like I was being carried. And there was a long corridor, and I thought I saw something silver on the walls shaped like a ... snake?"

He knew exactly what she was describing. And the one person who could possibly have brought her into his room. "Wait here."

"Wait? What do you mean—"

Turning on his heel, he didn't wait for her to finish as he strode out of his bedroom and crossed the living area to the main door. Yanking it open, he barked to the member of The Almoravid standing guard, "Find me the boy, and bring him inside."

The guard saluted him with a fist over his heart, then bowed as he ran down the hallway. It didn't take him long to come back, pulling along another figure, and pushed him inside the living room before closing the door with a loud thud.

The boy—almost a man, Karim reminded himself—looked up at him, his midnight eyes growing wide. He didn't need to ask. The look of guilt was plastered all over the young man's face.

"What have you done?"

Ramin's Adam's apple bobbed up and down his neck. "Highness. I had no choice."

"No choice?" Karim thundered. "You brought a woman—an outsider—into the city during our most sacred time and snuck her into the palace using the *azdaha* passage?" The tunnel that ran under the palace and led out to the city walls was a secret that only the royal family knew about. The woman had accurately described the long mural that stretched along its walls—the first Great One, with its long silvery body—which clued him in on who could have brought her in. "I told you about that passage in confidence!"

"And I have not told anyone," he protested. "I thought she was unconscious the entire time, Your Highness."

"And you brought her here? Why?"

Ramin's youthful face had turned dark, and the shadows he thought were banished from his eyes had returned. "She was in danger. I had to help her."

"In danger?"

"She was being attacked. I pulled the man off her, and I took her far away. He ... he would have dishonored her the way my mother was ... was... almost ...."

Fury rushed through his veins like the fire and flames The Great One spewed. Memories rushed back from nearly a decade ago. When he had been sneaking out of the palace and a blood-curdling scream had brought him to a house down in one of the poorer neighborhoods of the city. *That man*—Ramin's great-uncle—had beaten the boy's newly-widowed mother to death for refusing his advances. And Ramin had witnessed it all and would have been his great-uncle's next victim had Karim not intervened and had the man arrested and sent to prison.

And someone had tried to do it to that woman. No wonder the boy went crazy, the memories probably triggering him. By the fires of Gibil, he didn't even know her, yet he wanted to burn the world to ashes for what she had nearly suffered. And find the man who hurt her and let The Great One devour him.

"She needed help. Protection." Ramin gulped and lowered his gaze. "Highness."

"And so, you brought her here."

"You will protect her. The Great One protects all." Ramin dropped to his knees. "Forgive me, Your Highness."

Karim let out a string of curses under his breath. Arvin had been right—Ramin idolized him, for getting justice for his mother's death, for taking him in as his ward and providing for him. And now, he thought Karim could save everyone, too. He wanted to laugh. He was a prince yes, and the bearer of The Great One, but in truth, Karim knew, he was no noble protector. He was just another man.

But what to do now?

"How did you find her anyway? She said she was right outside our borders."

"I was out, Highness."

"Out?" Karim roared. "You know you are supposed to stay in the city just before the Easifat! What if the sandstorms arrived and you were locked outside?"

"I made it just in time. I saw you flying overhead and knew I had some time." Ramin looked up at him to meet his gaze. "Besides, the Almoravid patrol the borders during the Easifat."

"They are trained to do so and carry the necessary equipment to ensure they can navigate safely. You are not one of them." His teeth were gnashing together so hard, he thought he would grind them to the gum. "And you have not gone through the blooding ceremony," he said, referring to the ritual that all of the Almoravid endured to ensure they could effectively serve the royal family. "You could have been hurt."

"I took every precaution, Highness." He slipped something out of his pocket—sand goggles that were specially made for sandstorms, as well as a face mask to cover the nose and mouth. "The goggles allowed me to make my way back, and I put the mask on her to protect her lungs while I carried her back."

"How did you even—Never mind." Ramin was smart and resourceful, so he wasn't surprised he had gotten his hands on the special gear. And he had also saved that woman's life. The woman who was still in his bed, looking vulnerable, and at the same time, so alluring. Mentally, he shook his head. That was not the point. "Outsiders are forbidden in Zhobghadi during this time."

Ramin didn't say anything, but merely prostrated himself. "Forgive me, Highness. Don't send me to the dungeon, please."

Karim sighed. "Get up. Come, you have put us into this situation, and you will help me fix it."

CHAPTER THREE

Hanford on top of her. The blow to her head. Passing out. The sandstorm. Being lifted up. Her head knocking around and opening her eyes. There was no more sandstorm around her, but rather, she was inside. It was dark and humid, and the only light she could see were silver scales on the wall, shaped like a long, gigantic snake.

Deedee massaged the small knot on the side of her head. It wasn't bleeding and should be fully healed in an hour, so there was no need to try and soothe it, but it was like doing so would help her remember how she got here in the first place. Everything after she passed out was blurry, but bits and pieces of it was coming back. Someone had carried her here and put her into bed.

His bed.

That tall, hulking man with dark hair and those bright blue eyes.

A strange but vibrant chord struck into her as she thought of him. And the way his thick beard tickled her skin. And the way his mouth moved over hers, and his body.

"Ugh." She groaned and buried her face in the pillow. *Now, I really thought I'd never be in a mess like* this. Actually, in this case, *mess* was a complete understatement. Somehow, between passing out and waking up, she had been transported to another country.

Zhobghadi ... Zhobghadi ... Zhobghadi ... Why did that sound so familiar?

She scratched at the back of her head. That first injury now healed enough so it didn't bleed, but it did itch like a *motherlover*. Then she remembered her research.

Zhobghadi was a small, independent kingdom between the border of Afghanistan and Pakistan. She had wanted permission to dig in its northwest territory, but she didn't even know where to ask. Indeed, the notoriously xenophobic country had no embassy, no website, no presence abroad except for trade offices that dealt with their number one product—a pure silver metal that was used in 90 percent of the world's manufacturing industry, making them an extremely wealthy little city-state. When she tried to call those offices, they told her that it was impossible to get a visa or permission to enter their borders, especially when their king had recently died, and the entire country was in mourning. It was obvious she wasn't going to get anywhere, so she dropped it.

But how did she get here, and in the bed of—

A delicious shiver ran through her, and her cheeks felt like they were on fire. That man. Oh. Did she really ... did they ... Her nipples tightened at the memory of his mouth and his body on top of hers. And his splendid, naked body— all tanned taut skin over rippling muscles, broad chest, narrow waist and down his—

The door flew open again, and Deedee knew it was him coming back. Her wolf did too, and it let out a needy whine.

Not knowing what to do, she scrambled to her feet. *Oh dear.* She shook her head at her disheveled appearance. Though it was futile, her hands automatically smoothed down the wrinkled linen of her blouse. When she looked up, her gaze crashed with blue eyes the color of the sky. Dust seemed to swirl in her mouth, and her mind lost all thought. It was only now she realized how handsome he was, even with that great big scowl on his face.

"It seems I have solved the mystery of how you got here." His hot, smoky accent made her knees weak, and she had to lock them to keep from melting into a puddle on the ground. "My ward said he found you in the desert."

When he pulled someone from behind him, she realized they were not alone. Though he was taller and larger than her, his boyish face gave away his age—he couldn't have been more than sixteen or seventeen. He looked at her curiously, though he didn't say a word or move a muscle.

"Ramin carried you here, to save you, he said. And brought you to my room without my knowledge. He said you were attacked." His voice sounded tight for a moment, and she thought she saw his eyes flicker to a dark silver color."By a man who tried—"

"Thank you, Ramin." She gave the teen a weak smile. "I would have been lost under the sands without you." Stepping forward, she offered her hand. When he didn't do or say anything, she dropped it. "Do you speak English?"

"He understands some," hot scowling man said. "But does not know enough to speak it." He added something in a strange language that made the teen blush.

"Um, so, well, thank you so much for allowing me to stay. I mean, you didn't know ... but ... I really should be going now. My team will be looking for me. Perhaps you have a cellphone or computer I can borrow so I can send them a message?"

"No."

What kind of place was this? Maybe he was exaggerating, but then again, she had to remember not every place on earth had cell service or technology like they had in New York. "Oh. Maybe you can help me find some transport so I can get back to my team or to the nearest embassy? I'm happy to pay for—"

"No." His voice was rougher now.

"Excuse me?" She straightened to full height, which was nearly six feet if she stretched her chin up, but that was unlikely to intimidate him, because he still had a good eight or so inches over her.

"You are not understanding me," he began. "There is no leaving or entering Zhobghadi during this time."

"No leaving—surely you're joking."

He didn't look like he was joking. "The Easifat—those sandstorms you encountered—make it impossible to leave the country at this time. You could get lost or buried under the sand."

"In that case, I can send a message to someone. My team or my university."

"The storms have also scrambled all communication services at this time."

"What?" She took a step forward. "How can that be? There must be some way to—" When she tried to sidestep him, he simply blocked her way. "Sir, please get out of my way. I'm going to go out and find a—"

"You are not leaving."

She craned her neck back. "Excuse me?" The expression on his face was deadly serious. "You can't stop me from leaving your room!"

"I can, and I must," he said. "For it is forbidden for foreigners to be in Zhobghadi during our most sacred festival."

"Forbidden?" she echoed.

"Yes. It is the way of our people, the law of the gods for a millennium."

"I don't follow your gods, and I'm an American!" she shouted. "Let me out of here! You can't keep me locked up against my will." If he tried anything, she could shift into her wolf form. Technically, Lycans were not allowed to shift in front of humans. The moment their wolves manifested during puberty, they were taught to control it and only let it out if it was an emergency. Well, being kidnapped and held in a foreign land sounded like an emergency.

"If you are found, the punishment is death."

"Of all the—" These people were barbaric! "My embassy won't let you get away with executing an American citizen!"

"I wasn't talking about you."

It took a second, but his meaning dawned on her. She looked at Ramin, who had been staring at her wide-eyed the entire time. "You wouldn't."

"It's not for me to decide but the courts." He folded his massive arms over his chest. "Zhobghadi is a small place. When you are found wandering the streets, eventually they will trace your presence back to Ramin. Even if they didn't, someone will have to pay, most likely the guards on patrol at the border."

A sick feeling curdled in her stomach, and defeat made her sit back down on the bed. "You can't possibly keep me here forever. My team, my work ... my family will be looking for me."

"I'm not keeping you here against your will forever," he said. "Just until the Easifat has passed. Then I will arrange for you to go back to wherever you want."

"And how long will that be?"

"About a week. Ten days at the most."

"A week?" She shot to her feet. "I'm supposed to stay here for a week, and not contact anyone?" Oh God, if her father realized she was missing, he'd send an army to find her. Heck, he'd probably scour the desert himself. He was, after all, the world's only dragon shifter.

"I'm afraid that is your only choice." His tone sounded almost sorry.

"But what am I supposed to do around here? And where am I going to stay?" She would have to hide out for a week somewhere in this country. Where no one would be able to find her.

"You will stay here, of course."

"Here? In your house?"

"In my room."

The way he said that last sentence made something in her flare. "That's really generous of you," she managed to croak. "But I wouldn't want to get you in trouble or bother you. I can find another safe place."

"There is no place safer—"

Yeah, right.

"—than the royal palace, in the rooms of the crown prince."

She hoped her jaw didn't drop all the way to the floor, otherwise, her grandmother would have wasted the money she spent on her only granddaughter that entire year of finishing school in Switzerland. She scrambled her brain, trying to remember how to address royalty. "Y-you're a ... Your Highness?"

"Prince Karim Idris Salamuddin," he said.

She wondered if she should curtsey or bow. But before she could do or say anything, he spoke again.

"Now, Miss Creed—"

"It's Professor Creed," she bristled.

"Professor. You will stay here until the Easifat has passed. It is too dangerous to find you alternative accommodations, and no one enters or exits here without my permission. Ramin will bring you your meals and anything else you may need."

If he didn't sound like royalty to her before, he sure did now. Arrogance dripped from his words—or rather, his commands.

He turned around and swept out of the room without so much as a word or a backward glance.

Oh fiddlesticks, what had she gotten into?

If this were a movie, then Deedee surely would have hit the fast-forward button so many times that it would have worn right off the remote control.

But sadly, her life was not a movie, despite the current

plot twist she was experiencing right now. She not only wanted to get to the end, which she hoped involved getting out of this crazy country, but also get through the boring parts.

Boring was a mild word to describe what she was feeling right now. There simply was nothing to do inside the room.

She walked around the bedroom numerous times to keep busy and ate the three meals Ramin had brought her. There were a few books lying around, but none of them were in English, so she settled on sitting on the carpet, trying to entertain herself by reciting the first chapter of the ancient Egyptian *Book of the Dead*.

She checked all the walls, corners, and nooks and crannies for any sort of communication device. Nothing. Not even a landline, so there was no chance of calling out. There were two small windows on either side of the bed, but they were the kind that didn't open, and from what she could see, it was at least a hundred stories to the bottom.

There was no other exit except the bedroom door. Apparently, Ramin had taken Prince Karim's orders quite literally, and the teen stood outside the bedroom, making sure she couldn't even open the doors without alerting him.

It felt like ages since Prince Karim left, but in reality, it had only been a day, and outside, the sky had turned dark.

Prince Karim ... she racked her brain. The name sounded familiar. He was crown prince which meant he should be the next king. Maybe she'd read his name in the papers or something. But she wasn't really into gossip about royals, and she hardly watched live TV anymore. She was probably one of the few people left who actually read the newspaper in the morning for her news.

Her hand went to her scalp, where her once-bleeding head wound was now a deep scab. Thank God for Lycan healing, but that didn't really help the itch. And her head wasn't the only thing that was itching. She stuck her nose down her blouse. There was a bathroom here, but did she dare try to take a shower?

Slapping her hands on her thighs, she got up from where she was seated on the carpeted floor. "Well, I'm not going sit around and stay stinky for the next week." Surely the prince wouldn't mind if she washed up.

She padded toward the opulent bathroom and walked straight into the glass-enclosed shower. Her linen blouse and cargo pants were filthy too and needed a wash. She stripped them off, as well as her underthings, until they were a pool at her feet and turned on the tap.

"*Oohhhh.*"

Hot water blasted from the shower, making her scalp tingle. It felt amazing. There was also shower gel and shampoo, which she helped herself to, figuring it was the least Prince Karim owed her. It smelled just like him, of course, but she didn't care. She deserved this, after all she had gone through.

She eyed the massive tub in the corner enviously. A long, hot bath would be wonderful right about now. But she didn't want to be caught luxuriating in the prince's bathtub. *They probably had severe punishments for that, too.*

As she bent down to wash her clothes under the shower, she began to wonder for the hundredth time that day if Prince Karim was telling the truth. Surely, they weren't a barbaric people? From the impression she got from him, it sounded like their society was still living in the ancient times described in her textbooks and journals.

Try as she might, and no matter how many times she thought about it or argued with herself, the fact was that he didn't have any other reason to keep her here. Surely, if she had found a stranger in her home, she would have sent him packing?

Of course, there was that kiss ...

"Ludicrous." She shut off the shower tap and began to wring the water from her clothes. He was a *prince*, for God's sake. He had women falling at his feet. They probably snuck into his bed all the time, which is why he kissed her—he thought her some royal groupie looking for a night of fun. No, that couldn't be why he wanted to keep her here. Why would he, when he could have any woman on earth?

Her inner she-wolf growled.

Huh. Strange.

Except for warning her of danger, her animal mostly kept quiet. As she had learned to control it when it had first appeared, it was mostly a silent companion all the time. It was indifferent to anyone near her, even Cross.

She huffed, thinking of Cross. If he hadn't broken her heart, she wouldn't be in this mess in the first place.

"Stop." No, she had to take personal responsibility. It wasn't Cross's fault that she was here. Nor was it his fault he didn't love her back the way she wanted him to.

And speaking of personal responsibility, she wasn't just going to wait around for a week until that arrogant prince released her.

She was an independent woman, for crying out loud.

But how to do it without getting anyone in trouble?

With a deep sigh, she pushed the shower door open and reached for the towel on the hook. It was soft, thick, and engulfed most of her body. When she took a deep breath, she realized Prince Karim must have used it before her, because she could smell that unique scent he had—like sand, masculine musk, and ... she couldn't quite describe it, but the closest thing she could think of was a bonfire. It wasn't so much a smell as it was a sensation—warmth and coziness.

"Oh dear." She realized that her clothes—her only clothes—were drip-drying in the shower, and she didn't have anything else to wear. She supposed she could sleep with just a towel around her, but this was *his* bedroom.

The thought of having that hot body next to her fried her brain cells. But surely, he wouldn't be sleeping in there with her again, right? The thought made warmth pool in her stomach. No, mustn't think of that. Since Prince Karim said she was to stay here, he would probably find his own accommodations tonight. It was a palace, after all, and surely there were hundreds of rooms here.

Still, she'd never slept in the nude before, and it was a disconcerting thought.

Glancing around, she saw another doorway on the opposite corner, and walked over to peek in. Just as she suspected. It was his walk-in closet. Her eyes naturally adjusted to the dark, so she didn't need to turn on the light. The closet was huge, of course, filled with various clothing from luxurious tuxedos and suits to some robes and pants she guessed were traditional garb. She opened the first cabinet on her right.

"Ah, lucky guess." It was filled with more intimate apparel—undershirts, boxers, and pajamas. Well, since he didn't exactly provide her with anything else to wear for the next few days, she decided to borrow a shirt and a pair of boxers. Hopefully the prince wouldn't mind, but then again, she wasn't exactly a willing guest here.

Padding back to the bedroom, she wondered what else she was supposed to do. A yawn escaped her mouth. Despite not having had any activity the entire day, she suddenly felt tired. Probably the hot shower—a luxury she hadn't had in weeks living in a tent in the desert—and the prospect of being on a real bed that made her body crave sleep.

She let out a deep sigh of contentment as she eased under the luxurious covers in the ridiculously large bed. The last time she'd slept on a real mattress was in a dinky little hotel in Karachi, and they had only stopped there for two nights before they had to travel to the new dig site. After weeks in her pup tent in the previous site, the inch-thick mattress in the dank, humid room had been heaven.

But this ... it was a hundred times better than any five-star hotel she'd ever stayed in, and she wasn't exactly a stranger to those. After all, her father was a billionaire, and she grew up with every luxury she could ever ask for. Many thought it was strange that she would want to spend her days digging in the dirt when her trust fund was enough to fund her for the rest of her life, but she wasn't raised like that.

No, her father built everything he had from nothing, while her mother was a brilliant scientist who finished two PhDs before she was twenty. They taught her the value of hard work, and she wasn't going to live like some pampered princess. Besides, she'd fallen in love with archeology on her tenth birthday when Aunt Meredith had given her a book on

Egyptian mummies, and she knew what her career was going to be at that exact moment.

Another yawn escaped her mouth. It was probably late evening, and despite what she earlier thought about sharing the bed with Prince Karim, it was obvious he'd found somewhere else to sleep. She squashed that small bit of disappointment in her chest and closed her eyes. Maybe when she woke up, she'd be back in her tent, and this would have all been a nightmare.

However, it wasn't a dream or nightmare. Not when she suddenly woke up and felt the bed move. Was it an earthquake?

"Huh?" She quickly sat up. The room was pitch dark, but she could see slivers of early morning light peeking through the crack in the blackout curtains. And it wasn't an earthquake that woke her up. No, it was the very large person on the other end of the bed, thrashing about. Her instincts flared, and she knew who it was. Karim was near the edge of the mattress, his huge limbs struggling against sleep paralysis.

"Your Highness?"

His mouth opened. "*Mum ... Mum ...* please. No!" he cried, even as his lids stayed tightly shut.

The desperate tone made her heart wrench, and before she could stop herself, she was scrambling across the bed toward him. "Prince Karim!"

His handsome face was twisted in agony, and she couldn't help but reach out to touch him, her palms landing on his chest. The heat of his skin made her gasp. It was like he was on fire. She was about to pull away when his hands wrapped around her wrists and tugged.

"*Oommph!*" She landed on top of him, his arms wrapping

around her. Despite her attempt to struggle, he held her in a tight grip. "Your Highness?" Still, his eyes remained closed, and he stopped crying out and thrashing.

At least he wasn't having a nightmare anymore. Because that's what it was, right? He was having some kind of night terror. Her mother said sometimes Dad still had them, probably a PTSD episode from his time in the marines.

Minutes ticked by, but Prince Karim's arms remained around her like steel bands. With a soft sigh, she pressed her cheek to his chest. At least he was wearing clothes tonight. The T-shirt he wore didn't exactly hide much, seeing as it was stretched tight across his pecs, and she could feel the muscled planes of his body under hers. Her upper body was stretched out across his massive chest, which wasn't as uncomfortable as it sounded. In fact, it was actually comfortable. Like sleeping next to a hot water bottle.

Her lids started to feel heavy. Maybe if she closed her eyes for a few minutes, he'd eventually let go.

CHAPTER FOUR

SLEEP WAS STILL FOGGING HER BRAIN WHEN SHE FELT IT. Rough hands gliding over the naked skin of her stomach. It was a delicious feeling, like nothing she'd ever experienced before. Warm lips nuzzled at her neck, beard tickling her skin, and when she felt a hot tongue flick at the soft spot behind her ear, she groaned. Wetness flooded between her legs, and the mouth at her nape growled.

Holy smokes!

Her eyes flew open when something hard poked at her butt. But her limbs were too weak to protest. Or she just didn't want to, because those hands and mouth were doing things to her that made her feel so ... alive. She didn't want it to stop.

The large hand slid up, engulfing and cupping her breast and she couldn't stop her hips from pressing up against the hardness behind her or keep from moaning loudly.

He went still, and when he withdrew his hands, she nearly whimpered in protest. The loss of the heat of his body and his distinct scent made her wolf cry out, and it took all her might not to turn around.

But she did turn her head. The sight of his towering form stalking away from the bed and the bathroom door slamming shut told her that she wasn't dreaming. It *was* Karim. But what had he been doing?

Well, it was obvious what he'd been doing—but why didn't he find another place to sleep last night? And where had he been? And what was he dreaming about? And this morning ...

Oh dear. Heat rushed to her cheeks. *That was embarrassing.* He had probably been having a dream that he was in bed with some supermodel, and when he woke up and saw it was just her, realized his mistake.

Her wolf howled in protest at the thought of Prince Karim wrapped up in the arms of some other woman.

Oh, what's the matter with you, anyway?

The bathroom door flew open, and she quickly turned away, pressing her face against the pillow and shutting her eyes tight. His heavy footsteps told her he was walking toward the door, and when she heard it shut, she let out a sigh of relief she didn't realize she'd been holding.

What was it about his mere presence that seemed to command her attention? It was crazy; she hardly knew the man. Yes, they'd cuddled up in bed twice now, and even kissed, but both had been accidents.

"I'm going mad," she declared as she sat up. And it had only been twenty-four hours since she woke up in this crazy place.

I have to get out of here. But how?

Think, Deedee. You graduated magna cum laude from

Oxford. You finished your masters and published your first paper before you were twenty-five. Somehow, though, she doubted her thesis on *Techniques on Urban Archeology* would help her out right now. Archeology in real life wasn't like a movie, and Indiana Jones, she was not.

Well, she wasn't just a professor of archeology. She was a Lycan and the daughter of a dragon. If only her father's shifter side had manifested in her, she could sprout wings and fly away. But alas, it didn't. Sebastian Creed wasn't a born shifter, unlike the Lycans, so he didn't pass that on to his children. Something about his DNA remaining unchanged despite whatever accident had turned him. He didn't talk about it much, so she wasn't exactly sure how he came to sharing his body with a dragon.

But that didn't mean she couldn't escape. Her Lycan side would protect her from most harm, but she wasn't invincible. She couldn't jump out the window; the fall would kill her instantly. Even if it didn't, her injuries would slow her down and then she'd also have the sandstorms to contend with.

Somehow, she made it through the sandstorms and into the palace, which means there was a way out.

There was a tentative knock on the door, and she knew it could only be Ramin. Probably with her breakfast.

Ramin!

An idea struck her and she got up from the bed. "Come in," she said.

The door swung open, and as she thought, it was Ramin. The teen was carrying a silver tray with several plates, his gaze averted from hers. She knew he would set the tray down on the table by the door, but before he could, she grabbed the other end. "Thank you, Ramin." She cocked her head to try to catch his eyes. When he looked at her, his brown eyes grew wide with surprise. "Can you understand me?"

She saw a flare of recognition, an expression she knew from experience living abroad the past months when someone could understand English, but didn't have the confidence or practice to speak it. The trick was to speak slowly and use simple words. "I want to say ... thank you for saving me."

He gulped loudly.

"You ... you got ... saved me from the bad man."

There was something else in his face now. The briefest flash of anger before a dark expression took over. "Man ... hurt ... you?"

She shook her head. "No. Thanks to you." She smiled at him, which he returned. "How did you bring me here? Was it through that tunnel?"

The puzzled look on his face told her he didn't understand a word she said, and she cursed herself that she didn't even bother learning a few bits of the languages in the area. When Prince Karim spoke last night, she could pick up a few words of what sounded like Pashto, but that was it. The Zhobghadians probably had their own dialect or language.

"Ramin, you need to help me again."

No answer. Instead, he yanked the tray away from her and set it on the table. He gestured to the tray and to her, then quickly dashed toward the door.

Darn.

Ignoring the food, she crept toward the door and opened it a crack. Ramin was there, a silent sentry as he stood stiffly, his head facing forward.

Double darn.

The only people who would be seeing her were Ramin and Prince Karim. The former didn't speak any English and the latter was determined to keep her here.

"Well, now." She straightened her shoulders. There was no way she was going to sit on her behind and do nothing.

Walking over to the tray of food, she grabbed a piece of flatbread. It was hard to think on an empty stomach, and to be honest, the food they'd been serving her had been phenomenal, better than any Michelin-star meal she'd had.

She paced the carpet, munching on the bread as she brainstormed. Maybe she could scream her lungs out, but as far as she could tell, Prince Karim's bedroom windows did not face any other buildings, and she didn't know what was outside the doors.

Thought Ramin was well-built, she could probably outrun him with her Lycan speed. But then he might sound the alarms and then she'd not only get caught, but found out. While she might not know who would pay for her presence here, she knew they would be innocent, and she couldn't have that on her conscience.

Really, she could wait it out. Her team would have realized she was missing by now, and were probably trying to find her. And her family would surely know as well. Maybe she'd get lucky, and they'd send Uncle Daric to find her. Or Cross.

Dream on, Deedee.

Cross hadn't even cared to contact her after that disastrous night months ago. Clearly, he was not going to make the first move to patch up whatever had been destroyed between them when she confessed her feelings to him.

But oh, wouldn't that be romantic? Like a fairy tale. Here

she was, trapped by a beast in his castle and then Cross would rescue her and realize she was the love of his life all along.

I was wrong, Dee, he would say. *And I'm madly in love with you. Please forgive me.* Then he could carry her off into the sunset. It would be like the story her mom used to read to her about the beautiful girl who was trapped in the castle of that beast.

Wait a minute. Beauty wasn't rescued by the prince. The beast was *the prince and they fell in love—*

Oh, good Lord, the isolation was getting to her. She slapped herself on the forehead. This was not a movie or a fairy tale. And, she reminded herself, she didn't believe in fairy tales.

"There has to be a way." She sighed. A way to leave the palace and get to the border, then to her dig site. Surely the sandstorms didn't go on all the time? Even she knew that they eventually abated, if not shift around to other areas.

But how to get out of here without getting Ramin in trouble?

As she reached for more of her breakfast, the glinting silver tray caught her eyes.

Oh.

A plan began to form in her mind. The first part of a plan at least. But she could work with that.

———

Much like yesterday, Prince Karim didn't return to his bedroom at all during the day. *If that was a pattern, then that means he might not come back until tomorrow morning at dawn*. He had said there was some kind of festival, so maybe he was off doing his royal duties and attending parties and such.

Or maybe he spent his days with another woman.

"What the heck?" That thought came out of nowhere, as did the growl that rose from her chest. *Focus on the plan, Dee.*

She had all day to think and plan and get ready. First, she raided Prince Karim's closet and found the things she could use if she got caught in the sandstorm—swimming goggles, a ski mask, and a thin scarf. Then she dressed in her now-dry shorts and shirt. Somehow, she had lost her work boots, but if it was sandy outside then she wouldn't need them. Instead, she put on three pairs of the thickest socks she could find.

As a Lycan, she could keep walking for hours without food or water for a day or two and not get tired or dehydrated. Hopefully it shouldn't come to that. Ramin had managed to carry her all the way here through a sandstorm. That told her that her site was not too far away. But speaking of Ramin ...

Her stomach clenched, thinking of what she had to do.

"You're doing it for his own good, too," she told herself.

If she did get caught, then it would have to be obvious he had nothing to do with her being present here. Plus, she already had a convincing story—she had gotten lost in the sandstorms and wound up inside Zhobghadi. Besides, if Prince Karim wanted to alert everyone to her presence and send his guards after her, then that was on him. He was royalty, so surely, they wouldn't punish him if she was caught.

Her fingers curled into fists at her sides. "You're not going to get caught."

Ugh, this talking to herself thing was getting old. But

soon she'd be back at her dig site, and she could put this whole episode behind her.

With a determined shrug of her shoulders, she grabbed the silver tray from the table. She ate every scrap and drank every bit of liquid she could to prepare herself, in case she really did get lost for a while. There was also the flatbread she had kept from lunch, which she wrapped in some napkins and stuffed into the leather messenger bag she took from the prince's closet.

"You can do this." Okay, pep talk over.

The door was inches away, and she opened it, taking a deep breath. "Ramin? Ramin, come in here, please!"

The seconds crawled by as her heart beat a thundering rhythm in her chest. As soon as Ramin stepped inside, she swung the silver tray against his head, sending him to the floor.

"Sorry!"

She had spent the afternoon inside Prince Karim's closet, swinging the tray to try and get the right amount of strength. Too weak and he wouldn't be knocked out, but if she used too much of her Lycan strength, she could kill the boy. Bending down, she touched his pulse and breathed out a sigh of relief. He was fine. The headache he would have the next day would hurt like the dickens, but he would live. And she was almost home free.

There was no time to waste. She slipped through the door, and much to her surprise, she was in another room—a living room it seemed. *Of course.* His bedroom was part of a larger suite probably. Spying the ornate gold doors on the opposite side, she knew that had to be the exit. She tiptoed over and tried to filter out the sounds outside. Her Lycan hearing didn't detect anyone close by, so she grabbed the round crystal handles, turned them, and pushed.

A sigh of relief escaped her mouth. Thank goodness it was a hallway, and not another set of rooms. Of course, the corridor was just as ornate as the rooms, with beautiful blue, gold, and white tile work on the floor, latticework arches overhead, and ornate mosaics decorating the wall. *You're not here to admire the decor,* she reminded herself. But where to go?

Using the scientific method of *eenie, meenie, miney, moe,* she chose left and crept carefully down the hallway, following the path as it turned right and then left. Her enhanced senses were on full alert, as she tried to hear as far forward as she could, listening for any noise, avoiding areas where she could hear footsteps or murmuring, while her speed made her nearly invisible and silent as she darted through the hallways and down numerous sets of stairways.

So far, so good. But this palace must be huge, because it felt like she was never going to run out of hallways and doors. And the stairs. So many stairs. Didn't this place have any elevators? Perhaps this was intentional, to make it difficult to reach the royal family.

This was getting ridiculous though, she huffed as she stepped off the last set of staircases. She slowed down and then stopped completely, glancing around her. It looked like the hallway before it, decorated in the same pattern. Was she going around in circles? No, definitely not. The air here was different.

Lifting her nose in the air, she took a whiff. "Oh, wow." A delicious aroma hung in the air, like the grilled lamb and potatoes she had for dinner. But it was faint, like a trail.

Which meant someone had carried food through here from the kitchen. There would be people there, but it also could lead to an exit somewhere for workers and supplies and trash to go in and out.

She followed the scent of cooking food straight ahead, then turning right at the end through an arched doorway. The hallway inside became noticeably less ornate and more utilitarian, and she could hear the bustle of activity at the end where a wooden door separated it from the next room.

That had to be the kitchen. The scent of food was so strong, and the sounds of spoons clanking against pots, voices in a strange language, and the quick shuffle of feet came louder in her ears. She pressed her hands against the door and peeked ever so slightly inside as her heart hammered against her ribcage.

The room was definitely a kitchen, and she seemed to be in the rear part, as most of the stoves, tables, and workers were in the opposite end of the room. *But where—ah, there!*

On the wall perpendicular to where she was, a door swung wide open. A man came inside, dragging something heavy inside a sack. But that wasn't what caught her eye. No, it was the glimpse of dark blue sky and palm trees on the other side of the door. The outside.

Now or never.

Everyone seemed busy enough in the front of the kitchens. Even the man with the sack had gone to a far corner and began to argue with another of the staff members. After taking three deep breaths, she used her Lycan speed to quietly, but swiftly, dart toward the exit before it completely closed.

Cool, fresh air rushed into her lungs. The smell of the

outside nearly overwhelmed her, but luck must be on her side today because the courtyard she was standing in was empty. Another rush of adrenaline made her run toward the gated archway. The metal barrier opened when she pushed on it, and she ran into the darkness, not caring where she was going as long as it was far away from the palace.

Her eyes adjusted to the darkness, the light of the nearly-full moon making it an easy transition. She didn't dare look back, but kept walking and walking.

She was free! *Oh, my Lord, I really did it!* Who said archeology was boring? This was a real-life adventure and now—

"Holy ..."

Whatever word she wanted to use didn't come out of her mouth. In fact, she couldn't even remember what she meant to say. The sight ahead of her put her into a state of shock.

The sand swirled in the air, creating a wall that was over a hundred stories high. She could see the night sky, stars, and the moon above, but nothing in front.

Minutes ticked by, but the wall of sand never moved forward or backward. No, it stayed static, as if it were encased in an invisible shell. Whatever it was keeping it there, she knew it was not normal. Something like static electricity prickled over her skin, and she knew that feeling.

Magic.

CHAPTER FIVE

SOFT LIPS. SMOOTH SUN-KISSED SKIN. BOUNTIFUL breasts that overflowed in his hands. Karim had had his share of women, but nothing quite like *her*. Her sweet scent and lush body called to him like no other.

He tried to stay away from her, even thought to sleep on the couch in his living room. But when he came back after his evening flight over Zhobghadi to take a shower, he could practically taste her sweet scent the moment he walked into the room. The sight of her dressed in his clothes and wrapped around a pillow nearly shredded his control. It was a good thing he was tired, and the only thing he could do was dress himself and collapse into bed.

Desiree. Her name was apt, as she ignited desire in him like no other. Did he reach out for her again? Or maybe she came to him. It didn't matter, because he just wanted to touch and taste her skin. But once he was fully awake, he had gotten his senses back. Leaving her in bed was the most difficult task he'd had to face, but he needed to clear his head.

Not that it worked, because even until now, his mind was still fogged with lust.

And he wasn't the only one fascinated with the alluring woman. The beast inside him roared at him in fury the moment he moved away from her.

Ours. Mine. Claim.

What did The Great One mean?

"Your Highness? Did you hear what I said?"

Karim swung his head over to the right. The Minister of Energy's dark brows reminded him of two caterpillars butting heads, and his lips tightened so much, they were a thin line. "Yes, Minister Jamir?"

"So, don't you agree that we need to increase our output by thirty-five percent?"

Karim would rather be doing so many more things than being at this meeting. Well, just *one* thing. But he had duties to perform, after all. "Thirty-five percent. Of course." His disinterested tone made Arvin glare at him with warning, so Karim straightened his chair and cleared his throat. "You are most knowledgeable when it comes to Zhobghadi's needs, which is why you were appointed Minister of Energy. I trust that if you think thirty-five percent is what we require, then we shall have thirty-five percent." He glanced back at the rest of the council of ministers who were seated at the long table across from him. "If there is nothing else, then we should reconvene, and you can go home and spend time with your families on this blessed evening. I still have a long night ahead of me." He was about to stand up when someone spoke up.

"Er, Highness?"

Lakme, the only female minister on the council raised her hand. "Highness, one last thing."

"Yes?"

"About the coronation ceremony." There was a murmur among the other ministers. "When can we expect you to announce the date?"

All eyes turned to him. "I think that in these most sacred of days, such talk is inappropriate," Karim answered in his most diplomatic tone. "It is the time for reflection on the past, and how lucky we are that the gods have saved us."

Lakme didn't budge. "And so, you will announce it after the Easifat?"

"You can expect it." As soon as he stood up, everyone in the room followed suit. "Good evening to you all."

No one protested or said another word as he made his way out of the council room. He was eager to leave. Eager to go back to his rooms. To Desiree. That meeting ran way too long, all the way until after suppertime. He hardly ate the dinner served to them, but he was *hungry*. However, he knew Arvin was right behind him, fast at his heels as he stepped up to keep in stride.

"So, you are finally going to have the coronation?" Arvin inquired as they briskly strode away from the council room. "It sounds like you made a promise."

"I told Minister Lakme she could expect it." And she was expecting it, but it didn't mean he would do it. "So, technically, I did not lie."

"*Ay*, Karim." Arvin gently grabbed his arm, and they stopped. Karim didn't admonish him at the disrespectful way he was conducting himself, but didn't say anything else either. "*Your Highness*. Please, you must announce the coronation, and soon."

"I do not answer to anyone." His made his tone as chilly and authoritative as possible.

"Except the people," Arvin pointed out.

And Karim found he couldn't find a comeback to that, so he remained silent.

"They want a king. Their king. They want you," Arvin pleaded.

His jaw hardened. "My father has not even been in the ground a year."

"Yes, that's true, but the previous Crown Princes before you have had their coronation weeks after the previous king passed." His cousin lowered his voice. "And there's something else."

"Something else?"

Arvin looked around, then leaned forward and lowered his voice. "Karim, I've heard some talk."

What was he talking about? "What talk?"

"There is discontent among the ministers and certain people."

Karim snorted. "Of course there are."

"I'm not talking about the usual dissenters who clamor for the abolition of the throne," Arvin said. "I've heard whispers. There are certain people who think you are not worthy to be king."

The Great One roared in his head, and Karim felt his own anger rising with the fury of Ninurta. "Not worthy?"

"Because of your blood. Because your mother—"

"*Who* said these things?" he roared, making Arvin step back, his eyes filled with fear. "Apologies," he said quickly. "I know it was not you." His blood always boiled at the mention of his mother, and he could not help himself.

Arvin braced himself against the nearest wall and rubbed at his temple. "I've only heard them. And I have done my best to quell such talk."

"I know you would, thank you." Still, that did not abate his anger. Sure, it was one thing for him to doubt himself, but others? And because he was half-English, his mother's blood in his body, they think him not worthy? It made him want to release The Great One and raze the streets until he found the source of such treasonous talk.

But he knew that was not possible, so he calmed himself. "Arvin, you are my most trusted ... friend." Or the closest thing he had to one. "Will you find out for me the source of this talk?"

"Of course, Your Highness." Arvin bowed his head. "And what happens when I do?"

"You will report to me, and I will take care of them." The Great One agreed with a nod of its horned head.

Arvin raised a brow. "Ah, finally."

"Finally?"

His cousin's mouth quirked up into a smile. "Finally, I see the Karim I know. You've been acting strange since your return."

"What do you mean?"

"Just today, at the meeting." Arvin removed an invisible speck of dust from his robe. "You seemed bored. Like your mind was a million miles away."

Not a million miles. No, it was in the palace, in his bed, where a beautiful temptress waited for him. Gods above and below, if he did not have her soon—

"Highness?"

Karim shook his head mentally. "I need to prepare for the

evening flyover." He had a few hours until midnight. They were sharing a bedroom for the next week, Perhaps he could persuade her to share a meal with him. And if they shared more ...

It was obvious she wanted him as much as he wanted her, and why not make the time pass more pleasurably? He was experienced at seduction, and it would be easy enough to coax her. Surely the fact that he was a prince would flatter her, and make her even more eager. She was an American, after all, and they were all fascinated with royalty, something their country had never had. Besides, once she returned to her normal, everyday life, this would have been a grand adventure for her, something to brag about to her friends. That's what she wanted, right? That's what all women who came to him wanted.

"Good night, Arvin. And thank you."

"I'm at your service, Your Highness." Arvin bowed and turned on his heel, then walked away.

Karim proceeded toward the main palace, up to his living quarters. His steps sped up as he entered his living room, and he darted toward the door. He was so distracted at the thought of Desiree that he didn't notice the figure lying in front of door until he nearly tripped on it.

"You—Ramin?" He bent down. "Ramin! Ramin, what has happened?"

"H-H-Highness ..." Ramin hissed in pain as he touched his head. "She ... she ..."

Dread overcame him as he dashed into the bedroom. The trace scent of her was weak, meaning she was gone.

"No!" His roar was nearly inhuman, rumbling from his

chest. Where was she? How did she escape? There was no other exit except ...

His heart pounded like a gong as he raced to the balcony. The vision of her broken body lying at the bottom fueled his rage. But when he looked over, he could see no trace of her. Sure, she had been distraught that she had to stay here, but she didn't seem like the type of person who would commit suicide just to get away. But where was she?

The Great One roared again, and he could feel its claws raking at him from the inside. It was angry, but also frantic.

No! Ours. They are ours.

With a load roar, he allowed the beast to take over, a pillar of flame incinerating his clothes and engulfing his human body as it began to grow and expand. Soon, The Great One's humungous form filled the balcony, leathery wings flapping in the air as it took off.

Where are we going? Usually, he worked with his dragon form. They were one creature with the same mind and body. They always agreed on where to go, but now, it seemed too angry to listen to him and was wresting control of their body away. It veered left, then swung right, its large head moving side to side as its eyes scoured the grounds of the palace. *She could not have gone far. Maybe she might even still be in the palace.*

But the great beast didn't listen to him. It seemed to know where to look. But how? Zhobghadi was huge and—

There.

The voice called his attention as the beast's head cocked lower. The Great One's enhanced vision allowed him to zero in on a small, lone dot in the distance, not far from the rear of the palace. And deep in his heart, he knew it was her. Once they realized that, they were once again of one mind and body.

As their shadow loomed over her, she looked up. Her eyes widened in surprise, and she seemed frozen in horror. *Good.* She deserved to be frightened because of what she had put him through in the last few minutes since he discovered her gone. She had obviously escaped. Did she not know what danger she was in? If any Zhobghadian had seen her, they would have reported her to the authorities. Or worse, if the more superstitious and traditional citizens had seen her, they might take matter into their own hands.

The beast let out another roar as they swung around and flew lower, ready to grab her. However, as they came closer, Desiree ducked and stepped aside.

Inana's tits, how did she move so fast?

Swinging around again, their eyes searched for her. But she was gone. No, she wasn't. She was just quick. *Inhumanly fast,* Karim observed as the gray dot dashed away westward.

Well, that did not matter, because The Great One was bigger and had wings. They flew low, whipping up the sand in order to blur her vision. The gray dot stopped, and The Great One's mighty claws swooped in, digging into the earth under her so they could scoop her away.

It took much effort and concentration to execute a vertical takeoff, and their wings flapped with all their strength. They soared higher, then turned toward the balcony. Their little passenger struggled against the grip of their scaly hands. Not that it mattered. Their body was armored, and the teeth and claws were—

Teeth and claws?

No, no, no! What did we catch? Karim bellowed in his mind. *She has gotten away! We must go back—*

No, the beast protested. *They. Are. Ours.*

What was The Great One talking about? Obviously, they had taken some poor creature—perhaps someone's pet goat—and Desiree was still out there. But the beast would not listen.

Clawed, scaly feet landed on the balcony with a thud. As they began to transform back to his human body, their grip loosened on their unknowing captive, and they laid it down as gently as possible on the ground.

As he shrunk to normal size, the first thing he thought was, *that was one big pet.* He'd never seen wolves in real life, but he was sure they were not this large, like the size of a small horse. Despite the fight it put up as he carried it back, it stood there, unmoving, looking up at him with light green eyes. Familiar eyes.

No.

Yes, The Great One rumbled. *Ours.*

The moment he fully transformed back; the wolf dashed into the palace. He ran after it—her, or whatever it was—spotting a flash of gray fur as it disappeared into the bedroom. "Desiree!" He heard the door to the bathroom slam, but when he tried to yank it open, it didn't budge. "Unlock this door now!"

There was shuffling from the other side of the door, but it remained closed. He wiggled it violently. "So help me, if you do not open this door, I will—" Why was he even giving her a chance? This was *his* room, *his* palace, his godsdamned country!

Using all his and The Great One's strength, he slammed

into the door with his shoulder. The wood cracked in half, and he tore the remnants aside with his bare hands as he forced his way in.

Desiree stood in the middle of the bathroom; a towel clutched to her shaking body. Her eyes glowed brightly before fading back to their normal light green color. Even under her tanned cheeks, he could see the blood had drained from her face.

Her arms tightened around her towel, as if it could protect her. "What ... how did you ..." She gasped when he took a step closer. "What *are* you?"

CHAPTER SIX

"What am I?" Karim bellowed. "What are you?"

Deedee stood there, staring up at him. It was as if her feet were encased in cement blocks. She couldn't move. Couldn't speak. Couldn't breathe. Only one thought pounded in her head.

Karim was a dragon.

But how? The synapses in her mind weren't working properly, unable to make the connections. If Astrid were here, she would probably say that Deedee had literally blown her mind.

Her dad was the only dragon shifter in the world. That's what she knew growing up. What everyone assumed. And no way could he have fathered any other dragon kids because neither she nor any of her siblings were dragons. He was turned into a beast, and he had no other relatives. If there were others like him, surely, they would have known about it.

Yet, here was Karim, standing in front of her. Did he also have an accident that turned him into a dragon?

While trying to figure out how to get through the

sandstorm, she saw the dragon flying above. In her fright, she shifted, knowing that it was the only way she had a chance of escaping. But trapped between the magical sandstorm and a furious flying beast, she knew not even her wolf could save her. And so here she was, back where she started.

The silence stretched on between them, but neither spoke. Those cool, cerulean blue eyes held her gaze like magnets, and she couldn't look away.

She had shifted in front of him. Broken Lycan law. When her clan and the Lycan High Council found out, they would have to erase his memories.

Assuming she ever got out of here. For all she knew, Karim now had to get rid of her to protect his secret. Her wolf whined, and she quieted it with an audible *shush*.

"Do you talk to your animal?"

She nodded. "Do you?"

His face softened slightly. "Sometimes. It does not always speak in sentences, but I know what it is thinking." His brows drew together. "And you ... does your family know?"

She bit her lip. Obviously, he thought her a one-off. Of course, if he knew there were hundreds of Lycan clans around the world living among the humans, *his* mind might be blown.

But he couldn't know though. It was forbidden to tell humans.

And dragons?

Well, that was another thing. Though she had so many questions, practically bursting with them, it was best if she kept her cards close. "Yes." Technically, not a lie.

"And you were born this way?"

She huffed. "Why do you get to ask all the questions?"

Were she not holding onto a towel to keep her modesty, she would have crossed her arms over her chest in protest.

"It is forbidden for anyone outside Zhobghadi to have knowledge of The—to have seen what you have seen."

She swallowed hard. "Are you going to kill me then?"

A look of horror crossed his handsome face. "No! What do you think of us here, that we're barbarians?"

"And yet, I've been held captive for two days for no reason, and without any way to contact the outside world," she pointed out. "Even prisoners get one phone call."

He let out a string of what she assumed was curses in his language, then scrubbed his hand down his face. "I think we should talk, Desiree. Let's sit down, shall we?"

The way he said her first name made heat uncurl in her stomach. No one called her Desiree. "Fine, but, er, maybe we should both get dressed?"

She should win some kind of award for restraint as it took all her control not to let her eyes stray below his naked waist. Not that ogling the rest of him was any better. In the stark lighting of the bathroom, she got an eyeful of his well-formed chest, rock-hard eight-pack, and the deep V on his hips, not to mention all that glorious tanned skin.

He snorted. "My clothes burn when I transform, so I have always been comfortable with my nakedness. But I will put my robe on and wait for you outside. Put on anything you deem appropriate." He turned and walked through the door, or rather, what was left of it.

As soon as he was far enough, her shoulders slumped, and all the confidence she had drained out of her body. "Oh God, oh God, oh God." Her knees unlocked, and her limbs felt like jelly.

Somehow, she found the strength to force herself to walk over to his closet. What did one wear to a confrontation with a dragon? While her father was one, it wasn't like she ever had to take him on. Indeed, she'd been a good girl all her life, a papa's girl. None of that prepared her for the current situation she was in.

Fearing he might come in if she made him wait any longer, she grabbed one of his shirts and pajama bottoms. She was tall enough that she didn't need to roll up the legs too much. After a quick combing of her hair with her fingers, she marched out of the bedroom. To her surprise, the door was open.

"Your Highness?" she called as she peeked out into the living room. Again, she was taken aback, this time by the sight of Karim seated on the couch, pouring out tea from a pot into two glass cups.

"Have a seat, Desiree."

She padded over to the couch, deliberately choosing to sit on the cushions farthest away from him. "It's Deedee."

"What's a Deedee?" he asked with a frown.

"My name."

"No, you said it was Desiree. Professor Desiree Desmond Creed of New York University."

"Yes, but no one calls me Desiree."

"Why not?"

"Because ..." She wrinkled her brows. "Everyone just calls me Deedee."

"Everyone?"

"Yes. My parents, my siblings, my friends, colleagues—"

"And your boyfriends?" A dark brow had risen up.

"Yes. I mean, no." She shook her head. "No boyfriends."

God, why was she telling him this? "Anyway, you can call me Deedee."

"I prefer Desiree." Those blue eyes were like twin fires when he said her name, and the way he rolled his *r* sent her heart racing. As prince of this country, he could probably call anyone whatever he wished.

"So, you said we should talk."

He offered her a cup of tea, and though she hesitated, took it anyway. His fingers lingered as they brushed hers, and a spark of electricity tingled up her arm. *Must be the static.* This place was covered in carpets, after all.

"The knowledge of my existence is a secret that has been kept within our borders for a thousand years," he began. "Outsiders cannot know about ... my dragon. Zhobghadi has insulated itself, and kept out outsiders because of this, and every citizen is sworn not to reveal it, upon pain of death."

She gasped. "It's obviously an effective threat."

"It is law. Barbaric, you may call it, but it has kept us safe. Kept me and my ancestors safe." He took a deep breath. "One thousand years ago, Zhobghadi was about to be run over by invaders. In order to protect the people, the gods sent the Easifat, to act as a shield to protect us."

The gods? The skeptical scientist in her couldn't quite believe that. But then again, she could feel the magic from the sandstorm. That was definitely not natural. Mystical yes, but divine?

"But the Easifat could only shield us, not destroy our enemies. And so, they sent The Great One."

"The Great One?"

"The dragon, as you call it. Prince Hammam, my ancestor and the crown prince at that time, was the very first one to receive it. He transformed into The Great One, and defeated our enemies."

Surely, he didn't mean that literally? That his dragon was from the gods? Sure, while Lycans existed, they still believed in science and DNA. For the past decades, Lycan scientists like her mother worked to unlock the secrets of magic and of their nature. Of course, being an archeologist, Deedee knew that people in the past used allegory and exaggeration when trying to relay stories they could not explain with their limited knowledge. She needed to know more. "So ever since then, your ... family line has carried this dragon?"

"The Great One," he corrected. "Our records show that only one exists at a given time. The king and then his heir. While I had the beast inside me, I was unable to transform until my father passed away."

She chewed on her lower lip so hard, she winced. *Well, not quite, buddy.* There were two now. But she wasn't about to reveal anything to him. What would he do if he found out about her father?

"So ... if the king had other children, they won't be dragons? Why not?"

"This is the way it's been for a millennium. We do not know why. I was born with my beast, and when my father passed away, it became The Great One."

Hmmm. Lycans were in a similar situation, as only two Lycans could produce another Lycan, and even then it was difficult, and many couples often did not produce offspring. Their scientists have always hypothesized that perhaps it was some law of nature, to make sure the earth wasn't overrun with shifters and that humans were meant to be the dominant species on earth. Of course, there was one exception: True

Mates pairings, but out of their population, that was only still a small percentage.

"So, it's like a title?" she asked. "Like you becoming king."

His mouth set into a hard line and his nostrils flared. "Something like that."

Heavens, she didn't think this could be so fascinating, but it was. As an archeologist, it was like discovering a new ancient civilization. The academic in her couldn't resist. "What records do you have? How far back do they go to? Have you ever tried to have your DNA tested or sequenced?"

He looked rather horrified. "Of course not. But we do have many records." Picking up his own teacup, he gestured with it toward her. "And now, it's your turn."

"My turn?" *Oh, poop.* This was a tit for tat then. "I turn into a wolf. I always have. It's not controlled by the full moon every month in case you were wondering." She took a sip to stall, trying to choose her words carefully. "I'm faster and stronger than most hu—people. And I heal quicker too."

"And your family? Are they like you?"

The lie was on the tip of her tongue. But she just couldn't say it, not when he looked at her with those mesmerizing eyes. And so, she turned away from his oppressing blue gaze.

"You have your secrets too." He put the cup down. "One could say that this isn't fair, because I have revealed much to you."

"I didn't ask you to reveal the entire story of your dragon or your country's history," she pointed out. "You volunteered it. Had I known this was a sharing circle, I wouldn't have continued listening."

"True, and I defer to your superior logic." He sat up straighter, and she could see that arrogant, princely air again.

"But we are at an impasse. I cannot allow you to reveal our secret, and you cannot have yours out either."

An idea struck her. Maybe she could use this to her advantage. "The way I see it," she put the cup down, then looked at him straight in the eyes, "*you* have more to lose in this situation than me."

His eyes flashed silver, the color of his dragon's scales, and the air grew so thick, she struggled to breathe. Just like when her father's temper flared. It was eerie, really. There had to be a connection. If only she knew more about what happened to her father.

"And what exactly will I lose, Desiree?" The ripple of power from him when he said her name made her shiver. "My people know about The Great One, it's no secret here. So, the world outside will too, and what will they do about it? I am a head of state, and have immunity wherever I go. One nation cannot lock up the leader of another sovereign country. And everyone wants our silver, so they will always play nice. What about you, Professor? Can *you* afford to have everyone know about what you are?"

Her chest tightened, and her lower lip trembled. *Darn him!* But then she knew better than to try and play games with someone so versed in diplomacy and negotiation. She wished she had more of her father's cutthroat business sense. "What do you want?" Her voice shook, and she wanted to kick herself for sounding weak and backing down.

"There are still a few days left of the Easifat. You must not try to escape again. When the sandstorms die down, I shall arrange for your transport out of Zhobghadi."

Could she trust him? "And what about my family? My

team? They're probably going out of their minds, and they'll think I'm dead."

"I'm afraid I cannot do anything about that. As I told you, communications with the outside world are impossible. Even The Great One cannot penetrate the veil around Zhobghadi. The sandstorms make it too dangerous for anyone to try and venture out to get a message out, and I would not risk any of my citizens just to reassure your family, not when you will see them soon enough."

And she wouldn't either.

"People get lost all the time," he said. "In the news, there are people who go on hikes in the wilderness and encounter accidents." He scratched at his chin. "We are allies with a number of nomadic tribes around the region. Many of them camp along the border during the Easifat. We can simply say you were caught in the sandstorm, injured, and taken in by one of the tribes. I'll bring you to them myself and ensure their cooperation, then you can make the call to your family."

That sounded reasonable enough. But still ... a whole week! A whole week by herself. "I'm going to go crazy with cabin fever," she said. "You can't possibly leave me alone for a week without any stimulation." She blushed and tried really hard not to notice the way his face perked up at that last word. "I mean, mental stimulation. It's like being in solitary confinement. You probably don't have TV or the Internet, but how about books? Someone to talk to in English?"

He seemed to consider this for a while. "Books I can provide, but I have very few in English. Most of them are in the library. And as for someone ... I may have an idea. There is someone I trust with my own life. But," he got up from the couch, "it is nearing midnight, and I have duties to attend to."

What kind of duties needed to be done at midnight? "Wait! One more thing." Oh dear. How was she going to say this?

"Yes?"

"Er ... you really don't have any other bedrooms available? I mean, I'm happy to sleep on this couch."

"No!" He blinked and cleared his throat. "I mean, this living room leads directly to the outside hall, and a servant or guard could come in any time. I would have Ramin guard the outside, but you have put him out of commission for a while."

She winced. "Sorry about that. Is he okay?"

"He'll live."

"Isn't there another bedroom around here?" She looked around the massive living area.

"No, just mine. And it's the only place in the palace where no one else is allowed to enter."

"Well, we can't possibly keep sharing a bed!" Her cheeks flamed, but the words flew out of her mouth before she could stop it. "Er, you don't suppose you could sleep here?"

"It is *my* bed," he said. "Why should I leave it?"

Was he being obtuse? Twice now they'd almost ... in his bed. Didn't he remember? Did he want her to say it aloud, that unspoken thing between them that even now was like the elephant in the room?

"Are you afraid of me, Desiree?" His tone turned low and sensuous, and his usually cool eyes turned molten. "Or perhaps of yourself? That you might actually want—"

"Fine!" She shot up to her feet. That bed was ridiculously huge anyway. "I'm putting a pillow in the middle and you're going to stay on your side." She pivoted and marched into the bedroom, and when she heard him chuckle, slammed the door shut.

"Argh!" Throwing herself on the bed like a child in a snit, she punched the nearest pillow she could reach, imagining it was Prince Karim. She shoved it aside, positioning it exactly in the middle. "You better not cross that line," she said, as if he were present in the room. Pulling up as close as possible to the edge of the bed, she got under the covers and closed her eyes, willing herself to sleep.

Hang on and wait, she told herself. In a few days, this would all be over. Prince Karim was right that she couldn't afford to have her secret revealed, because it wouldn't just be her real nature that would be exposed. It would be her mother, brothers, their friends, the whole New York clan, not to mention her Alpha, Lucas Anderson, one of the most powerful and richest men in the world. Lycan law compelled her to do anything and everything she could to keep their secret. All she needed to do was coast along the next few days, it would all be over, and she could leave this place and never see Prince Karim again.

Her wolf, on the other hand, didn't seem to like that and whined at her.

Oh, shut it, she told her animal. *We are going to sleep.* One more night over and she'd be closer to freedom.

CHAPTER SEVEN

WARM. SO WARM. HER CHEEK WAS PRESSED UP AGAINST a hot, firm pillow, while the smell of musk, sand, and fire overtook her senses.

What?

Her eyes flew open, and she realized her "pillow" was Prince Karim's chest. His very naked chest.

An undignified squeak escaped her mouth as she scrambled away from his torso. Her wolf protested at the loss, wanting to be near him and his warmth and scent. She ignored the little hussy and instead slapped him on the leg. "I said to stay on your side!"

"Eh?" One blue eye opened lazily, followed by the other. He let out a sigh, then gestured to his body. "And so I did, Desiree."

"You—" Her face grew hot with embarrassment as she realized that he was right. His body was still on his side of the bed. It was she who had rolled over the pillow and plastered herself to him.

"The next few days will be long and lonely." The smile

he flashed her made heat rush through her veins. "If you want, I'm happy to—"

She rolled off the bed and dashed into the bathroom to escape his sensual, searing gaze. Of course, his mind was on sex. He was a man. And he was probably used to seducing women all the time. Or having them seduce him.

"Argh!" She pulled at the sink handle angrily, letting the water gush out of the tap, hoping to drown out any sounds she made. If only the water could drown *her,* because she wanted to die of humiliation. How could he even suggest ... or think she would willingly want to ...

Well, you did wake up in his arms, for the third night in a row, a small voice inside her head countered. *And it felt so good to touch him ...*

How did he even invoke such a response from her? She'd never felt that way for anyone. Well, not that she would know how that *felt.*

Because, while few may believe it, she, Professor Desiree Desmond Creed, was still a virgin at thirty years of age.

It was embarrassing really. And not her intention. Yes, she'd had a crush on Cross since she was sixteen, but she wasn't saving herself for him. In fact, she had thought it would have been more prudent to gain experience before she settled on one man, whoever that may be. However, with a dragon for a father and two protective brothers—not to mention a whole extended family consisting of Lycans and hybrids—the few boys who weren't intimidated by her height were eventually chased off. And by the time she was eighteen, she was so consumed with her studies, first for her undergrad degree then her masters, that she didn't have time for relationships.

Then the offer for a position in New York University came, and she rose to the top so fast that now men her age were even more intimidated by her.

Of course, she wasn't totally untouched. She'd done ... *some* things with men. *Most* things. Just *not* everything. She'd even been prepared, making sure she took her birth control shots regularly. But she just couldn't seem to find the right person, someone who she'd be sure wouldn't ridicule her inexperience.

A knock at the door made her jump. "If you could be so kind," said the muffled masculine voice, "I would like to get ready for the day."

She bit back curse words wanting to burst from her mouth. Really, she hated cursing, but this man seemed to inspire it from her. "Just a minute."

After rushing through her bathroom routine, she walked out of the bathroom with as much dignity as she could muster. Though she kept her gaze straight ahead, she could definitely feel his eyes on her. Thank goodness, he went straight inside, and as soon as the door closed behind him, she let out a breath.

What to do now? She plopped herself on the edge of the bed, her toes digging into the soft carpet underneath her. Three—no, it had been four days since she got here. Prince Karim said it would be about ten days until the sandstorms subsided, so that meant she had a week here at most. Hopefully she didn't go crazy until then. Maybe that was why she was acting strange around him. It wasn't lust or desire, just that he was the nearest warm body around.

"Desiree."

She hated that she reacted to the sound of his voice like a

puppy hearing its master, but she didn't even realize he had left the bathroom.

"Yes?" She cleared her throat and turned around, then let out a silent groan. She didn't know if seeing him dressed was worse because he looked so uncommonly handsome in his well-tailored, all-black outfit. The tunic had a very military-like style that molded to his wide shoulders and chest, which showed off a number of ribbons and medals.

"I have matters to take care of today," he said. "But, as promised, I have found some way to keep you entertained. I have spoken with my Aunt Zafirah, and she will take you to the library and have your meals with you when she can."

"Your aunt?"

"Do not worry, she can be trusted. She is family." He frowned. "However, seeing as you are what you are ... can I trust you?"

"Trust me?"

"Not to ... harm her. In your other form."

She let out an undignified squeak. "Of course. I don't just ... I can control my wolf."

"Good." That seemed to be enough for him. "Now, come," he gestured toward the door. "She's already waiting."

"Hold on." She looked down at her outfit, which still consisted of his shirt and pajamas. "You want me to meet your aunt looking like this?"

"You can put on my robe, if you like. But I have nothing else that can fit you."

She huffed out a breath. "Fine." As she marched toward the door, she grabbed his robe and yanked it around herself. God, what was this woman going to think? That she was one of Prince Karim's lovers? Maybe she was used to him bringing women in and out of his bedroom. He was the prince, after all.

He went out first, and she followed behind him. "Good morning, Aunt Zafirah. Thank you for making time this morning."

Deedee stopped short right beside Karim, and turned her gaze toward the woman who rose from the couch. As she turned around, Deedee couldn't help but stare at her. If she was Karim's aunt, then she must be older, but she had that ageless beauty few women had. Her dark hair was pulled up into intricate braids and curls, while her smooth, milky skin didn't betray her years, save for the crow's-feet in the corner of her light hazel eyes and smile lines around her mouth. Though it was obvious she was surprised at Deedee's presence, she sent him a sly look.

"Good morning, Your Highness." She gave a small nod. "I am at your service, as always."

"Aunt Zafirah, this is Professor Desiree Desmond Creed of New York University," he said. "Desiree, this is Princess Zafirah Fatima Al-Fyahh Salamuddin."

"Your Highness." Desiree curtseyed automatically, which made Princess Zafirah laugh, but not in a mean way.

"My dear." A hand touched her elbow to help her get up. "Please, we do not curtsey here. It's a quaint British tradition, but not something we practice in Zhobghadi."

"Er ... should I bow then?"

"That would be more proper, but under the circumstances, we can be more casual." Princess Zafirah raised a brow at her nephew. "I'm so terribly sorry for what has happened to you. To be attacked like ..." She gave a shudder.

Deedee turned to Prince Karim, her brows furrowing together. What had he told his aunt? "I'm quite all right now," she assured the older woman.

"Aunt Zafirah is one of the most trusted members of the royal family," Prince Karim declared. "She will keep your presence here a secret."

Princess Zafirah nodded. "The old ways ... they have their uses, but they are so pedantic that there are no exceptions, even in the dire circumstance. I've always said they could use some updating." She laughed. "When I was younger, many thought I was too radical and non-conformist, especially when I insisted on learning to speak English, French, and German. 'What use are those outside languages to us?' my father would say. But now, everyone in the royal family knows these languages."

"You were always very forward-thinking, Aunt Zafirah. Now," he placed a hand on her shoulder. "I trust you have cleared this wing of servants for the day?"

"Yes, I told them that no one was to go in and out of the family rooms. The meals have all been prepared, and the boy will be the one to bring them up."

"Thank you, Aunt Zafirah." He leaned down to kiss her on the cheek. "The troops await. I will see you later."

Deedee didn't know to whom he meant to say that to, and maybe her brain really was fried, because it made her shiver.

Princess Zafirah turned to her. "Now, Desiree—"

"Deedee."

"Excuse me?"

"Please, call me Deedee, Your Highness. Everyone does."

"Except Karim."

She shrugged. "Have you ever tried to make him do something?"

"Unfortunately, yes," the princess said with mirth. "All right, but then you must call me Zafirah."

"But—"

"Bah," she said with a wave of her hand. "If I am to be your only companion for the next week, then it would be good if we start on more friendly terms. As far as I am concerned, you are a guest. It was not your fault you were brought here."

"Why are you doing this?" The question came out of nowhere, but Deedee couldn't help asking it. Zafirah seemed nice and wouldn't hurt a fly. But Deedee felt like her world had turned topsy-turvy, and she didn't know who to trust.

"Because my future king asked me to," she replied bluntly. "But also, because I am an old woman and growing bored." She sighed. "After I gave birth to my son, my duty and destiny were fulfilled. And since I have been widowed for decades, there's not much use for an old woman like me."

"I'm sorry. About your husband. And I don't think there's no use for—"

"Oh, don't you mind me. I'm just a silly old lady." Her smile brightened, before dimming again when she frowned. "Oh dear, did my nephew not find you any proper clothes?"

"Er ..." Heat bloomed in her cheeks, and she clutched the robe tighter. Dressed in Karim's clothes, she felt like a hobo, especially compared to the princess, who wore a beautiful dark blue tunic dress with silver embroidery and loose pants. "Mine were ... destroyed." Zafirah hadn't mentioned anything about her being a shifter so maybe Prince Karim didn't reveal her secret.

Zafirah tsked, then cocked her head toward the plates on the coffee table. "Have some breakfast first. I'll be right back."

As the older woman left the room, Deedee sat down on the couch, and reached for the pot of tea, pouring a cup for herself and nibbled on some freshly-baked bread. So now, one more person knew of her current predicament. Prince Karim wasn't stupid, so he wouldn't have told his aunt about Deedee if she really couldn't trust her. And Zafirah seemed nice enough ...

"Here we are." The princess breezed into the room; her arms piled with green fabrics. "These were mine when I was much younger. They may be a tad short for you, but it should fit."

Deedee took the offered clothing. "Thank you. I'll go put them on."

A few minutes later, she emerged from the bedroom. "Are you sure I can borrow these? They seem way to nice for just lounging around all day." Before putting it on, she thought it would be the same outfit Zafirah had, but it turned out to be a kaftan-like dress that fell mid-calf with gold embroidery around the torso and chest.

"You look stunning, my dear," Zafirah exclaimed. "I knew this would suit you." She motioned to the couch. "Come, let's finish our tea and then I will take you to the library."

"Oh!" She clapped her hands together. "That would be great. I've been so bored here." She took the empty spot on the couch next to Zafirah. "Thank you so much. I'm really about to go crazy in here."

"I completely understand." The older woman poured herself some tea. "I have lived my whole life in here."

Deedee was about to drink from her cup, but stopped

halfway. "Wait a minute ... you've never gone outside the palace?" What kind of place was this?

Zafirah laughed. "Oh, you misunderstand. I have been all over Zhobghadi, once or twice to one of our neighboring countries or when we meet with the nomadic tribes." She put the cup to her lips and looked at Deedee from over the rim. "I can leave if I wish, but where would I go? My life is here, watching over my son. He is grown, a man over forty years of age, and is the Royal Vizier, but still, I am his mother, and I cannot leave him. And of course, if I were to go, the Princess Amaya would be left alone as well."

Princess Amaya? Her heart clenched at the name of another woman. A woman who apparently lived in this palace. With Karim.

"Prince Karim is very busy, and will be even busier when he is king." Zafirah put the cup down. "Princess Amaya will be even lonelier."

I bet. She chewed on the inside of her cheek so hard she tasted the coppery tang of blood.

"She's his only *sister*," Zafirah said with an emphasis on the last word, "and does not get much company outside her tutors."

"Sister?" He never mentioned having a sister. Not that they'd had much time for getting-to-know-you questions.

"Yes. Half sister, actually. She's only eleven years old." Zafirah offered her a plate with bread, cheese, and honey. "Why don't you finish your food, and we can be on the way?"

"Thank you." As she ate her breakfast, Deedee couldn't help but wonder about Prince Karim's sister. Ten seemed so young to have lost her father. But where was her mother? And for that matter, where was his?

When she told Zafirah she was done eating, the princess led her out of the living room. "Don't worry," she had assured Deedee. "I've instructed the staff that no one was to come in this wing of the palace, except for when Ramin brings us our noon meal."

They walked down a few hallways, which were all similar to the ones Deedee had seen during her attempted escape. Zafirah stopped at the end of one particularly long hallway and opened the door. "This is the king's personal library."

As they entered, Deedee couldn't help but gasp. Though the room wasn't very big, it was richly decorated. Rows of shelves occupied most of the room, while a small sitting area was set up on the opposite side, with thick carpets and cushions, but also couches and chairs. "It's beautiful."

"My late brother, King Nassir, did love to read. He loved knowledge of all kinds, really." Zafirah turned her face away from Deedee as she ran a hand down a well-worn leather wingback chair.

Poor Zafirah. She didn't want to show the grief in her face, which was why the older woman was still looking away. Deedee couldn't even imagine what it was like to lose a close family member. Why, if it were Bastian or Wyatt ... despite the shortcomings of her younger brothers, especially that pompous youngest brother of hers, she didn't want to think of what it would be like if they were suddenly gone.

"Nassir was also very radical for his time. He was always speaking out about opening our borders and such, much to the consternation of our father. He, on the other hand, was very much rooted in the old ways." Zafirah gestured for her to follow her to a row of shelves at the other end of the room.

"Here you will find books in languages other than Zhobghadian. They were from Nassir's personal collection."

"Thank you." She looked at the books and found a few in English. Her French and German, unfortunately, were too rusty to even begin reading in those languages for pleasure.

There were mostly classics on the shelves—Shelley, Dickens, Shakespeare, Carrol, and much to her surprise, Mark Twain and Joseph Conrad. She grabbed a copy of *A Connecticut Yankee in King Arthur's Court*, because, *why not*, and then headed to one of the comfortable couches in the main reading area. Zafirah had also picked up a book—a title in Zhobghadian—sat regally on the leather wingback chair. There was a mysterious smile on her lips, which made Deedee curious as to what she was reading.

A few hours had passed and Deedee was lost in the world of King Arthur until the door swung open. As she looked up from her book, she saw Ramin enter the room, carrying a large tray.

"Ramin." She placed her book down and walked over to him. "I'm so sorry about what happened the other day."

The young man looked up at her, obvious hurt in his eyes, and Deedee felt about two inches tall. "I didn't mean to hurt you. I mean, I sorta did but ..."

Ramin ignored her and began arranging the plates on the table.

"Will you translate for me, please?" she asked Zafirah. "Tell him I'm deeply sorry for hurting him, and I'm glad to see he has recovered. And that I'm still grateful he rescued me from ... from that man who tried to hurt me."

The older woman nodded and spoke to Ramin. His body grew stiff, but turned to Deedee and gave her a slight nod.

However, he did make a big deal of taking the silver tray with him as he left.

"I suspect he hasn't forgiven me," Deedee said glumly.

"Give him time," Zafirah said. "He's very much like Karim you know. I'm sure one of the reasons Karim took him was because he saw much of himself in the boy. That, and the fact that both their mothers—" Zafirah stopped short. "We should eat before the food gets cold."

His mother what? Deedee desperately wanted to know more, but was afraid to pry. In any case, what use was it to know about Prince Karim's mother? Soon, she'd be leaving this place.

After lunch, Deedee continued to read, and by the time she reached the end, the sun was already low. "Wow, I don't think I've ever spent a day just reading. This almost feels like a vacation."

Zafirah closed her book. "Perhaps it's better for you to think of it that way. Like ... one of those retreats where you are forced to withdraw from the world to examine yourself."

Deedee got up and stretched her hands over her head. "I suppose that's one way to view it, rather than being trapped in a foreign country because of freaky weather. Zafirah, may I take another book so I can read with me in bed?"

"Of course. Karim said that you were free to borrow any book in the library."

"Thank you." She walked back to the row of shelves Zafirah had brought her to and returned her book, then began to scan the spines. Mary Shelley's *Frankenstein* caught her eye, but it was on the highest shelf, which she could only reach by tiptoeing, despite her height. Her fingers brushed the end of the cover.

C'mon ... ah. Her forefinger hooked the underside of the spine, but when she pulled, it sent the book—and several others—tumbling down over her head. "Ow!"

"Deedee?" Zafirah called. "Are you all right?"

Oops. "Yes," she called out as she got to her feet and grabbed Frankenstein, along with some of the other fallen books. Placing them under her arm, she walked back out to meet Zafirah. "Okay, I'm ready. Are we going to have dinner first?" She rather liked the older woman, and if she got to spend a few hours with her, the next few days would pass by much quickly.

"My apologies, my dear." She placed her hand over her heart. "But I'm afraid as a member of the royal family, I have duties during the evening festivities. But your dinner should be ready for you back in Karim's rooms."

"Oh."

"He will not be back until dawn, so you will have some privacy before then."

"The festivities go on until dawn? Must be some party."

Zafirah's face turned serious. "Yes, there are parties, and Karim must make his appearances. But then at midnight, he must take the shape of The Great One and fly all over Zhobghadi."

From the older woman's tone and expression, it was obvious that the fact that Deedee knew her nephew turned into a giant fire-breathing dragon wasn't a surprise. In fact, she sounded almost reverent. "So ... Prince Karim flies over the entire country from midnight until dawn?"

"Yes. It is tradition. Every bearer of The Great One has been doing it for a millennium."

She remembered him telling her the story about how they

were saved from invaders. "So, they recreate the events from a thousand years ago?"

"I suppose you can say that. Since the gods send the Easifat each year, so The Great One must also watch over our nation. And he will do so until the sandstorms subside."

Huh, so that's where he was every night. Flying over his kingdom, protecting it. A tiny part of her was glad that that's how he spent his nights, and not in the arms of some woman.

She mentally shook her head. Where did that come from?

"Were you satisfied with the selection of books here?" Zafirah asked.

"Oh yes. I'm sure I'll be pretty occupied." She paused. "Is the history of Zhobghadi written down anywhere? Do you think you could translate some of the texts for me?" When Zafirah gave her strange look, she added, "I specialize in Archeology. So all this is fascinating to me."

Zafirah raised a dark brow. "I suppose I could, but I must warn you: there is nothing about The Great One in our written texts."

"Why not?"

"For the protection of Zhobghadi and the royal family of course," she said matter-of-factly. "The story is passed down orally, all schoolchildren know it. But it is not written down officially."

Deedee said nothing as Zafirah led her back to Prince Karim's rooms. As she promised, her dinner was already there—if the scent of spiced grilled meats, buttery pilaf rice, and warm fresh bread wafting into her nose was any indication. "Oh, that's really good."

"We have some of the best chefs in the country," Zafirah

said. "Now, Deedee, I must bid you goodnight, and I will see you tomorrow."

She thanked Zafirah as she left, then sat down cross-legged in front of the low table to eat her dinner. As she bit into some bread, she tried to think more positive thoughts.

Really, it was like a holiday—albeit a forced one. She was in a beautiful palace, could sit and do nothing the whole day, have delicious food brought to her, and she also had a handsome prince in bed.

The last sentence made her choke on her rice and she had to gulp down a whole glass of water to clear her airway. *Don't think of him,* she chided herself. To distract herself, she reached for the pile of books she had taken from the library, grabbing the first one on top.

"Huh." She held up the leather-bound volume, which didn't have a title on the spine or the cover. It did, however, had some kind of coat of arms embossed on the front in silver depicting two eagles on top and a sword going through a shield. Placing it on her lap, she opened it to the cover page.

"*The History and People of Zhobghadi,*" she read aloud. "By Lord Nigel Brandon, Earl of Crawford." The date on the bottom of the type-written page was over thirty years ago. But Zafirah said there was no text about Zhobghadi in English. Did she lie?

She flipped through the pages, and based on the age and quality of the paper and printing, this was more of a manuscript than a published book. That's probably why Zafirah didn't know about it.

As she ate her dinner, she began to read through Lord Crawford's manuscript. While most people probably wouldn't have thought it riveting dinner time reading, Deedee couldn't stop. The Earl of Crawford was obviously a trained anthropologist, and his writing was so organized, yet vivid and descriptive. It seemed he either learned to speak Zhobghadi or had a translator, because half his manuscript was devoted to the events of the last five hundred years, though as Zafirah had said, there was no mention of The Great One.

She flipped through the rest of the book, and based on his outline in the table of contents, Lord Crawford must have spent years on this manuscript, because he was able to devote pages and pages to the people of Zhobghadi and the workings of their society.

Lord Crawford had really done a great job, especially at tracing back the history of Zhobghadi. For one thing, he had noted that the way they counted time and dates was different. For example, that when people said "a thousand years" it just really means a very long time ago, which made her wonder: when Karim told her that The Great One came to them a 'thousand' years ago, did he mean that literally or was it actually way older?

She was deep into how the first Zhobghadians processed the silver found in the deposits deep in the mountain range in the southern border when a loud roar made her start, the book dropping to the carpeted floor with a muffled thud. The hairs on her arms and the back of her neck stood on end and she knew why.

Dashing toward the balcony, she stood outside, and saw him—Karim—his massive scaly body casting a shadow over the palace as he flew by. Though she'd seen her own father transform into his dragon many times, the sight of Karim still made her shiver.

What would he do if he found out that there was another dragon like him?

It didn't matter because he wouldn't. No, she would make sure that her secret—and that of her family and clan—would be kept safe. They were counting on her.

With a loud yawn, she stood up and walked to the bedroom. After showering and changing into a fresh set of pajamas, she crawled into bed with Lord Crawford's manuscript. She must have been more tired than she thought because a few pages in and her eyes were drooping. After tucking the book under her pillow, she laid her head on top of it and closed her eyes.

———

Deedee was having a dream about a tall British man with a monocle, dressed like he was going on safari, traipsing about the sand dunes, shouting, "I found it! Gads, I found it!" Then his face turned into a piñata for some reason and then a mariachi band started playing ...

"Huh?" Her eyes fluttered open. *What a strange dream.* "*Oh.*"

Oh indeed.

Arms like bands of steel wrapped around her waist. And warm lips were clamped to her neck, the soft hairs of Karim's beard tickling her as his mouth roamed over her neck. *Not again.*

Her wolf yowled with happiness, practically rolling over and showing its belly as his hands reached up to cup her breasts. *Tramp.*

But really, maybe *she* was the tramp because she was enjoying this far too much.

"Karim," she whispered when his thumb and forefinger found her nipple. He responded by sinking his teeth into her neck, and lust and heat shot straight into her belly. Karim must also have an enhanced sense of smell because the moment she felt the wetness between her thighs, he growled and rolled over her, pinning her body, mouth covering hers.

Oh, maybe she should just stop fighting it. They were consenting adults, and she had a week of nothing better to do. She wanted him too—badly—and maybe this was her one chance to finally rid herself of her virginity. Besides, when else was she going to have a chance to sleep with a handsome prince who would make every fantasy she didn't know she had come true?

The nip at her lips told her that Karim was not happy that she was lost in her thoughts and unresponsive. So, she opened her mouth, allowing him to dip his tongue between her lips. Oh dear, he even *tasted* hot. Hot and masculine and all ... Karim. His hips ground to hers, and the hardness pressing against her heated core made her groan.

A hand thrust into her hair, pulling her head back to open her mouth more. He kissed her, devoured her like a man who had been lost in the desert without water and she was an oasis.

"*Karim!*"

Deedee froze, and so did Karim. The high-pitched voice wasn't someone's she'd heard before, but based on the soft curses that he bit out, he knew who it was.

Quickly, he rolled off her and the bed, his hand reaching

for his robe. "What are you doing here? You know not to come into the rooms of the Crown Prince without invitation."

The other person replied in Zhobghadian, sounding annoyed.

"You know you must practice English when you are speaking with me, German with Aunt Zafirah, and French with Arvin. Now, tell me why you think you can just come in here?"

"I haven't seen you in so long." The words were slow and deliberate, tinted heavily with an accent, and the voice young and feminine.

"That's not an excuse."

"But Karim—"

"No buts," Karim said. "No excuses, no exceptions, not even for a princess of Zhobghadi."

It was Karim's sister. *Princess Amaya.* She bit her lip and shut her eyes tight. Maybe if she kept still, the princess wouldn't notice her.

"Why haven't you—oh! What's that in your bed?"

Despite the cool temperature, a bead of sweat formed on her forehead. *Oh no.*

"Amaya?" Karim exhaled. "Amaya, get away—no!"

"I knew it!" Princess Amaya exclaimed. "I followed Ramin and he keeps bringing food up here. When I saw him leave your rooms this morning, I came in. What are you hiding in your bed? Did you finally get me that puppy I've been asking for?"

A puppy? Well, considering what she was—

"Amaya—no!"

But it was too late. The covers pulled away from her body. Slowly, she opened her eyes.

Standing next to the bed was a young girl, maybe ten or eleven years old. She was dressed in a similar tunic and pants as Zafirah had been wearing, but in a soft pink color. Her light brown hair was loose and matted, like she had just woken up from sleep, while her eyes and mouth were wide open.

"Hello!" she greeted, her voice pitching higher in excitement. "Karim! Did you bring a friend home? Why didn't you tell me? Oh, she's so pretty." Amaya jumped on the bed and peered closer at Deedee. She began to twitter in Zhobghadian as she tried to touch Deedee's hair.

"Amaya, stop, I order you," Karim commanded, making the young girl freeze.

As Amaya's face fell, Deedee felt sympathy for the young girl. "Prince Karim," she said, giving him the stink eye. "It's all right. I don't mind."

"But—"

"Your Highness." Deedee helped Amaya off the bed and she did a little curtsey. "My name is Deedee Creed from New York. It's nice to meet you."

"New York?" Her eyes went wide. "I've always wanted to see New York! The Big Apple!" Turning to Prince Karim, she said. "Why is your friend sleeping here? We have so many guest rooms." Her eyes lit up. "Oh, can she sleep in my room tonight? Please?" She tugged at Deedee's hand. "I have so many stuffed animals. You can choose any one of them to sleep next to. I'm sure you'd much prefer that than sleeping next to my brother. He snores."

"Uh ..."

"No, she will not be sleeping in your room," Karim said. "She will stay here."

"But why not?" Amaya whined. "Why do you get to keep her? I want to play with her too!"

Deedee felt her face flush, thinking that Karim and Amaya had two very different definitions of *playing*. "Um, I'm afraid I need to stay here, Princess," she soothed. "You see I'm ... er, you can't tell anyone I'm here."

Amaya cocked her head. "So, it's a ... secret?"

"Yes, Amaya," Prince Karim said as he came closer. He knelt down to her level. "A royal secret. So only you and me and Aunt Zafirah can know. We need to protect Deedee."

"Oh." Her eyes went wide. "Someone wants hurt her?"

"Yes," Deedee supplied. Technically the truth.

"You came here to hide from some bad people? And my brother is protecting you?"

That, she didn't have the heart to lie about, so she was glad when Prince Karim spoke. "You are so smart, little one. Now, you will go back to your rooms and never speak a word to—"

"No!" Amaya's pretty little face scrunched up and she stamped her foot on the floor.

"No?" Prince Karim stood up to full height, towering over the girl.

"No!" Her mouth curled up into a smile. "I want to spend the day with her, so she can tell me about New York and America."

"Amaya, no—"

"Please?" Amaya grabbed her brother's hand and looked up at him with her big dark eyes. "For me, brother?"

It was obvious from the way Karim's broad shoulders sank that he was giving in, and Deedee's heart went flip-flop the moment she saw his tough exterior crumble down. He ran his fingers through his hair, muttered something under his breath, then nodded.

"*Wheee!*" She hugged Karim. "This is better than a puppy."

"She's not a pet, Amaya," Karim groused.

"I know." She looked up at Deedee with those great big eyes that seemed to take up half her small face. "Even better. She is a friend."

A pang of something hit her in the heart—what kind of lonely existence did this little girl lead? "I'd be happy to be your friend, Your Highness."

"Hooray! Do you like playing with dolls and animals?" she asked.

"Amaya," Prince Karim began. "Will you go to the living room? I need a moment with Deedee."

"But—"

"It's all right, sweetheart," Deedee urged. "We'll be right out."

Amaya hesitated, but nodded and turned toward the door. When she disappeared into the living room, Karim closed the door.

"Well, I really should get dressed." Deedee made her voice as casual as possible as she tried to breeze past him.

He was too quick, however, and grabbed her forearm. "Desiree."

The rough sleep-hewn quality of his voice made her knees weak. She swallowed hard. "Yes, Your High—oh!" She was pulled against his hard body, and all the air rushed out from her body.

"Had we not been interrupted ..." His mouth pressed against the side of her forehead, branding her.

"But we were," she said weakly. When he tipped her head back, she couldn't help but look up into those cerulean blue eyes and get lost in them.

"Next time, we won't be." There was a promise in his eyes that made a dizzying current run through her.

"I look forward to it."

That seemed to stun him enough to let her go. Deedee walked as normally as she could to the bathroom, but she really wanted to do a victory dance. For one, she finally found a way to shock him, if the way his blue eyes turned a dark silver were any indication. And for another .... well maybe this *vacation* was finally about to get enjoyable.

CHAPTER EIGHT

I LOOK FORWARD TO IT.

All day, the words had repeated in Karim's mind when he had a moment. Gods above and below, not even when he had one to spare could he forget it.

I look forward to it.

He couldn't remember if a woman had ever had this effect on him. In fact, he couldn't even recall any of the women he had before. He was sure of one thing: None of them brought him to his knees with five simple words.

I look forward to it.

Had he not had a full day or if Amaya had not been in the other room, she wouldn't have had anything to look forward to because he surely would have ravished her right then and there.

Of course, she was no ordinary woman. She was not even human at all. Apparently, she also transformed into a beast. A beautiful one, but a beast nonetheless. Like him. Was that why she was so alluring? Did she possess some magic to enchant him?

The Great One growled in displeasure. *Claim them. Now.*

Patience, he told his beast. Desiree Creed was not a woman who deserved a rough tumble. No, he was going to enjoy her delectable body, explore every inch of her, make her moan out in mindless desire until they were both sated.

And then he would do it all over again.

"Your Highness?"

"What?" he snapped at his secretary, Mustafa. When the young man gulped, Karim sighed. "I was deep in my thoughts. Apologies."

"None necessary, Your Highness," Mustafa replied quickly. "But you did call me in here. Was there anything else you needed."

Karim glanced toward the clock. "Do we have any more appointments for the day?"

"None, but there are some people who wanted—"

"Good." He stood up. "I'm done for the day."

"Done, Highness?"

"Yes. I'll be having supper in my rooms. Make sure I am not disturbed."

"Of course." Mustafa bowed and placed his hand over his heart. "Have a good evening, Your Highness."

Oh yes, I will. He relished the thought as he headed toward the residential wing and took the steps to his rooms two at a time. It was still hours before he had to make his flight. What better way to while the time away than in the arms of a willing, beautiful woman?

His blood was on fire by the time he entered the door to his suite. His cock twitched in anticipation. He would strip her of every bit of clothing and—

"Oh hail, the King, Amenhotep the Third!"

Amaya. The familiar, youthful squeal was enough to douse the flames of his desire. For now. With a deep sigh, he strode into the room and headed straight to the middle of the living area where two figures sat on the carpet.

The low table had been pushed to the side, and various stuffed animals and dolls had been laid out all over the floor. Neither Desiree nor Amaya had noticed his presence, so he remained silent as he watched them.

"And now," Amaya's voice had turned solemn. "King Amenhotep is dead, and so we must prepare him for his mummification and burial in the great pyramid. Prepare the canopic jars!"

"Yes, High Priestess." Desiree handed Amaya three plastic teacups, which his sister accepted with a reverent nod. Picking up a fork, she raised it in the air. "I will now heat the hook, insert it into his nose, and take out the brain—"

"Ahem."

Two heads turned toward him. Desiree was suppressing a smile, but the blush on her cheeks made her embarrassment evident. His sister, on the other hand, brightened when she realized he was there.

His sister waved him over. "Karim, you are just in time."

"In time for what, little one?"

"For the mummification of King Amenhotep the Third." Amaya gestured to the toy giraffe by her feet, laying on its side with a cloth over its eyes. "We're getting to the best part."

"You mean, where you pull his brains through his nose with a hot poker?"

"Exactly," Amaya cackled.

He moved toward them, removing his shoes as he walked

over the carpet. "And how many mummifications have you done today?"

Her brows wrinkled and then she turned around. Behind her were several more dolls and stuffed animals, wrapped up in what appeared to be toilet paper. "Let's see ... Ramses the Second, Ramses the Third, Akhenaten, Hatshepsut, and ... Thutmose the Third." She turned to Desiree. "Did I get the names right, Deedee?"

"You did, Your Highness, good job," Deedee said proudly.

"You taught my sister how to mummify a body?" Karim asked.

"Er, I was telling her about ancient Egyptians and then ..." Her cheeks flushed. "Our little lessons just kind of ran away. I'm sorry—"

"Well, looks like you've got quite the talent, Amaya." His sister beamed. "You should be, er, proud."

"Oh, thank you, Karim!" She rushed over to him, then dragged him toward their little circle of toys, and pulled at him to sit down. "We're not done yet. We can't let King Amenhotep be buried without his organs. He'll never make it to the underworld."

"Of course we can't," he said in a serious tone. "Now, High Priestess, tell me what I need to do."

As they went through the ritual, Karim did his best to pay attention to his sister, but he couldn't help but glance over at Desiree. She seemed quite proud of her little pupil, but when their gazes met, she blushed furiously and turned away. Had she changed her mind about them? He sincerely hoped not.

They were burying Amenhotep in his great pyramid—in

this case it was Amaya's toy box turned over—when the door opened and Zafirah entered. "My, my, what's going on here?"

"Aunt Zafirah!" Amaya greeted. "Come, I want to show you something."

"Er, maybe you can show her something else," Desiree said, her tone embarrassed.

Karim was not surprised his aunt had come. This morning he spoke with her and told her about the situation with Amaya, and she didn't seem worried. "She is a child," Zafirah had said. "And even if she spoke about Deedee, no one would believe her."

"Actually, I am here to let you know that dinner is ready."

"Ready?" Karim asked.

Zafirah's gaze darted to Desiree, then to him. "Since you have no official duties tonight, I thought it might be nice if you had dinner with Amaya and Deedee in the private dining room."

He frowned, not wanting to share Desiree. Not tonight. "I don't think—"

"Oh, Karim, can we, please?" Amaya begged.

"But—"

His sister turned those pretty dark eyes up at him again, like she was some kitten or lost puppy and, curse the gods, it worked on him every time. "Fine. No need to follow my wishes." He huffed out. "I am only crown prince after all."

His sister's squeal of delight and her small arms wrapping around his neck as she jumped toward him, however, made it all worth it.

"Since you will be dining out," Zafirah began. "I thought you might want to wear something more appropriate." She handed Desiree a bundle of yellow cloth. "There are slippers in there too. Now, Princess, let's get you dressed up for dinner, shall we? Karim, why don't you escort Deedee to dinner. Say, in twenty minutes?"

"Of course, Aunt Zafirah."

"I—thank you. I should get dressed so we won't be late." Desiree said, before she headed into the bedroom.

Karim raised a brow questioningly at his aunt, but the older woman merely gave him a mysterious smile. "You seem presentable enough," she said. "But do comb your hair. It looks like you've been pulling at it the whole day."

Yes, with frustration, he said silently. "I'll see you at dinner, Aunt Zafirah."

"Of course." She bowed her head and then offered her hand to Amaya. "Come along, Princess."

Karim sat down on the couch as he waited for Desiree to emerge from the room. Minutes ticked by like hours, and he could hardly sit still.

How had he come to this? All he wanted was for her to stay put for a few days. Then this morning, things had changed, and he thought an understanding had passed between them and that tonight—

"Uh, I hope this is okay."

Merciful mother Nammu.

Desiree looked at him shyly as she stood in the doorway. The traditional kaftan she wore covered most of her, but somehow, the way it clung to her curves made her even more alluring. The yellow was a contrast to her caramel hair and light eyes, making her skin glow. There was something missing ...

Jewels. Gold. A voice inside his head rumbled. *Adorn her.*

Yes, she needed to be draped in jewelry. Maybe even just jewelry as she lay naked on his bed and—

"Prince Karim?" She cocked her head to the side. "Did I put it on backwards or something?"

"No, no." He stood up and cleared his throat. "You look ..." What word could do her justice at this moment? "Perfect."

The blush under her fading tan deepened. "Th-thank you."

"We should go," he offered her his arm and gestured toward the door. "I'm hungry." *But not for food.*

———

Karim couldn't remember the last time he'd seen Amaya so happy. In fact, he didn't know the last time he'd enjoyed a meal so much, and he wasn't talking about the food. Aunt Zafirah had gone all out, preparing the finest Zhobghadian dishes, but he couldn't quite concentrate on the meal, not when Desiree sat opposite him looking like some goddess in her yellow tunic, her hair tumbling down her shoulders, her eyes sparkling as she spoke.

"What most people think of when they say American Indians are usually the Crow or *Apsáalooke,*" Desiree said when Zafirah asked her about American tribes. They had been having a discussion about archeology, and his aunt had been interested about the Native American civilizations. "They lived in teepees made of buffalo or elk hide, wore moccasins and feather headdresses. But there are so many indigenous people and tribes all over the Americas. They lived anywhere from caves to houses made of red clay."

"Such a rich history," Zafirah commented.

"Do they also practice mummification?" Amaya asked.

"Amaya ..." Karim warned. "I don't think that is proper conversation for the dinner table."

"But, Karim," Amaya whined.

"I think your brother is right," Desiree said. "But tomorrow, I'll tell you about the Aztec mummies."

"Really?" The young girl seemed mollified when Desiree nodded. "I will remind you so you don't forget."

"Maybe it's time we give Desiree a rest," Karim said. "She's been telling you so many stories non-stop."

"I don't mind," she replied. "I rarely get such an enraptured audience."

"Why don't we tell Desiree a story?" Amaya suggested. "I ... oh!" She clapped her hands together. "I know, how about I tell you the story of the The Great One?"

Karim was going to protest, but when he saw her face and his sister's face light up, he didn't have the heart.

"A wonderful idea," Zafirah said. "You can use the murals to tell the story."

"Murals?" Desiree asked.

Amaya stood up from her seat at the low table and gestured around her. "See? The murals around you, painted in the walls."

Desiree's plump lips opened, and her head swung around. "Oh my. I didn't notice ..." Her face turned into an expression of curiosity, and he could practically see the cogs in her head moving as she soaked in the murals. He had to admit, to see her like this, so caught up in history and knowledge, was strangely turning him on. But then again, everything about her incited lust in him.

"The murals start there." Amaya pointed to the east wall. "And move this way." Her hand moved around in a counter-clockwise moment. "Tell her, Karim."

Desiree fixed her gaze on the east wall where there was a painting of a walled city. It looked like shadows were climbing the walls.

Karim hesitated for a moment, but he supposed it wouldn't be so bad, to tell her the story. Clearing his throat, he began. "One thousand years ago, a plague had arrived in Zhobghadi. The oubour, a race of monsters whose only purpose was to consume, came upon us. They were set to devour the entire nation when the gods answered our prayers."

In the next panel of the mural, three giant figures representing the Triad of Heaven—An, Enlil, and Enki—were depicted behind the walled city.

"Enki intervened on behalf of our people and pled to An and Enlil to help Zhobghadi. So, Enlil sent the Easifat that blew away the oubour." The next panel depicted swirls of sand surrounding the city, and the shadow monsters being tossed away.

"But the sand storms could only shield us, not destroy our enemies. And so An, the supreme god, sent his greatest weapon—The Great One." That portion of the mural showed the said god pointing to Zhobghadi and the form of a giant dragon flying toward them.

"The Great One is a spirit, but could not exist without a body. Prince Hammam, the oldest son of the king, volunteered to become the bearer of The Great One, and so he went through the ritual." The next panel was quite gruesome. It showed a man—Prince Hammam—strapped to a table as a priest in brown robes stood over him. The priest held up a curved knife in one hand that pierced Prince Hammam from left ring finger to his heart—the vena armoris. In the other hand, he held a jar where he poured a liquid over the wounds. "For thirty days and nights, the prince endured the ritual as his body and blood were infused with the spirit of the The Great One. After the ritual was completed, he became one with The Great One and defeated our enemies."

"Wait, let me tell the next part." Amaya interrupted. The last panel showed a giant dragon breathing fire and destroying the oubour. "And ever since then, the Easifat comes once a year and the bearer of The Great One flies over the entire nation to protect it." She brushed her palms together. "The End."

"That was a lovely story," Desiree said. "Well done, Your Highnesses."

"Indeed, a nice story," Zafirah agreed. "Now, how about dessert?" She stood up and took a silver tray from a table in the back, then lay it on the table.

On it was a baked pastry made of honey and nuts, a delicacy that was Karim's favorite. Of course, he could hardly concentrate on it when Desiree finished hers and licked the leftover honey from her forefinger. He groaned inwardly. *Marduk's beard,* did she have any idea what she was doing to him?

Finally, as they were having tea, Amaya let out a yawn.

"I think it's time for bed," Zafirah commented.

"But, Aunt Zafirah—" Amaya's eyes drooped as she let out another yawn.

"You need to be up early tomorrow for lessons," Karim said.

"Lessons?" she whined. "But I wanted to spend the day with Deedee again."

"Oh no, little one," Karim said. "Tomorrow is the start of the school week. So, lessons it is for you."

Amaya let out a cry. "Please, please, can I not have lessons just for tomorrow?"

"How about you come after lessons?" Desiree suggested. "And I can tell you more about those Aztec mummies then."

Amaya looked up at Karim with those big camel eyes, and before he knew it, he said, "Of course you may."

His sister let out a whoop of triumph. "Can you tuck me into bed, Karim? Please."

"Of course." It had been a long while since he had done that. In fact, he couldn't remember the last time Amaya asked to be tucked in. *Probably before Father died.* Nassir had doted on her as much as he did, after all.

"I'll take Deedee back to your rooms," Zafirah said.

"Thank you." He nodded to both women and then took Amaya's hand as he led her back to her quarters. Her room was all the way at the other end of the residential wing, and she was getting so sleepy that he carried her in his arms all the way. Again, he couldn't remember the last time he had done this, and of course, she was much bigger and heavier now.

He supposed for now, it was all right if she didn't brush her teeth before bed. He pulled back the covers of her bed, took her shoes off, then covered her with the blankets. "Good night, little one," he whispered as he kissed her forehead. Deep in sleep, his sister didn't stir.

Quietly, he crept out of her bedroom so as not to disturb her. As he made his way back to his rooms, anticipation thrummed in his veins. Was Desiree still looking forward to it?

The answer, perhaps, came in the form of the woman in question, who lay invitingly on top of the bed, still dressed in her alluring yellow gown. She was holding a large, leather-bound book, but as soon as he entered the room, she quickly put it down on her lap and looked up at him, those light eyes piercing right into him.

"Is she asleep?"

"Yes," he replied. "Thank you for indulging her today."

"My pleasure," she said. "Amaya is a bright child, so curious, and very mature for her age. You should be proud of her."

"She is used to the company of adults, and I do not think she has had a chance to be with other children. I sometimes wonder if I'm keeping her too sheltered." He drew closer, watching her face and enjoying the way her eyes subtly changed shades. "However, she still plays with toys and dolls. Surely, girls her age don't do that anymore?"

She let out a delicate snort. "If you ask me, kids these days are growing up way too fast. You'd be doing her a favor by letting her hold on to childhood for as long as possible. You should think about—"

"Desiree?"

"Yes?"

As he came nearer, he began to unbutton his tunic. "I don't really want to talk about my sister anymore."

"What—" Her eyes drew down to his chest, which was now exposed as he shrugged off his tunic. "*Oh.*"

A delicious blush grew in her cheeks, and he wanted to see more of that. *Everywhere.* He knelt on the mattress and crawled over to her, stopping as he loomed over her prone body. "Are you still looking forward to this?"

"Oh." The redness deepened. "Yes."

That was all the answer he needed. He swooped down, cupped her chin, and took her mouth with his. The urgency to have her was driving him to the edge, and he may have been too rough, but she didn't protest. Oh no, she kissed him back eagerly, met his lips with as much passion as he did. When her lips parted and he tasted her sweetness, he thought he would expire then and there.

His hands moved down the slim column of her neck, moving lower to the tops of her breasts. Reaching around, he fumbled, looking for a zipper or snaps, but there were none. How in Nabu's name did she get into this thing? And more important, how was he going to get her out?

She let out a needy moan, and so, unable to wait any longer, he ripped the damned thing right down the middle.

"Oh no!" she gasped, clutching her hands to her chest, attempting to put the torn cloth together again. "Your aunt will—"

"Shh." He put a finger on her mouth. "I told you, no more talk of my family."

Her mouth clamped shut. Good. He didn't want to hear her make another sound unless it was, *yes, Karim; more, Karim;* or *harder, Karim.*

He leaned back and pulled her hands away from her chest. That beautiful blush tinted her cheeks again, but he couldn't make himself turn away from her. The tanned skin ended just below her neck, and the rest of her was untouched by the sun. And her breasts ... they were generous, and he knew they were more than a handful for him, but he didn't realize how gorgeous they were or that her nipples were so large and pink.

Adorn her. The beast inside him said. *Claim her.*

Yes, gold and jewels would look good against her naked skin. Rose gold, maybe, to match those delicate nipples. A delicate chain with pink diamonds between her breasts. He traced a finger down between them, imagining it.

"Karim," she whimpered. Gods, his name on her lips—not Prince Karim or Your Highness, but just Karim—was like music to his ears.

"You are so beautiful," he said as he leaned down to capture a nipple in his mouth. The shiver she gave from such a simple touch made him preen like a peacock. He licked at the sensitive nub, feeling it harden. She squirmed underneath him, and her hands slid up his chest, fingers teasing him as she moved higher, digging her fingers into his shoulders to pull him closer. With a groan, he straddled her, capturing her thighs between his knees. His cock strained against his trousers, and so, to give himself some relief, pressed against the apex of her thighs. However, there was something else between them. Something else that was hard.

A protesting moan escaped her lips when he released her nipple. Looking down, he saw the book that was on her lap. Grabbing it, he had meant to toss it aside but then he froze when he saw the coat of arms embossed on the cover.

His blood cooled, and all thoughts of lust washed away. He didn't know how long he'd been staring at it, but it must have been long enough because she wiggled underneath him. "Is, uh, everything all right."

Is everything all right? How could she—

"Where did you get this?"

"Karim?" Her voice trembled. "What's wrong?"

He rolled off her and got to his feet, holding the book up. "I said *where did you get this?*"

Desiree scrambled to sit up on her knees, her hands crossing over her chest. "What do you mean? That?" She nodded to the book in his hand. "It was in your father's library."

"And you just took it?" He could barely hold on to the rage wanting to escape.

Her expression faltered. "Yes. I mean, you said I could borrow any book."

"But not this!" He wanted to toss the damned thing away. "How dare you?"

"I didn't know," she cried. "I'm sorry. I wouldn't have—"

He turned on his heel, the blood roaring in his ears blocking out her pleas as he slammed the door behind him when he flew into the living room. This damned book. The silver embossing of the crest seemed to wink at him in mocking. He knew what this was of course. What it *really* was. It wasn't Desiree's fault, but he couldn't stop the anger or the memories from flooding his mind.

The darkness of the room.

Moonlight pouring in through the balcony doors.

Fabric whipping in the wind.

Mum ... Mum ... please. No.

He closed his eyes, trying to block it all out. He tossed the book against the wall and dashed toward his balcony. The tightness in his chest was threatening to consume him, and he had to let it out.

He wasn't angry at Desiree. No, he was angry at *himself.* For taking things too far with her, letting his feelings run away. There was no way he was going to ... he just *couldn't* let that happen to her. To have her meet the same fate as his mother.

He called on The Great One. It wasn't happy with him; he could feel its displeasure. He knew what it wanted. Who it wanted. But he couldn't bring himself to give in.

"Go," he shouted into the wind. "Just go."

As the flames devoured him, he closed his eyes, allowing the beast to take over and take control of their body and mind, letting its fire devour his memories.

CHAPTER NINE

DEAR GOD, WHAT HAVE I DONE?

It took Deedee a moment to process her thoughts, but when the door slammed shut, she jumped out of bed and followed Karim out the door. When she saw the door to the balcony open and the loud roar that made her chest constrict, she knew that he was gone.

Sinking down to the carpet, she tried to make sense of what happened. One moment, they were in the throes of passion, and the next, he was hightailing it out of the room.

And all because of that book.

Because that had to be it, right? Karim wanted her, he was touching and kissing her all over until he saw that darned book.

Dejected, she marched back into the bedroom. She looked down at the tattered remains of her dress, wondering how she was going to explain it to Zafirah.

Her heart ached as she went to Karim's closet, trying to find something to wear for bed. Everything here reminded her of him, of course. And it smelled of him in here too. All masculine musk and warm sand. Her wolf yowled with unhappiness. She could sense its confusion too, and she tried her best to calm it. *I'm sorry, I don't know what happened either.*

She slipped off what remained of the dress and hid it under the growing pile of laundry in the corner. Then, she picked out a shirt and pair of boxers to wear and trod off to bed. Not that she could sleep, because all she could do was stare up into the empty ceiling.

No matter how much she thought about this whole thing, examined it, turned it around to look at every angle, she still couldn't figure out what happened. Why was it so bad she read that text? Were they really that xenophobic here that they didn't want anyone to know about their history and people? As far as she could tell, there was nothing about dragons in the manuscript.

She stayed up waiting for him. Lying on her side, she kept her eyes on the empty space next to her on the bed. Hours passed, and her eyelids grew heavy, but she fought sleep.

When dawn came and there was no sign of Karim, she just didn't have the energy to fight sleep. She woke in the same position some hours later with the sunlight streaming through the windows, and the empty spot next to her undisturbed. Regret weighed in her stomach like a heavy stone, but she forced herself to get up.

"Karim?" She padded out carefully into the living room, just in case he'd decided to sleep on the sofa. But, no, the living room was empty. As she sat down at the low tables, she saw that food had been set up, but the pot of tea had gone cold, so it obviously had been in there for a while. Not that she wanted to eat, because the thought of food made her stomach turn.

"Deedee. Finally, you are awake." Zafirah stood in the doorway, teapot in hand. "I brought some fresh tea."

"What time is it?"

"Ten o'clock."

That late? Well, she was up until dawn after all. Zafirah sat next to her and poured some tea into a cup. "Thank you," she murmured as she accepted the drink.

Zafirah was obviously hesitant as she said, "I hope you don't think I'm prying, but ... did anything ... significant happen last night after dinner?"

She stopped halfway as she was bringing the cup to her lips. "Huh?"

"It's just that ..." Zafirah folded her hands in her lap. "Karim ... Karim has asked that some of his things be moved into one of the guest quarters."

Her stomach lurched even more, and she put the cup down. "I ... I don't know, Zafirah." What could she say? Did the older woman already guess something was happening between her and Karim? She didn't seem surprised that they had been sharing his bedroom. Did she already think they were lovers?

"That's not all."

What more could there be? "What do you mean?"

Zafirah took a deep breath. "Karim said that no one was to see you except for Ramin, when he brings your meals. Not me. Not Amaya. She doesn't know it yet, but I know she will be upset. And the only reason I am here now is because I browbeat Ramin into letting me inside. I told him I would accept the consequences for defying Karim's orders."

And so that was how it was to be. She really was a prisoner now. Her throat constricted, but she refused to cry. Not in front of Zafirah and certainly not for *him*. But she at least deserved some answers, right? This might be her last chance. "Zafirah, do you know a Lord Nigel Brandon, Earl of Crawford?"

Zafirah's eyes grew wide, and she clasped a hand to her chest. "Where did you hear that name?"

Deedee told Zafirah about how she found the manuscript in the library and took it back with her to read. "And then last night when he ..." Hopefully Zafirah didn't see her blush, but she continued. "He saw me reading the book and he went crazy. He just ... he kind of froze, and it was like he'd seen a ghost." Her father had often described such a look as a "thousand-yard stare". He said it was common in veterans who returned from war zones. "Then he ran out and shifted into his dragon, and I haven't seen him since."

"Oh, my dear, it's not your fault." Zafirah placed a hand over hers. "I just ... I don't know how to begin. And I'm not even sure if it's my story to tell."

She could see the hesitation in Zafirah's face. "Please ... I just want to understand."

"All right." Zafirah looked around, as if there were other people she didn't want to hear. "Lord Crawford is ... Karim's grandfather."

Did she hear that correctly? "Grandfather?"

"Yes. He was an academic, just like you. Nassir wanted to learn about Western History, but our father, King Eshan, would not permit him to leave Zhobghadi to study it, and so he had Lord Crawford brought in. In exchange for tutoring Nassir, he was allowed to learn about our culture and possibly publish a book if my father was able to review his writing before final publication."

"So, your father didn't like what Lord Crawford wrote in his manuscript, which is why it wasn't published?"

"Not quite. You see, Lord Brandon had been here a few months and he hadn't gone back to England. He was missing his only family—a daughter, Grace. So she came to visit while she was on summer holiday. Nassir said he fell in love with her on the spot."

"Oh." She didn't realize Karim was part English.

"Nassir wanted to marry Grace, but Father forbid it. He said that Zhobghadi could not have a foreign queen. They fought about it, screaming at each other so loud that it was a wonder An himself didn't come down from above to complain at the noise."

"But your brother got his way."

Her face fell. "Only because our father died."

"Oh no. I'm sorry."

"It's ... it is what it is. But, anyway, since he was now king, Nassir could do whatever he wanted, and so he married Grace. Lord Crawford was ecstatic, of course, because now he had even more leeway to continue his research. They had Karim, and she was happy ... for a time."

Dread filled her. She didn't want to know, but at the same time ... "What happened?"

"They say ... they say she hated being queen. She was a great mother and wife, but she despised the trappings of royalty. And Nassir wanted to accomplish so much to establish his legacy—expand the silver exports, and maybe even open up Zhobghadi to foreigners. Queen Grace was lonely. Lord Crawford traveled back and forth between

England and Zhobghadi to meet with his publishers so he wasn't around much. Yes, she had Karim to take care of, but even then, he was always going to various tutors so he could be prepared to be king. So, she sought comfort in the arms of one of her personal guards."

Deedee covered her mouth in shock. "She cheated on Karim's father?"

"Yes ... and I'm sure you've heard the rumors. Most of them are ... true. She was caught with her lover, and Nassir was in a rage. He was about to confront her, but rather than face him, she threw herself off the balcony. Karim was there. He saw it all. And he was only eight years old."

"No!" She couldn't stop herself from crying out this time. That poor woman. Poor Karim. Was that what he was dreaming about when he cried out for his mother? Tears burned at her throat.

"Nassir was grief-stricken. He wouldn't ... he withdrew from everyone for weeks. And the scandal it caused ... Lord Crawford was bitter and angry over his daughter's death and blamed Nassir. He went back to England, but Nassir wouldn't let him take Queen Grace home to be buried or publish his manuscript. So, he talked to all the newspapers, talk shows, anyone who would listen to him. He insinuated that Nassir killed her in a jealous rage."

Desiree's instincts flared. There was something about the way Zafirah said it that seemed like there was a grain of truth there. *Ludicrous.* She shook the thought out of her head. "And so that's why Karim went crazy when he saw I had the book."

"Yes. Nassir had all of Lord Crawford's papers and books tossed away. I don't know how that book survived but ..." She sighed. "Karim ... he'd gone through so much, and Nassir never really recovered. He married again, but she was never elevated to queen, just consort. I think ... despite what she did, he still loved Grace."

Oh, that poor man. "What happened to her, the consort? That's Amaya's mother, right?"

"Fatima was in love with Nassir, despite their age difference. She was broken-hearted that Nassir would always see her as second best, and so when she became ill, she just couldn't fight. She died when Amaya was just three years old."

So much tragedy in one family. Amaya. Karim. "I think I understand." She brushed the tears from her cheeks with the back of her hand. "I just wish ... I wish I could tell him I'm sorry for opening those wounds again."

"He ... has carried them all his life, and he is strong. Perhaps he just needs time."

"Time," she echoed. "How many more days until the Easifat ends?"

"We should be halfway through, so maybe four or five days?"

"And he really doesn't want to see me?" she asked. The look on the other woman's face told her the answer she didn't want to hear. Her wolf yowled in despair. "Zafirah ... if you do see him, please tell him I'm sorry I upset him."

"I will try." The older woman stood up. "My time is running short. I wish you well, Deedee."

She stood up and embraced her. "You too, Zafirah. And tell Amaya ... tell her that I hope she does well in her lessons."

"I will be able to tell her that, at least. When she finds out that she has been forbidden to see you, she will be distressed."

Deedee didn't want that, but she didn't have any choice in the matter. "Goodbye, Zafirah. And thank you."

She gave Deedee a slight nod and then left the room. Now all alone, Deedee sank into the couch. Her "sentence" here was halfway over, but it seemed like a million years away.

She wanted to hate Karim for locking her up and leaving her alone like this. It wasn't like she wanted to hurt him and remind him of the past. But she couldn't bring herself to hate him. Not when all she could think about was the eight-year-old boy who had seen his mother plunge to her death. And she so desperately wanted to reach out and comfort him.

I'm a fool. It was better this way, for them to be apart before things got too out of hand. *Soon, I'll be home.* Maybe a few days in New York wouldn't be too bad. Her best friend, Astrid, should be giving birth any time soon, and she'd been pestering Deedee to come visit once the baby was born because she had been assigned as Godmother.

Yes, it would be nice to go home, to her house and her own bed. She could see her family and then put this whole thing behind her.

———

Despite everything that had happened, a small part of Deedee had some hope that maybe, *just maybe,* Karim would cool down and come to her again. However, as the day wore on and she spent it alone, it was getting more and more evident that he was not coming. When Ramin had come to clear the remains of her evening meal, she knew she would be spending the rest of her time here alone.

The young boy seemed even more angry at her now. She could see it in the stiffness of his stance and the way his lips pursed together tight whenever he came into the suite. Not that she cared much for what he thought. It was his fault anyway that she was here in the first place.

It was a good thing she had brought the other books with her from the library, so she at least had those to read for the next four or five days. Also, while she paced around the living area, she found Lord Brandon's manuscript on the floor where Karim had presumably tossed it. She couldn't bear to touch the vile thing, and so she left it where it was. *That Lord Brandon ...* sure he'd been grieving, but King Nassir was still his grandson's father. And Karim had seen his mother jump off the balcony, so the king couldn't have killed his wife, so she could only imagine how dreadful it was for him knowing his grandfather was spreading those lies.

There wasn't anything else to do after dinner, but she couldn't bring herself to go back to the bed she had shared with him. So, she curled up on the sofa with a blanket and read until her lids were heavy and she fell asleep.

It was sometime in the middle of the night she suddenly woke up. It was her wolf, yipping at her restlessly. What was going on? Her animal had been quiet and desolate all this time, and now it was excited.

No, not excited.

It was fear and worry. And she didn't know why, but she shot to her feet, her blood going cold.

And then she heard it. The loud shriek from a distance.

Karim!

"No, no, no, no." She dashed out onto the balcony, running all the way to the end. Her hands gripped the cement handrail until her knuckles grew white, her eyes searching.

There!

In the distance was a blur. A large silver one, falling down to the ground.

"Karim!" she cried, her heart twisting in horror. Dear Lord, what happened to him?

Her wolf howled in despair, and it was like her body went into overdrive. She dashed out toward the living room and toward the door. "Ramin!"

The young man had been sitting on the floor, leaning on the door so when she yanked it open, he fell over.

"Ramin!"

He let out an annoyed grunt as he rubbed his eyes with his hands.

"Ramin," she repeated, helping him to get up even as he glared at her. "I ... Karim ... he's in danger. He was in his dragon form, and he was flying and ..."

But he was just staring at her, his brows wrinkled in confusion. How was she going to make him understand her? "Please ... Ramin. It's Karim. Karim ... danger. Hurt!"

He cocked his head at her.

"We have to help him! I saw him falling!" She put her hands together like they were wings, making them fly across the air, then falling down.

He seemed to understand some of it, because he started chattering in an excited tone. Oh Lord, this was taking too long. "I'm sorry," she said. "I have to do this."

She pushed him aside with all her might and then dashed

away. Ramin's indignant yells echoed down the halls, but she paid him no mind. With her Lycan speed, she was able to outrun him anyway.

She tried her best to recall the path she had taken to escape the first time, but she had taken so many turns back then and didn't really do anything to keep track. Her best bet was to find an exit and figure out where he had fallen.

I can see the sun rising from the windows in the bathroom, she thought as she rounded the next corner. *If the balcony is directly in front of the living area then—*"Oomph!"

There was something solid in her way, and she staggered back. However, as she brushed her hair back from her face, she realized it wasn't a something. It was a *someone.*

The man in front of her was tall—not as tall as Karim, but still two or three inches taller than her. He had a shock of midnight hair on his head the same color as the thick beard that covered half his face, but his eyes were a light hazel. His face went from surprise, to shock and anger, as he spouted out a string of angry words.

"Please!" She held her hands up. "I don't have time to explain, but Karim's in trouble."

His mouth formed into a perfect O. "You are English?"

"American," she corrected. "I know about Karim and The Great One." He let out a snarl. "He was out for his nightly flight. I was looking out of the balcony, and I heard him cry out and saw him fall from the sky." She bit her lip, hoping he wouldn't ask her exactly how she saw and heard him from such a long distance.

"How did you ... wait, you say The Great One fell?"

She nodded.

His brows wrinkled. "I do not ... I cannot believe you. You are an outsider and you should not even be here."

"Please, I beg of you." She narrowed her eyes at him. There was something familiar about him. He had a similar facial structure to Karim, but those eyes ... "Ask Princess Zafirah."

His expression turned to hot anger and he seized her arm. "How do you know my mother?"

"Karim trusted her with my secret. She knows about me ... you can ask her. But it might be too late for Karim. We have to get to him, *now*." Urgency made that last word almost an inhuman growl. "I swear to you, I'm not lying."

The man hesitated for a moment. "If you are, then I will ensure you pay for it," he said through gritted teeth. "Where did you see him fall?"

Relief washed over her. "I was standing on the balcony outside Karim's rooms and he was far away ... that mountain range was behind him. I think it was south."

"Southwest," he murmured. "The Grand Balcony has a direct view of them. You say he fell between the capital city and those mountains?"

"Yes. What's in that area?"

His eyes went hard. "Nothing but vast amounts of sand."

Which meant no one would have known he was gone if she hadn't seen him fall. "Then we have to go. We can't waste any more time."

"Come." He tugged at her arm, leading her down the long hallway. Hopefully there would be no one around, but she didn't really care right now. All she wanted was for Karim to be safe.

They walked swiftly through the darkened palace, down

a maze of hallways and a large set of staircases. When they stopped outside a humungous metal door, he put his finger to his lips to indicate that she should stay silent, then pushed the door open and stepped inside.

Through the small crack, she saw him talk to two burly men. After exchanging a few words, the two men disappeared from her view. His head turned back, and he crooked a finger at her.

When she stepped inside, she realized this was some kind of garage. Several cars, ranging from luxury convertibles to hulking SUVs, were parked in a line.

The man was already walking toward one of the vehicles, and he pointed to the armored Humvee. "Inside."

She did as he said, climbing into the passenger seat as he slipped into the driver's side. "We will drive toward the general area you indicated. This vehicle is heavily tinted, and there shouldn't be many people out here, but if you do see any, duck and hide."

"I will," she said. "Um, who are you?"

He switched the ignition on, and the engine came to life. "My name is Arvin," he said without looking at her. "Karim is my cousin. But shouldn't I be the one asking questions? Like who *you* are and what you are doing here?"

That's right, he said Zafirah was his mother. "My name is Professor Deedee Creed." She gave him a concise version of what had happened to her and how she ended up in Zhobghadi and that Karim had been keeping her presence a secret.

"I can't believe Karim would ..." He muttered something unintelligible under his breath. "We will have to deal with this once we find him."

She agreed. Once they find him. Not *if*.

The rest of the drive went by in silence. She couldn't help but stare out of the vehicle as they passed the near-empty streets of the capital city. It was strange, to have been in here for a few days, yet to have never seen the sights. And much to her surprise, everything around them looked modern. Sure, the buildings were smaller and the architecture was different from western cities, but the roads were clean and paved, the streets well-lit, and even in the middle of the night, it all looked safe. There were also a lot of trees, and they passed a large park on their way out. It was vastly different from the cities and towns she'd passed by in the last six months.

As they passed over the large walls at the end of the city, Arvin stepped on the gas. "You said you saw him fall between the end of the city and the mountains? From the balcony?"

"Yes," she confirmed. Now that the adrenaline was starting to drain out of her, she finally realized something. "Has he ever fallen before?"

"Not that I know of," Arvin answered. "And as far as I know, The Great One cannot be taken down by any normal weapon." His lips pursed tight. "But then, it's been less than a year since he became the bearer of The Great One."

Dragon scales were bulletproof, though they weren't completely invulnerable, as her father had told her. She supposed something like a rocket launcher could injure a dragon's wing, but surely, she would have heard an explosion of sorts? Of course, there could be another way a dragon could be taken down, but she didn't want to reveal to Arvin what she knew of magic.

"Do you think someone may have ... harmed him?"

"There is only one road out of the city that heads to those mountains where the silver mines are located, and this is it." His fingers gripped the wheel tighter. "If anyone were lying in wait for him, they would have had to take this road."

"And Zhobghadi doesn't have any other cities?"

He shook his head. "A few small towns scattered about. Our country is small, the city is about the size of Berlin, and beyond that, there's not much. If Karim did fall where you say he did, then we should be able to—there!" His hand flung out, pointing toward her window.

She immediately saw it—a large, silver lump in the distance. When Arvin revved the engine and the vehicle lurched off the road, she clung to the grab handles in surprise. As the Humvee sped forward, the silver lump began to grow larger and larger, and she could make out its shape—the long neck, large horned head, the tips of its wings, great claws reaching out like it was struggling to get up, its shrieks growing louder. How badly was Karim injured?

The Humvee stopped a few feet away, right by the dragon's massive head. Arvin unbuckled his seat belt and dashed out, and Deedee yanked the handle of her door and followed him.

"Is he hurt?" she asked. "What did—" She sucked in a breath. There was something covering the dragon, like a thin net. "Is he caught in something?"

Arvin's body stiffened, then he leaned down. "Zhobghadi silver," he stated. "But how ..." He shook his head then knelt down beside the dragon. "Quick! We must get this off him!"

Deedee ran to the opposite end and grabbed a corner of the silver net. "It's no use, he's too big. Why can't he move or take this thing off?"

Arvin's shoulders sunk. "Zhobghadi silver is the only thing that can hold The Great One," he stated. "It's a ... necessary precaution."

"Precaution?" she echoed.

"Our history with The Great One is over a millennium old," he began. "And not all the princes and kings of Zhobghadi have been wise or just. This is a safety net."

A literal one. "So, this ... silver can hold The Great One? But why doesn't Karim just transform back?"

"I do not know how it works exactly, but if the bearer is bound with the silver, then it affects his ability to call upon The Great One." His dark brows knitted together. "But I have never heard of The Great One being trapped while in this form. Perhaps the effect is the same."

"So ... Karim is trapped in there, unable to change back?"

"That's the only explanation I can think of."

Dread filled her. "We have to find a way," she said. "Can you call and get some help?"

"I could, but ..."

"But?"

"This ..." He nodded to the beast, who had stopped struggling, "is a sign of weakness. Karim's standing is shaky enough as it is, this might put his status in peril. There are some people in high places who want him gone from the throne."

Karim was having problems within his government? She had no idea. But what were they supposed to do? The only way they could get this off him was with a crane or if Karim shifted back. This was hopeless.

Suddenly, her inner wolf yowled and yipped, scratching at her. *What do you want?* It seemed to go on and on ...

Not sure what else to do, she followed her wolf's instincts. She knelt down by the beast's gigantic head the size of a small car and reached inside the net, rubbing a hand on its snout. "Karim."

A gigantic eye snapped open and looked up at her, the thin-slitted pupils focusing. A shiver ran through her, and while the great silver orb was nothing like Karim's eye, she couldn't help but feel he was looking out of it.

"Karim," she repeated. "Please. Please, come back. We want to help you, but you need to come back. Oh ... Great One, let him have his body back."

The air went still, and the silence was ringing in her ear. Her wolf let out a deep, longing howl, and she jumped when the scales under her palm turned hot.

A hand pulled at her shoulder, tugging her back as the dragon was suddenly engulfed in fire. The blazing form grew smaller and smaller, though the heat of the flames were still scorching. When the fire dissipated, a naked, prone form lay underneath the net.

Karim.

He let out a strangled cry that made her blood freeze.

"We must take it off him." Arvin grabbed one end of the net and began to drag it across the sand. "It will not harm us, but the chains are hurting him."

Karim's anguished moans made Deedee scramble to her feet and grab the nearest chunk of netting she could. In no time, she and Arvin managed to remove the silver net over Karim's body, freeing him. Arvin removed his tunic and covered Karim with it.

"Karim!" She knelt down next to him. "Oh, Karim."

Unable to stop herself, she threw her arms around him, her heart still pounding madly in her chest.

"I ... Desiree?" He inhaled deep, his nose in her hair. "How did you ..."

"Are you hurt?" She winced as she pulled back, seeing the crisscross burns across his skin.

"They will fade," he assured her. "I just ... how did you ..."

"Karim, I'm glad to see you."

He looked up. "Arvin! But," he looked at Deedee and then back at him again. "I can explain."

"You better," Arvin huffed. "But for now, we must bring you back. Dawn is breaking." In the distance, hints of ink and orange were streaking the sky.

"Yes, we need to get back to the palace." Karim got up on his knees and hauled himself up. Deedee slipped a hand under his elbow, and though he let out a grunt, he didn't push her away when she helped him toward the Humvee. Her Lycan strength allowed her to take most of his weight. The two of them sat in the back, Karim slumped against her, his breathing becoming even as they drove back in silence. The adrenaline rushing out of her almost made her forget that he was half-naked. Well, almost. His delicious scent and warm skin tickled her senses, and it was difficult not to reach out and rake her fingers through his hair.

Though she was desperate to know what was on Karim's mind and what he was planning to do, she was glad no one spoke, because frankly, she didn't know what to say. She was only glad that Karim was here and alive, and as he said, the burn marks on his skin were already fading.

Soon they were within the capital city's walls and then

making their way into the palace. It was still dark, but the city was slowly waking up as there were now more vehicles in the street.

"I have made sure the guards will not be back here," Arvin said as they arrived in the same garage where they had come from earlier that morning. "But I will scout ahead just in case."

As they left the garage, she and Karim let Arvin walk ahead, following his lead and only turning corners when he gave them a signal that it was safe. After what seemed like hours of roaming the palace, her heart ready to jump into her throat at every moment, they finally arrived in Karim's rooms.

"What happened?" Arvin barely waited for the door to close before he spoke. "How did you fall out of the sky?"

"I ..." He raked his fingers through his hair. "I was flying overhead and then I heard this loud sound ... like something flying toward me. Before I knew it, I was covered in that net."

"Zhobghadi silver," Arvin said. "The Great One's weakness."

"Someone is out to get me," Karim added. "They knew The Great One could be taken down with Zhobghadi silver, and they made that net to capture me and some sort of device to shoot it at me. This was planned." His eyes blazed with the silver of his beast. "What you told me the other night about those who are against me taking the throne. Have you found out anything else?"

"Nothing significant or anything that talked about actually harming you." Arvin's expression darkened. "But I will endeavor to find out more, now that I know that talk has turned to action."

"Thank you, Arvin," Karim said. "I also have much to explain to you."

"But not now." He glanced at Deedee quickly. "Your lady looks like she will faint at any moment."

"I'm fine," Deedee protested, but her voice was annoyingly shaky.

"And you need some rest," Arvin added. "We will have time to talk later. For now, I will investigate further. I will go back and find the silver net. That may be a clue to uncovering who tried to kill you tonight. Time is of the essence, and when you show up for your morning duties, they will know they did not succeed."

"I owe you a lot," Karim said.

"I am your loyal subject." Arvin bowed. "But also, your family." With one last nod at Deedee, Arvin turned and left the room.

"Someone's trying to kill you," Deedee stated matter-of-factly.

"It seems so."

"How can you be so calm?"

"I am a prince and future king. I always have a target on my back." He let out a deep sigh. "How did you come to be with my cousin?"

"I ... I saw you fall," she began. "I was sitting here, and I heard your dragon. It must have been just as you were caught in the net. I went out, tried to talk to Ramin but he couldn't understand me. I ran away and bumped into Arvin and explained what I saw."

"You saw and heard me fall from this distance?"

Her wolf was the one who figured out he was in trouble. But how? She didn't know how to explain it, except maybe it was her animal's keen hearing and sight. "Enhanced senses." She tapped on her ear. "Anyway, we found you and brought you back here."

"You shouldn't have ... you could have been discovered."

"And you could be dead by now," she said. "Anyway, you should get some rest. You've been up all night and you need sleep, especially after what you've been through. I'll ... I'll stay out here."

"I ..." As he moved toward her, he swayed forward. She shot to her feet in an instant and helped him get steady.

"You're still not well," she sighed. "Let's get you to bed so you can rest."

She helped him walk to his bedroom, all the way to the bed. "Get some sleep. I'm going to sleep on the couch, and I'll see you later."

"No."

"No? But you were practically falling over."

"No."

She blinked at him in confusion. "Are you well, Your Highness? Should I call—*oomph!*" Before she knew it, Karim grabbed her hand and pulled her into bed, then rolled over her.

"No. You will not be sleeping on the couch and I will not see you later," he growled against her mouth. "You will stay here."

CHAPTER TEN

Desperation made him act impulsively, but Karim was not going to let her get away. No, she would stay here, in his bed, where she belonged.

They said that near-death experiences always made one's entire life flash before one's very eyes. But, as he was plunging to earth, Karim had only one thought: Desiree Desmond Creed. How she offered her sweet body up to him. And then how he pushed her away in anger over something that wasn't her fault. He prayed to all the gods listening to him that if he survived that fall, he wouldn't squander his chances again.

Despite what he did, she was the one who saw him, came to his rescue. He was a brute, he kept her here and then seduced her, then discarded her. He should leave her alone, yet, now that she was back here in his arms ...

"Karim," she whispered. "Karim, I'm sorry."

"It is I who should be sorry." He pushed a lock of caramel hair off her forehead. "You had nothing to do with what I felt when I saw that book. It was all ... me."

She sucked in a breath. "Zafirah told me. About your grandfather. Oh, please, don't be angry with her." Her hands pressed up against his chest. "I thought I would never see you again, and I just wanted to know. I ... I made her tell me."

"I'm not angry." He thought he *would* be angry. That she had known his deepest, darkest secret. But no, he only felt relief. Like a big weight had been lifted off his shoulders. It wasn't totally gone, but the burden was lighter now. And more than that, she didn't run away from him. In fact, she came running toward him, in the face of danger, to save him.

All the more reason he should toughen his resolve to stay away from her. To not let the darkness of his past touch her.

But he just couldn't, not when she lay under him, so yielding and sweet.

"Karim?" Those light eyes looked up at him, so full of an unnamed emotion.

"She was so beautiful, my mother." He didn't know how or why the words came out from his lips, but they just did. "She was full of life. From what I knew of her, there was no way she could have been unhappy. Yes, my father was busy running the kingdom, and she might have been lonely, but she always put on a brave face for me."

I love you, Karim, my pet. She said all the time. Love him. Loved him.

"It was the middle of the night when I heard some voices and footsteps. I got up and followed the commotion to my mother's rooms."

His blood froze in his veins, but even if he wanted to stop, he couldn't.

"I saw her, standing out in the balcony. I called out to her, but she ..."

Mum ... Mum ... please. He shut his eyes tight. Everything was a blur after. Someone lifting him and taking him away back to his rooms. His father, telling him that Mum was gone. The funeral and—

"Karim. Oh, Karim." Fingers sifted through his hair. "I'm sorry."

"Maybe if I had been there sooner. If she saw me, then she would have changed her mind—"

"No," she said in a half growl. Her fingers dug into his scalp and pulled his head down lower, so close he could feel her breath on his skin. "Maybe she was already lost, and there was nothing you could do about it. If she changed her mind, she would have done it before she stepped out on that balcony. Karim. Karim, look at me."

Opening his eyes, he found himself lost in the depths of her light green gaze.

"What happened wasn't your fault. It was *never* your fault."

Who had ever told him that, in his entire life? No one. He kept the shame deep inside. He was the Crown Prince, future king and bearer of The Great One. No one coddled him or allowed him to cry. They wouldn't even let psychologists or therapists near him, for fear of showing any sign of weakness in the bloodline.

He tried to roll off her, but her legs locked around him. "Don't go," she said. "You want this."

"Yes, I do." Oh, how he wanted. "And I know you wanted me until I made a mess of things."

"You didn't—"

"Yes, I did." And he still would. He didn't even have to

try, and he could make a mess of things. Ruin her. "Desiree, I cannot ... I cannot promise you anything."

"Then don't." She wrapped her arms around his neck, her grip surprisingly strong. "I don't need any promises."

"Desiree ..."

It was too much; *she* was too much, and a man could only resist temptation until he could fight no longer. He captured her mouth in a fierce kiss, ravaging, taking, plundering her sweetness. As her delicious burnt sugar scent filled his nostrils, he let out a growl of need. Need to touch her all over. Taste her. Be inside her.

His hands pushed at her shirt, lifting them up over her breasts, his fingers plucking the buds to hardness. She gasped into his mouth, then moaned in protest when he pulled away. "I need to taste you." He pulled one tip into his mouth. She was sweet, sweeter than anything he'd ever tasted. As her body squirmed underneath his mouth, he moved a hand down, slipping under the pajamas, moving lower to cover her mound.

Gods above and below, she was already wet and hot. His fingers skimmed her nether lips, feeling how slick she was. It was so easy to slip a finger in her. She made a needy sound and thrust her hips up.

"Easy," he mouthed against her nipple. She was tight, too. So tight. He eased another finger into her, and she bucked up against his hand. Twisting his hand around, he found her clit, already hardened with arousal. He worked his thumb against it.

"Karim!" Fingers tugged at the roots of his hair as her slickness drenched his fingers. He knew he needed a taste there too.

He moved lower, trailing kisses between her breasts, down her abdomen, and finally, over her mound. His heart pounded in anticipation as he spread her legs and pressed his lips to her.

"God!" she cried. "Karim. I ... I should ... *Nggh!*"

His tongue spearing into her made her clamp her thighs around his head. He eased them apart gently, not ready to give her nectar up yet. His tongue lashed at her pussy lips, teasing, tasting, drinking in her sweetness.

Switching around, his mouth found her clit, teasing her there, as his fingers sought her tight, wet, and hot cunt. Her inner walls clamped around him, and he knew she was close.

Come for me, Desiree, he said in his mind, as if she could hear him. He wanted it so bad—

"Karim!" She whimpered as her body shook with her orgasm. Gods, her scent was even more overpowering now, bursting around him mixed with her arousal. His cock, which was already straining against the mattress, was practically leaking, begging to be let in her.

He wanted to make her come some more. Again and again, until she begged him to stop. Maybe another time, because he'd waited long enough.

He crawled up her body, which was still shaking from the aftershocks of her orgasm. His knees nudged her thighs apart, and he positioned himself at her entrance. "Desiree."

"Please," she moaned, lifting her hips. "I need ..."

He knew what she needed, and he was going to give it to her. Right now. "Gods, Desiree." He slipped his cock in slowly, as he feared he might come right there and then. He held his breath, pushing in. "You're so ..." Tight. So unusually tight. When he gave a strong push, he felt something give way.

No. She couldn't be.

She whimpered, and he gathered her close in his arms. He felt wetness at his neck and tasted the salt in the air. "Desiree ... you're a ... you've never ..." He pulled back, making her take a deep breath. Staring down at her, he saw that track of a single tear down her cheek.

"It's fine." Her mouth trembled. "I ... I know it's ... unusual in this day and age. But, really, it's fine."

"It is not fine," he said sternly. "I've hurt you. Why didn't you say anything?"

Those mesmerizing eyes stared up at him. "If I told you, would you have stopped?"

Enki could have come down himself and he wouldn't have stopped. "No. But I would have given you more time."

"Time?"

"Yes. To think about it. To think hard if I am worthy enough—"

"Shush." She put a hand to his lips. "The idea that virginity is a gift to be bestowed is human construct, don't you know? It's not that I haven't had a chance. I just ..." Her plump lips pursed together. "Anyway, Karim, I don't need more time. I just need *you*."

She needed *him*. Not his riches, his title, his power. Just *him*. The idea shook him to the core.

"Karim?" She raised a brow at him.

"Are you still in pain?" he asked, not knowing what else to say.

"I ..." A small sigh escaped her lips. "No ... it doesn't hurt.

I just feel ... feel so full. Of you." Her hips wiggled and then she tightened around him.

Gods, was she trying to kill him? "Desiree ..." he moaned and steadied her hips. "Slow. We will go slow." For your sake and mine. "And if it hurts, tell me to stop."

She nodded.

He had no experience with virgins, so he thought that was the way to go. Slowly, he pulled back and then pushed back in again. Her heat and slickness were driving him mad, but he didn't want to hurt her.

She inhaled a deep, sharp breath, but said nothing. He must be hurting her. So, he put his weight on his right elbow and leaned his head down to capture a nipple in his mouth. He sucked and mouthed at her, his tongue swirling around the bud. She shivered, and he felt her relax.

His free hand moved between them where their bodies were joined, and he touched her clit, teasing and coaxing at her until he could feel her hips moving up at him.

He told himself to be gentle. But when her hips arched, he knew she wanted the same friction he did. She angled upward, and he found himself burying deeper into her.

She writhed against him. Over and over. He withdrew his hand from her and cradled her ass. "Yes, Desiree," he urged as he lifted her up. "Yes."

He didn't even have to do much, as she continued to move up against him. Slowly, again, he thrust into her. She didn't tense or wince, but instead, let out a needy, breathy moan.

"Yes," she said. "More. Please, Karim." Her hands went up to his shoulders, digging into them.

He buried his face into her hair. "So good, *habibti*." It was beyond good, but his words were escaping him. He moved, setting a rhythm that pushed deeper into her with each thrust. She opened up to him, yet the clasp of her was enough that he wanted more and more.

"Come for me," he gasped. Her legs wrapped around him, pushing him deeper into her tightness. Death now would be easier, but he couldn't ... not yet. Not until she ...

"Karim." It wasn't possible, but she tightened even more around him as her body shuddered. He held on for another few heartbeats, until she was over that crest before letting go. Pleasure drained from him, his seed filled her, but he couldn't stop. His body shook with aftershocks as he felt all the strength drain from his body.

He had never spent so quick with a woman. Usually, he'd make his partner come at least two more times in different positions before he allowed himself to come. But with Desiree ... it was like he had no control over his own body. But then again, it was her first time, so she needed time for her body to adjust.

First time. Gods, she had never been with ... no one had ever been inside her. It shouldn't have mattered to him, but somehow, it made something in him rejoice with pleasure.

"Karim ... you ..." She let out a small sound and gave him a push.

Of course, she was probably uncomfortable and sore. He held his breath and slowly slipped out of her. She gave a small wince, but other than that, didn't say anything.

"Stay here," he commanded as he rolled off her. It was silly, because where would she go? Still, it felt right to say it to her.

He strode into the bathroom, cleaning himself up quickly

as he ran the bath, filling it with warm water and the scented oils he never used.

When he walked back to the bedroom, Desiree was still in bed. Early morning daylight filled the room, bathing her in an unearthly glow. Her hair spilled over his pillows, smooth skin against the sheets, and those plump lips swollen with his kisses. She'd never looked more beautiful.

"Karim, I—" She let out a soft whoop when he hauled her up into his arms. "Where are you taking me?"

"A hot bath should sooth your aches," he said.

"You could have just said so. I can walk, you know."

"I know." He set her down by the tub. "But where is the fun in that?"

A deep blush colored her neck and cheeks, and she cast her gaze toward the water. "Oh. That looks divine. I've been wanting to soak in it, but I was afraid there was some kind of law against bathing in the prince's tub."

He chuckled. "Perhaps, but you have my permission now."

"Thank you." As she stepped over the side of the bath, his gaze roamed over her naked figure, and though he wanted her again, he controlled himself. For now, at least.

"Ohhh." She moaned as she sank in, the water level not quite covering her breasts. The round globes bobbed up and down teasing him and making his cock twitch painfully. "Thank you … this feels … amazing."

"I should go and let you—"

"Join me." A wet hand grabbed onto his arm. "There's plenty of room."

How could he say no to this desirable Venus? With a quick nod, he joined her, the lavender-scented water rising up as he lowered his body. The tub indeed, was large enough for both of them, yet he gathered her up and held her close to his chest, her head resting in the crook of his arm. She sighed again and nuzzled up at him.

They lay there in silence, allowing the warmth of the water and the scent of the oil to soothe them both. When the water began to cool, he motioned for her to get up. Grabbing a fluffy towel from the rack, he helped her out of the tub and buffed her dry, giving himself a once over before carrying her back to the bed to lay her down.

Mine. Ours. The Great One's voice was clear. *Adorn her.*

"Wait a moment," he said and turned back to dash into the bathroom and into his closet. He saw something glinting out of the corner of his eye. A chain hung from one of the many jewelry cases inside his vast wardrobe. This particular chain, however, was very special to him. He would never give it away, except—

Adorn her.

He grabbed the chain. It was delicate, made of the finest white gold. *Perfect.* Padding back into the bedroom, he got into bed behind her.

"Karim, what are you—" She gasped when he slipped the chain over her head. "I ... what's this?"

"It's for you." He kissed her shoulder.

"Me? Why?"

"I don't know ... it just felt right." This felt right too, holding her in his arms. If he wasn't careful, he could get used to this. Maybe he should remind himself of what he said earlier, about making no promises.

"It's beautiful." She lifted the chain to eye level. "I can't possibly—"

"You can," he said firmly.

"Thank you."

The chain glinted against her skin and The Great One rumbled in delight.

Delight?

"Karim ... I ..." She twisted around to face him. "I wanted to assure you of something."

"Assure me?"

"Yes, see ... you didn't use any condoms and ..."

Yes, that was careless of him. "Oh." The implication of her words became clear. Normally, he would have broken out into a cold sweat. She would not be the first woman to make a claim, but really, she would be the only one where that would be even possible.

"So, I wanted to let you know that I'm safe."

"Safe?"

"Yes." She smoothed a hand over his shoulder. "I've always used birth control, and my kind ... we don't reproduce easily."

Her kind. Had he forgotten what she was? That like him, she also had a beast inside her. Would they even be compatible? Would any offspring of theirs be like her or have The Great—

Gods above and below, offspring?

It seemed he spent his life avoiding women who wanted such things from him and now he was the one thinking these thoughts.

"Karim?" Her voice was sleepy now. "Do you have time to nap, or do you have to get up soon?"

The hour was growing late. He should get dressed and

attend to his duties, but ... "No. Arvin will anticipate that I need rest and will cancel my morning appointments."

"Oh."

Was that a sigh of relief? Or disappointment. He wasn't sure because the rise and fall of her chest became even, and he knew she was fast asleep.

He held her closer, feeling the warmth of her body. *Danger*, his mind warned. No promises, they'd said. But the question wasn't if she could stick to that agreement. It was if *he* could.

CHAPTER ELEVEN

DEEDEE WOKE UP FEELING SORE. IN A GOOD WAY. As soon as she opened her eyes, the first thing she thought was, *I'm not a virgin anymore.*

She sat up and looked around. Karim was gone, of course. Part of her was miffed, but another part of her was relieved. Because, really, what was one supposed to do after a night of sex? Or in their case, it was morning. And it was just the one time.

Was there going to be more? A delicious shiver ran through her, thinking of Karim. Her lover. *Lover,* she repeated in her mind. *L-O-V-E-R.*

Swinging her legs over the side of the bed, she made her way to the bathroom, wincing as she got up. When she looked at herself in the mirror, she tried to examine if there was anything different about her. Really, she should have paid more attention to herself before she was deflowered, as now, she didn't know if there was a difference between the old Deedee and the new.

You silly idiot. Her hand slapped on her forehead. She

was acting like a teenager, not a woman of thirty with a promising academic career.

White gold glinted between her naked breasts, and her hand immediately went to the chain Karim had given her. Oh, it really was lovely, and no man had ever given her such a gift. *Hmmm* ... she recalled her mother having a similar chain around her neck.

A longing hit her all of a sudden. Her family, her friends ... *They must be worried out of their minds by now*. Her mother would be distraught, and her father would be combing the earth looking for her. And then there was Cross.

Hmmm. When was the last time she had thought of him? Frankly she couldn't remember. For someone who had occupied most of her thoughts for the last year, he had suddenly disappeared from her mind.

It was strange, really. While she didn't plan for Cross to be her first lover, she had always imagined it. But now, it seemed almost like a childish dream.

Maybe what they said was right. The best way to get over someone was to be with someone else. Or *do* someone else, she thought wickedly. And it seemed she'd hit the jackpot with Karim. He was just so sexy and hot, and he did all the right things. It had hurt like the dickens, much more than she'd thought it would, but after the pain had subsided ... it was all so good. Her nipples puckered now, thinking about it.

Oh dear, hopefully she could get him out of her system by the time she left. After all, he had told her that he couldn't make any promises. And she agreed, because she didn't want to repeat history. She had let her feelings run away with Cross, and she wasn't ever going to let herself fall in love with someone who could never love her back. It was better that she and Karim had an understanding now before things went too far.

Her stomach growled loudly, making her jump in surprise. It had been hours since she'd eaten. Hopefully Ramin would be setting her breakfast—or lunch?—out soon.

After getting refreshed and putting on one of Karim's shirts and loose pants, she walked out to the living room. The smell of food made her stomach grumble, and she saw that Ramin was indeed putting food on the table.

"Oh, that smells good. What is it?" She didn't even wait for the young man to finish before she grabbed a skewer of meat. "*Mmm ...*"

Ramin looked like he was trying to hide a smile as he picked up his tray. Deedee wasn't distracted enough by the food to notice that he didn't give her his usual glare or have the air of animosity around him. In fact, he looked downright friendly. It unnerved her.

Placing the skewer down, she walked to him. "Ramin, I'm sorry about last night. Making you chase after me. You understand that Karim was in trouble, and I had to help him."

There was a glimmer of comprehension in his eyes. "You ... save ... Karim."

Oh, so he knew. "I ... guess ..." She nodded. "Do you know who could have hurt him?" Her she-wolf growled, wanting to know the answer too.

He said nothing back, but placed his hand over his heart as he gave her a short bow. Then, he turned and left her.

Strange. But then again there was nothing normal about the past few days, right?

Her stomach clamored for attention again, and this time, her wolf joined in.

"Oh, all right." She sat back down at the low table and began to heap a plate with food. Fragrant garlicky flatbread. Meat skewers with exotic spices. Fresh, crisp salads. And a divine pastry with pistachios, honey and fresh cream. Before she knew it, she had finished almost everything on the table.

"I'm glad to see you have a healthy appetite. But did you not leave any for me?"

She was about to wipe her mouth with a napkin when she heard that familiar, low baritone. "Karim!" It was hard not to scramble to her feet or let those trills of excitement run up and down her spine. "I didn't know you were coming for lunch, or I would have saved—"

He was so close to her, she nearly collided into him. "I was joking, Desiree." He steadied her by wrapping his hands around her arms.

It was like the full force of his handsomeness hit her right in the gut. He was wearing that military uniform again, cut so well to fit his form, and those medals seemed to glint at her. And goodness, that smile on his face—so full of sensual promise.

"I have already eaten with the generals," he continued.

"Oh, did you find out anything about who could have attacked you?"

A line of worry furrowed between his brows. "Arvin and I are keeping that to ourselves for now." His shoulders tensed. "But we will find out who tried to harm The Great One."

"And you," she reminded him. She wanted to find out too, and so did her wolf. It seemed to relish the thought of raking its claws down whoever tried to hurt Karim.

"Do not fret. I will take care of it." His face softened. "But I stopped by to see how you were feeling." He brushed his thumb against the corner of her mouth. A bit of cream and honey came off, and he popped it into his mouth, his tongue darting out to lick at his lips. "Delicious."

Deedee would have melted into a puddle right then if he wasn't holding her up. "Karim ..."

He lowered them both to the plush carpet. "I had to come and see you. I couldn't wait until tonight."

Oh dear, now he was crawling over her, and she had no choice but to lie back and let him cover her with his body. He nudged her knees apart and settled on top of her, his hardness pressing against her thighs. "Oh ..."

"Desiree." He devoured her mouth like a man aching with hunger, the force of his lips sending a shockwave of desire rippling through her. "Desiree ... I want you again."

A delicious shiver tickled her spine. "Oh ... yes."

"But I don't want to hurt you."

"You won't," she growled against his mouth. "I just need you."

His eyes flashed silver, and he swooped down again to take her mouth. A warm palm cupped her breast through her shirt, his thumb teasing a nipple. She spread her legs, pushing her heat up against him, making him groan. "Oh, Kar—"

The door slamming against the wall made them both freeze.

"Deedee," came the youthful voice. "I came to see if you were feeling better. Aunt Zafirah said you were sick yesterday and—" Amaya let out a gasp. "Karim! What are you doing?"

He mouthed a few choice curses against her mouth before letting out a sigh. In one quick motion, he got up and lifted Deedee up with him. "Amaya, what are you doing here? Where is your tutor?"

"I just finished my noon meal, so he let me go and play, but I came here instead to check on Deedee." Her small eyes narrowed at them. "What were you doing to her?"

Oh dear, she wanted to sink into the ground right then and there.

"Er ..." Even Karim seemed at a loss for words. "Desiree was having a hard time breathing." He scratched at the back of his head. "So, I was helping her."

"By getting on top of her?" Amaya asked in all her wide-eyed innocence. "And breathing into her mouth?"

"Yes," Deedee added quickly. "He was. Thank you, Karim," she said.

The corners of his mouth quirked up. "I'm at your service." He turned to Amaya. "Now, it's time to go back to your lessons."

"Karim!" she protested. "But Deedee hasn't told me about the Aztec mummies yet."

"She will, tonight at dinner. If your tutors are satisfied with your work."

Dinner? She raised a brow at him, but he ignored her as Amaya let out a squeal of delight.

"I can't wait!" The girl rushed to Karim and hugged him, then did the same with Deedee. "I promise to finish my lessons and homework." And just as fast as she breezed in, Amaya was gone.

Karim cleared his throat. "Apologies for the interruption."

"It wasn't your fault," she said. "And I'm glad to see Amaya. She really is a great kid."

He shoved a hand into his pockets, then took something out. "Here," he held his palm open. "For you."

"What?" She peered down at his hand. On it lay a necklace with a pink diamond pendant the size of her thumb. "Oh my. No, Karim, no." But he was already placing it around her neck. "I can't accept—"

"It suits you." His eyes gleamed that silver color again. "I got it just for you."

"I ... thank you." The two chains—the diamond pendant and the necklace he gave her last night—clinked together as she twisted them in her fingers. "I didn't think ... did you mean it about tonight? Dinner again?"

"You seemed to enjoy yourself the last time." He traced a finger down the side of her face. "And ... you should enjoy your time here."

Her heart thudded in her chest. "During dinner."

"Yes." His thumb brushed against her lips. "And after, as well."

"I—"

His kiss was quick, a soft sweep of his mouth against hers. But oh, the heat rushed through her like wildfire. "I ... I should go. I shouldn't have come in the first place but—"

"You have duties," she pointed out. "Your people need you." *I need you*, she wanted to say.

His eyes smoldered, as if he heard her, but then he gave her a small nod. "Until tonight."

She stared after him as he left the suite, her body still aching with need. No promises, they had said. But his words sounded like a thousand promises he intended to keep.

CHAPTER TWELVE

That evening, they all had dinner in the dining room again. Since Karim had already explained the reason for Desiree's presence to him, Arvin had joined them as well. Though his cousin had railed at him for risking so much by keeping her here, he had agreed that there was no other way to have handled the situation that didn't involve dire consequences to Deedee or Ramin.

"So, Professor Creed," Arvin began as he took a sip of his wine. "Is archeology as exciting and a glamorous field as they show it in movies? What was that famous film where the adventurer is chased by a large rolling boulder and then escapes in an airplane?"

Desiree laughed. "Oh no." She wiped her mouth with her napkin and then put it back on her lap. "I'm afraid except for the scene where he's in the classroom teaching uninterested students, archeology's nothing like that at all. The actual academic work is very tedious, mostly."

A vision of Desiree in a prim white blouse, tight skirt and

glasses popped into Karim's mind. No, that didn't sound very boring at all. He grabbed his wine glass and took a sip, hoping the fleeting buzz would help dull the ache of desire in his groin.

"And what were you studying when you arrived here?" Zafirah asked. "Surely our little part of the world wouldn't interest someone as accomplished as you. Wouldn't you have rather gone to someplace like Egypt or maybe Rome?"

"Perhaps, but so many other archeologists are already studying those places," Desiree said. "But really, this region has fascinated me for years. I've devoted most of my research to it after finishing my master's thesis five years ago, just when I started teaching. Actually, I received a grant earlier this year for my research. After writing to a couple more foundations, I finally had enough funds to do an extensive trip. I've been out here since about the beginning of the year."

"The state of the academe is such a sorry one." Arvin shook his head. "I can't imagine it's easy to find funding."

"It's hard, definitely. There's so much money in the world, yet I can't even get a grant for newer tools or more people." Her jaw clenched. Big universities in the US often focused on more glamorous pursuits, like sports, not very un-sexy ones like archeology.

"Then why not stick to teaching?" Zafirah asked. "It's much safer, too, right?"

She rolled her eyes. "I don't know which is harder, getting corporations or foundations to part with their cash or getting students to pay attention." She gave a little laugh. "They're all obsessed with scrolling on their little screens or the latest celebrity gossip."

"You must really love this research of yours," Arvin

commented. "To come so far away and for so long, be away from your family and peers. You don't want to go back home soon?"

"I, uh ..."

Desiree's hand shook as she put her fork down and for a brief moment, she looked perturbed. It sent alarm bells ringing in Karim's brain. Did she look flustered or was it his imagination?

"I'm not done with my research." She seemed to have composed herself as she popped a piece of bread into her mouth, chewing it slowly and carefully.

"And what have you found out?" Zafirah inquired.

"Oh, some really good things," Deedee answered. "But, I'm not quite ready to reveal them yet, not without sitting down and sifting through the data."

"What about Zhobghadi?" Zafirah prodded. "Did you find anything interesting about us?"

"Actually, I wasn't allowed to do any research here." Deedee shrugged. "Or I couldn't find any resources to get permission. You don't have any embassies abroad or any representation other than trade offices. I sent an inquiry, but I didn't hear back."

Karim didn't realize that she had known about Zhobghadi before, but he supposed if she was doing research in the area, she would have heard of their country. "You do understand why we keep our borders shut?"

"I do," she said. "And really, now that I think of it, I probably wouldn't have been able to find anything useful to my research because I study the movement of the people in the region, but Zhobghadi seems to be trapped in this time capsule where very little has changed. I mean, even your religious and cultural practices are vastly different from the other countries in the region. I would say it's more similar to the earlier cultures here, like the Assyrians or early Mesopotamians. And the people here, at least from what I've seen, look like they're of Persian or even Caucasus descent than of the other people in the area, perhaps even older than most civilizations we know of."

"And you don't think that's worth studying?" Arvin asked.

"Oh, I find it fascinating. It's actually like a starting point of humanity in this region, where it all began."

"Maybe you could stay here and study Zhobghadi!" Amaya popped in.

Karim felt a strange twinge in his chest, but ignored it.

"I could be your assistant," Amaya continued. "And we can go in the desert and dig for artifacts. Maybe even find some mummies."

"Is that so?" Desiree smiled at her. "What else would we do?"

"We can go on adventures, and fight off our rivals while we go searching for gold...."

Amaya continued to chatter on, and Karim was relieved that his sister was mostly talking the sort of nonsense children her age would prattle on about. Because really, it would be an absurd notion. Desiree stay here? She would have to be suffering some sort of Stockholm syndrome to want to remain in Zhobghadi. Most likely, after she left, she would walk away, and they'd never see each other again.

That twinge in his chest came back, this time, stronger. "I think it's time for dessert." He wanted to hurry this dinner along and have Desiree to himself again. Yes, that's all he craved from her—her sweet delectable body. His damn chest could twinge, pluck, or pang all it wanted, the only spasm he was going to relieve tonight was the one in his trousers.

The meal, thankfully, did not last much longer. Amaya was once again drowsy by the time they were finishing their tea and coffee. She only agreed to go to bed if Desiree came with her and Aunt Zafirah to tuck her in.

"Are you sure I should go?" she asked him.

"It is all right," he said. "The entire residential wing has been cleared of staff and guards." Normally, they would be crawling with the Almoravid at least, but since it was the Easifat, he felt less worried about security inside the palace. He had, however, told Captain Fariba that he wanted security outside to be doubled and that only the most loyal staff were to come inside the palace, and no one at all in the residential area. "Go ahead." His gaze flickered over to Arvin, and his cousin acknowledged the silent signal with a short nod. "I will meet you back in my room."

When the three females had gone, he turned to his cousin. "Walk with me." Arvin nodded, and they began to make their way back to his suite. "Have you any more information about the incident from last night?"

"I'm doing my best to look into the matter discreetly," Arvin said. "I didn't have a chance to go back to the desert until this afternoon. When I did, I found that not only was the net they used to capture you gone, but it seems whoever took it back erased their tracks."

"You should have taken it with you when you came to get me."

Arvin raised a brow. "Apologies, I was busy trying to save

your life and also escape in case your captors were still around."

Karim cursed inwardly. His cousin was right, of course. Desiree had been there as well, and if she had been captured ... "What else?"

"I've begun by inquiring into the whereabouts of your staunchest critics that night."

"And?"

"I ... have a list of five people whom I think would be bold enough to harm you."

He stopped in his tracks. "Who are they?" he demanded. "Tell me their names and I will—"

Arvin held a hand up. "This is just a preliminary list. And I do not want them to get wind of my suspicions, especially if you start to act strangely around them."

"Strangely?" He echoed. "What do you mean?"

"I do not want you treating them differently," Arvin said in a hushed tone. "We want whoever is trying to harm you to get confident and think he can succeed. Otherwise, if he knows we have suspicions, then he'll withdraw before we can gather more evidence."

Godsdammit, he hated to admit it, but Arvin was right. Setting off any suspicions would send his enemy scurrying back into whatever hole they crawled out of. Or make them more crafty and harder to find.

"All right." They stopped outside his door. "Thank you, Arvin. For your help and advice. As always, I know you cannot steer me wrong."

"I am your humble servant, Your Highness." When he looked up at Karim after he bowed his head, he added. "And may I advise you on another matter? As your family?"

"What about?"

"The nature of your relationship with Ms. Creed."

"That is not up for discussion," he snapped. Did Arvin suspect anything? Of course he did, otherwise, he wouldn't have brought it up. But this was not something he was going to go into detail with him.

"I only wish to *advise* you to be cautious and prudent." Arvin bowed his head and placed his fist over his heart. "Good evening, Your Highness."

Karim didn't bother to return the pleasantry, nor wait for him to turn and leave before yanking the door to his suite open and slamming it behind him. *Of all the nerve.* Arvin dared to inquire into his personal affairs?

He walked briskly to the liquor cabinet and took a bottle of Three Wolves Whiskey, a gift from his friend Duncan, made in their family distillery, and poured himself a measure. The liquor did not make him drunk, but he did enjoy the way it went down his throat so smoothly. And of course, it brought back the memories of spending time at Kilcraigh Castle, Duncan's family's home. He had met Duncan MacDougal back when he studied at Eton, the two of them becoming fast friends because they were both foreigners and hated by the snooty English students. While his father didn't permit him to visit them while he was in school, once Karim went on to University in London, he went home with Duncan to visit his family during shorter breaks and even once during Christmas.

With the MacDougals, he felt like a normal person. Not a crown prince, or the bearer of The Great One, but just him. Karim. No responsibilities, no kingdom, no obligations, and the only thing he was worrying about was if the paparazzi was on his tail. Out there, he could just be him, doing whatever he wanted, anywhere he wanted to be.

"Karim?"

Or be with anyone he pleased.

"Desiree." He turned to face her. He had been so deep in his thoughts he didn't hear the door open. "I hope Amaya didn't give you any trouble."

"Not at all." She laughed, her voice like bells tinkling. "She was pretty tired and was down in seconds."

He wondered if it was a mistake, to let her spend so much time with Desiree. Amaya would be distraught when she left. "I have something for you." He fished a box out of his pocket. "Here."

Her brows knitted together, but she accepted the box anyway. "Karim ... this is beautiful." Her eyes went wide. "I can't—"

He plucked the box out of her hand and took out the contents. It was a decorative gold comb, studded with diamonds that formed the shape of a flower. In the middle of the flower was a yellow-green diamond that matched her eyes perfectly. The jeweler he had visited had two more of the same stone, and he bought them as well, thinking he might have earrings fashioned for her. "Here." He placed the comb in her hair, the stones winking at him. "It pleases me to see this on you."

The Great One rumbled in his chest in agreement.

"I ..." She touched the comb self-consciously and stared at her feet. "I wouldn't know where I would wear it."

His fingers skimmed down the side of her face, tracing her jaw, and tipped her chin up. "To bed, with me," he rasped. "It would please me even more to see this on you and nothing else."

As their lips met, he pushed away all other thoughts that were bothering him. Because Desiree deserved his utmost attention, both body and mind.

CHAPTER THIRTEEN

DEEDEE HAD NEVER BELIEVED IN FAIRY TALES. EVEN AS A child, she knew those stories about princes and princesses were just that—stories. Made up to make hearts flutter. But she couldn't help but feel giddy when she thought of Karim.

In the last two days, they had fallen into a routine—dinner in the evenings with Amaya and Zafirah, then a few hours of glorious, heart-racing sex before midnight when he had to leave. When he came back at dawn, he woke her for another round before getting an hour or two of sleep so he could wake up refreshed for his duties. During the hours they were apart, she was thinking of when she would see him again, and when he did appear, her heart went flip-flop, like a high diver jumping off the board.

That's not giddiness, she scolded herself. *That's horniness.*

Yes, that was it. Just sex. Surely, it was just intimacy, and she would feel the same with any future lover—

Her wolf growled at the thought.

Ugh. Her stupid she-wolf was acting weird again. Maybe

she should feed it more food. Certainly, she had eaten so much in the last few days that it should be satisfied. Last night during dinner, even Amaya had noticed that she ate three plates of food.

"Desiree?"

Oh, his voice never failed to make her shiver. "Karim," she greeted as she stood up from the couch.

Their routine seemed ingrained in her that she knew to be dressed for dinner by the time the sun was setting in the distance. Tonight, Zafirah had brought her a more daring outfit—a green western-style gown that had a low V-neck.

Normally, she'd feel self-conscious in such a dress, but it showed off the simple gold chain Karim had given her. Sure, he'd also given her other jewelry since that night—sapphire earrings, a gold bracelet studded with diamonds, a necklace with an emerald pendant, plus some thick bangles decorated with all kinds of precious stones—but for some reason, she loved the simple chain most of all.

He probably did too, as his eyes immediately zeroed in on the chain that lay between her breasts. "You look ..." His Adam's apple bobbed up and down. "Exquisite."

She *felt* exquisite, especially with the way his eyes devoured and undressed her. "Thank you. I think it's too fancy for dinner with Amaya, but Zafirah insisted."

"We are not having dinner with my sister."

"We aren't?"

He took her hand and pressed his lips to her palms. "No, I have something else planned." Before she could ask anything else, he tugged her toward the balcony. "Come."

They walked hand-in-hand with Karim leading her

outside. She was wondering what was going on, until she saw it. "Oh my ..."

A large carpet had been spread out in the middle of the balcony, and several cushions and blankets were laid out on top. A low table on the side was overflowing with food, and a bottle of champagne chilled in a silver bucket next to it.

"Ramin prepared it while you were getting ready." His arm slipped around her waist and he pulled her to his body. "I hope you like it."

"It's so ..." *Romantic?* She bit her lip. "It's wonderful, Karim, thank you. Is there a special occasion?"

"You can say that." He guided her toward the spread, leading her to the middle of the carpet where they sat down and reclined on the cushions. "Tonight is a thanksgiving of sorts."

"Thanksgiving?" As he opened his arm to her, she automatically moved into his side, cuddling up against him.

"Yes. The Easifat is fading, and Zhobghadi has once again survived the worst of it."

"Oh." She plucked an imaginary piece of fluff from the cushion beside her. "That's wonderful."

He motioned to the sky. "And so tonight, we celebrate."

The sun had set long ago, and the night was dotted with hundreds of stars. Deedee stared up, mesmerized, wondering when was the last time she'd seen such a sight. "It's beautiful out here."

"It is." When she turned her face to his, she realized he'd been staring at her. His finger came up to her collarbone, lazily caressing it. "Everyone will be out in the streets tonight, celebrating. There will be music, dancing, and—"

He was interrupted by a loud whistle, followed by a

brilliant burst of light in the sky. "Fireworks," he finished. "Looks like they are doing some tests."

"Looks like it." She did her best to sound casual, but the implication of what he had said was weighing on her. With the end of the Easifat came the end of her time here. Soon, she'd be on her way home.

"You must be hungry." He reached over to the table and began to put food on a plate. "Come, let's eat and enjoy this feast. The fireworks won't start for a while."

She accepted the plate as Karim began to explain the various traditional dishes prepared only during the Easifat. It seemed fascinating from the way he described it, but the words didn't quite sink into her head, and the food itself tasted like sand in her mouth.

I should be celebrating, like the people of Zhobghadi. Because they had survived the sandstorms, and she had survived her time here.

"Champagne?" He offered her a flute. "I cannot get drunk, a side effect of being the bearer of The Great One, but I do like its taste."

"Thank you." She accepted the glass and put the rim to her lips. However, something about the smell of the bubbly drink made her nauseous, and she stopped halfway before the liquid reached her lips.

"Are you well?" he asked.

"Me?"

"You seem quiet."

She let out a laugh, hoping it sounded casual. "Oh, you know, just tired." Placing the champagne flute on the floor beside her, she turned to him. "You've been keeping me up and waking me so early."

He placed his glass next to hers and then snaked his arm around her waist to pull her on top of him. She chuckled even as she struggled to balance against his chest. "Karim ..."

"You didn't seem to mind staying awake with me before I take my evening flight. Or welcoming me back when I returned." He nuzzled at her temple.

"Now, I didn't say I minded."

"Is that so?" He flipped her over, so she lay back on the cushions and he was on top of her. The heat of his body burned through his clothes and hers, and those intense blue eyes bore into hers with the intensity of the sun. Reaching between them, his finger traced a path down her neck, between her breasts, to the chain that lay between them. "The emerald would have matched this dress."

"I know," she said. "But I like this most of all." It was the first one he gave her, after that first time. And when she left, she might even be tempted to keep it. Because there was no way she could accept all those extravagant gifts.

His eyes flashed silver briefly. "I like it most of all too."

Her heart did that strange flip-flop as he lowered his head to hers. His mouth was warm as it brushed over hers. Oh, how did such firm lips kiss so tenderly and make her knees turn to jelly?

The kiss deepened, his tongue seeking entrance into her mouth. She opened up eagerly, wanting to taste him just as bad. He tasted of champagne, heat, and something that was just *him*. Once again, his scent was threatening to overwhelm her, and she didn't know how much she could take. How would she be able to forget him once she left this place?

It was wrong, *so wrong* to think of an ending to this story that didn't involve anything else but a goodbye. No promises, they had said, and she tried so hard not to let her emotions run away again. Her brain screamed at her to stop her heart from running into the unknown. *Turn around right now and never look back*, it said to her, *that is, if you ever want to leave here whole.*

As Karim began to trail kisses down her jaw and neck, she lay back on the cushions. *Let me have this*, she said to nothing and no one in particular. *Just this night. Let me have this.* It would be enough. It would *have* to be enough.

He pulled the shoulders of her dress down, baring her breasts to him. Her nipples tightened in the cold night air, and she let out a moan when his mouth covered one bud. The heat of his mouth and the cool air were a maddening contrast, sending pleasure signals across her body.

A hand moved under the skirt, pushing swathes of silk aside until it landed on her inner thigh. The simple touch, and the anticipation made heat and wetness rush to her core. He must have known, smelled her arousal as he slowly teased his way up. Fingers brushed along her skin at an achingly slow pace, caressing her in every place but the one where she wanted to feel his touch.

She whined, digging her fingers into his shoulders to catch his attention. He lifted his gaze up to her, his mouth still on her nipple, hand under her skirt. Though she pleaded at him with her eyes to give her what she wanted, he only narrowed his gaze, as if to say, *no, I'm in control now.*

Infuriating man.

He switched his attention to her other nipple, and finally, his fingers reached up higher. The rough pads of his thumb brushed against her slick lips, and she nearly wept. His mouth suckled deeper as a finger pressed against her sex, slipping in easily.

"Karim."

Her eyes nearly rolled back into their sockets as his thumb found her clit. Pleasure shot from her hardened nub, up her spine, and all the way to her brain. She couldn't think of anything else except chasing that exquisite feeling. Her hips arched, wanting more. So much more.

Her body tightened, then exploded as her orgasm washed over her. Karim bit her nipple gently, sending her reeling again into another crest. It was too much, and she scratched her nails down his arms, marking him.

"My she-wolf does have claws," he said as he popped her nipple out of his mouth.

The possessive words and his gaze made the fire burn in her. She wanted him so much. That greedy side of her wanted *everything.* "I'll show you claws." Hooking her leg around him, she used his weight to flip him over so that she was now on top.

"Now, this is interesting." He stretched his arms over his head, then clasped his hands behind his head. A lazy smile curled up his lips. "Go on then."

Oh yes, she would go on. She quickly unbuttoned his tunic, exposing his muscled chest and all that glorious golden skin. Leaning down, she let her hair fall over him, and she relished the stifled groan he bit out. They had only been lovers for a short time, but she had come to know his body and his likes and dislikes. Not that he had many dislikes. It seemed as long as it involved any part of her body and his coming together, it was definitely a like.

She pressed a kiss to his throat and then made her way

down. His skin tasted so masculine and warm, the muscles underneath hard and coiled with power. She grazed her teeth down across one pec, her tongue peeking out to lick at a nipple. His torso tensed, and a strangled groan escaped his mouth.

Oh, definitely a *like*.

She continued her exploration—or perhaps torture, if she were to ask Karim—lower still, her hands and mouth roaming over those hard eight-pack abs. Her fingers made quick work of his pants, untying the belt that was only in her way. Pushing them down, she exposed the deep V-cuts of his hips —the Adonis belt—and sank her teeth into it.

He growled, but she wasn't done yet. There was one more place to explore, after all.

She lowered his pants, exposing his erect cock. Despite her inexperience, she knew he was magnificent. The shaft was thick and heavy, and the bulbous head already had a pearl of moisture. She licked her lips as she looked up at him.

"Desiree ..." he said in a warning tone.

Yes, they'd done so much ... but she had yet to do this. Her fingers grasped the base of his shaft, and he tensed.

Slowly, she stroked him, just the way he liked it, with a strong grip and steady motion. He was biting his lip, staring down at her with those cerulean blue eyes glinting like sapphires, but didn't make a sound, until she lowered her head and engulfed the head of his cock with her mouth. He let out a strangled cry, and his fingers dug into her hair, kneading into her scalp.

Oh, he tasted ... interesting. Her tongue licked at the underside of his shaft, as her lips tightened around him. She looked up at him again, and seeing him practically losing his mind, knowing she had this much power over him, made her bolder. She moved lower still, taking more of him inside her mouth.

"Desiree." The tug at her scalp was not so gentle. "*Habibti*, I cannot ..."

She let go. As much as she wanted to continue, the ache between her thighs wasn't going to go away until he was inside her. But she wasn't done yet.

"I want you." She stood up, and pushed the rest of the dress off, shucking it aside.

"Then take me."

The words made her shiver, almost scaring her. But she found her courage and knelt down over him, her knees on either side of his. She wrapped her hand around his cock again, pointing the mushroomed tip at her entrance.

"Desiree ... Desiree ..." he repeated as she sank down on him. She was already so wet, it was easy enough to slide all the way down, seating him in her.

God, she never felt so full as when he was inside her. It still took her a while to stretch around him. When she finally did feel comfortable, she braced her hands on his abs and began to rock back and forth. She angled her hips so that his pelvis hit her just right, the friction making her tense and wanting more.

Her pace quickened, her hips pistoning against him in a mad rhythm. *Oh, so close ... almost.* Karim was grunting through gritted teeth, and his hands reached up to grab at her breasts. When his fingers pinched her nipples, her orgasm ripped through her in a violent wave.

She was barely coming down when he sat up and flipped her over so she was on her back, never leaving her. He hauled her up against a cushion and began to pound mercilessly into her.

"Karim!"

Lights burst across her vision. Exploding into a dazzling, illuminating display. The fireworks had begun, and she cried out as her own body burst apart in orgasm. Tears pricked at her eyes, the sweetness and joy of the moment mixed with bitterness as she tried to capture that feeling, that moment and tuck it away deep in her memories. Yes, this moment would have to be enough.

Karim whispered things in her ear, words she couldn't understand in that low, guttural tone of his native language. Then his words turned into a roar as his movements became jerky and irregular.

His hands gripped her ass so tight they would surely bruise. His mouth clamped down on her neck, his teeth biting into her soft flesh so hard they would leave his brand. His body shuddered, and he thrust into her one last time, his cock twitching in her as she felt his warm seed gush into her, marking her on the inside.

And that's how she felt. Bruised. Branded. *Marked.*

She shut her eyes tight, trying to swallow down the burning sensation in her throat. When she could finally breathe again, she opened her eyes. It felt like time had stopped, but she knew that wasn't true because the fireworks continued lighting up the sky, a brilliant, blinding show that did nothing to fill the darkness creeping inside her.

Karim rolled away from her, heaving as he lay on his back. He reached for her, as he always did, and gathered her to his side.

They lay in silence, watching the stunning display before

them. It was beautiful, but each burst of light seemed to count down her limited time here. Soon, she would be putting this place behind her. Putting Karim behind her.

"Do you still have to fly tonight?"

"Yes, I do. Until the Easifat completely fades." He kissed her temple. "But do not worry, we have time enough."

And for just that moment, she chose to believe his words.

CHAPTER FOURTEEN

Time was running out.

Karim could feel the Easifat fading down to his bones. In the past, he didn't feel it as keenly as he did now. Maybe it was because now he was the bearer of The Great One, he was much more connected to the magic in the sandstorms.

Or maybe it was because as the Easifat wound down, so did his time with Desiree. Slipping through his fingers like grains of sand.

"You should get some sleep."

Her soft, warm body was curled up against his side, an arm thrown over his chest. They had just finished another vigorous lovemaking session. He thought he would surely get enough of her by now, but his desire only seemed to grow stronger. As soon as he came back from his flight this morning, he woke her up. He wanted to see her wrapped in jewels and gold, and so he took every piece of jewelry he had given her and placed it on her, then made love to her, the precious metals and jewels on her bare skin only fueling his lust. As they lay together in the afterglow, he couldn't bring himself to sleep, knowing that when he woke up, it would be another day closer to her departure.

"Karim?"

"I'll be all right; I don't really need much rest."

She sighed against him. "I guess that means I won't be getting any sleep either. I think we should do something more productive." Her fingers drummed across his collarbone.

"Oh?"

It still surprised him, on many levels, how passionate she was. Her enthusiasm more than made up for inexperience, and if he were honest, he enjoyed teaching her and seeing her reactions knowing that no one else had made her feel that way.

"Yes," she said. "Like breakfast."

"I see. So, I guess that means you don't have any other needs to be satisfied."

"I wouldn't say *that* ..." Her fingernails raked down his chest, the motion sending blood all the way down to his cock. "Maybe after we eat ..."

He reached for her, but she rolled away from him. Not that he minded much, because then he could admire her shapely form as she stood up. He had explored every inch of her body by now, but still, the sight of her naked skin and curves made his desire surge. The memory of last night had been burned in his mind, and he knew he would never forget it. Her full breasts bouncing as she rode him. Her sweet mouth around his cock. And the tightness of her as she clasped around him. For as long as he lived, he would never find anyone like her again.

Mine. Ours. Mate.

The voice of The Great One rang clear in his mind.

His father never told him that The Great One spoke to him. What did this mean? Was it the next evolution in his transformation as the bearer?

And theirs? What was theirs? And ...

Mate. Keep.

No!

The Great One rumbled in displeasure.

No, he hissed again.

Keep Desiree? Was the damned thing mad? Didn't it know what happened to his mother? How unhappy she was? No, he wasn't going to let that happen to her. If only there was another way.

"Karim?"

Her soft voice cut into his argument with his animal. He saw that she was sitting at the dresser, taking off the jewelry he had adorned her with. He wasn't sure why, but seeing her bedecked in gold, silver, and jewels pleased him and The Great One so much. It was like a way to mark her, and make her his. And now she was removing them from her body, one by one. He did not like that one bit.

"Why are you taking those off?"

"Hmmm?" she hummed absently as she unclipped the earrings and placed them on the table. "I can't wear these all the time."

"And why not?"

"Don't be silly, Karim." She combed her fingers through her hair, as if trying to put some semblance to her mussed locks. "They're heavy, and I'm just sitting in here the whole day. Besides, Amaya or Zafirah might notice them. I don't want any questions, and I don't want your aunt thinking I'm stealing from the treasury or something."

His fists curled around the sheet at his hips. "And why would she think that?"

She motioned to the pile of jewelry. "Because where else would you get these?"

"I bought them. For you. We do have stores in Zhobghadi."

Her hands stilled, caught in the tangles of her hair. "You ... bought them?"

"Of course." He rose up from the bed and began to walk toward her. "You think I would give you something that others had worn? No, I would not do that."

"But ... but why?"

He stood behind her, meeting her gaze in the mirror. "Because I enjoy it. Because I like seeing you adorned in jewels. Because you deserve it. Because they belong to you." *And I gave them to you.* His fingers brushed aside her hair and caressed the simple chain around her neck, the only piece she didn't take off. In fact, he couldn't recall if she ever did, as he loved to see it glint between her naked breasts when he was making love to her.

Her pulse jumped in her throat. "Karim, you can't mean for me to keep all these once I ... once I ..."

Emotions swirled inside him at the way her voice trailed off. She couldn't say it either. "Of course you will keep them all." He leaned down to press a kiss to her shoulder.

"It's too much, Karim. All of these ... it must have cost you thousands of dollars!"

"The cost means nothing to me." As he tried to kiss her further up, she brushed past him and grabbed the robe hanging from one of the bedposts.

"Still," she said as she wrapped the robe around herself. "I can't keep it. It's not right."

"Yes, it is." The words escaped his mouth before he could stop them. But they felt right.

She let out a sigh, and her shoulders dropped. "Karim, we need to talk about this. The Easifat is over, and it's time for me to leave."

No! The Great One screeched in his head. *Ours. They are ours.*

There had to be a way. A way for her to stay, but not be corrupted and burdened with the heavy responsibilities of the throne. "What if you didn't have to go?"

"Are you joking?" Her grip tightened on the sash of the robe. "You're going to keep me here like a prisoner?"

"No, that's not what I meant." He raked his fingers through his hair. "Live here with me. Stay in the palace."

"As what?"

"Whatever you want. I can employ you as Amaya's tutor. You can even start your own school. Dig holes in the desert, I don't care. As long as you are with me. I promise, I will take care of you."

Her face was still for a moment, before twisting into ... anger? "Stay with you? And then what?"

"What do you mean?"

"And then what happens after? What if we decide that we aren't compatible or that we're not happy with this little 'arrangement' and want to part ways? I can't just jump back into my career, you know."

His first impulse was to tell her that he would never make her unhappy and want to leave him. As long as she didn't have the burden his mother did, it would never happen. "I will not abandon you. I will provide for you no matter what."

"Oh my God!" She threw her hands up. "Are you seriously saying this? You want me to stay here, make up some official position so I can be on the payroll, and then dismiss me with a pension when you're done with me.?"

Anger burned through him. "I would never—"

"You want me to be your mistress, is that it?"

"That's not what I meant—"

"Really? What did you mean, *Your Highness*? Because that's exactly what it sounds like." Her nostrils flared. "Besides, you're going to be king. You know what that entails, right? You need to produce heirs."

What in the name of An had happened in the last five minutes? He had been so elated once he realized there was a way she could stay and that she would be safe from his mother's fate, but then she spurned him? What was the matter with her? Talking about dismissing her and being done with her and him producing heirs. Unless …

"Surely you don't think you could be queen?"

Her face faltered. It was just for a moment, but Karim saw it. And if he had any sense, any pity in him, he would have stopped there. But he was so livid at her rejection that he continued.

"It must be so tempting for you," he sneered. "You think it is all glamour? Do you even have any idea what this life is like?" He scrubbed his hand down his face. "To be forever owned by the people and never yourself? To have to keep up a perfect facade, keeping your emotions in check all the time, never showing anger or sorrow or weakness? To be burdened with responsibility, and to always have to put yourself and your family last? To be consumed by loneliness, devoured by it that you would do anything to escape?"

His mother's dress whipping in the wind ...

Her slender frame swaying as she stood on the bannister.

Mum ... Mum ... please.

Begging her silently. Wishing that he could be enough of a reason to stay alive.

He tipped her chin up with a finger. "Tell me, is that what you want, Desiree?"

Desiree's lips trembled, but she remained stiff, her spine straight, and her head held high.

"It doesn't have to be complicated. You can have riches beyond your wildest dreams without any responsibilities. I can erase your debts, your worries."

She winced and turned away. "You don't know anything about me."

But he could already guess what her life was like, seen her clothes when she got here. Like most Americans, she was probably drowning in student loans. That, and combined with the fact that educators were the worst-paid professionals in the world, she probably had to watch every penny she spent. "Do you want to be struggling your entire life, teaching ungrateful, spoiled students for a chance at tenure, when I can make you more than comfortable for your entire life? I can fund any expedition or dig you want; you'd never have to beg for grants again." His thumb brushed her jaw. "I can give you *anything.*" *But don't ask me to make you my queen.*

She slapped his hand away. "How dare you! Are you trying to buy me? You think ... you think I would exchange m-myself for money? For security?"

Gods above and below, he was making a mess of things. "This is not what—"

"Let me tell you something, *Your Highness!*" She marched toward him, with all the flame and fury of Gerra. "I would rather struggle my entire life doing something that gave my existence meaning than to accept your offer of 'security.' Because being beholden to you would never bring me security."

Her rejection stung deep, slicing into him like a dull sword. Maybe she was holding out. Playing the long game. Hoping she would get the bigger prize, push for more. So he upped the stakes. "I could give you the world on a silver platter."

"And I don't want it. I don't want *any* part of this world you offer."

And damn him, he believed it. Saw it in her eyes. No trace of greed, or selfishness. In fact, for a moment, he saw only an intense emotion that was soon swallowed up by another more powerful one—hurt.

At that moment, he would have given up everything, even his own soul, to be able to take everything he said back. But he could not—would not—ever let her go.

"Desiree," he said, his voice cracking. "Don't—"

The door to his bedroom burst open. "*Your Highness!*"

"How dare you?" he bellowed, without even knowing who it was. He swung around and came face-to-face with his ward. "What are you doing here?" Remembering who he was talking to, he asked the question again in Zhobghadian.

"Highness!" The boy's voice was high-pitched and frantic. "We are under attack."

His muscles tensed. "Under attack? By whom?"

"Highness, please!" Ramin grabbed his arm. "You must come!"

Why wouldn't the boy say anything? Why was he so terrified? "Where?"

Ramin's eyes slid upward to the ceiling. "From above. Highness ..." He turned his eyes toward Deedee, vitriol evident. "The Gods must have been angry enough to send ..."

"Send what?" He stared Ramin down, but he wouldn't talk. They were under attack, but by whom? Perhaps it was the same people who had caught him in the net the other night. Did his enemies tire of palace intrigue and decide to stage a coup? He should have been spending more time trying to find the traitors within his government, but he had been distracted.

A cold shiver went through him. If they came in here and discovered Desiree ... "Go to Captain Fariba now. Tell him I want as many of the Almoravid as he can spare guarding my suites. I want no one to get in," his gaze flickered to Desiree who was still standing in the same spot, unmoving, "or out. Do you understand? This is the most important thing I will ever ask of you."

Ramin pounded his fist to his chest. "Yes, Highness." He turned on his heel and marched to the door.

When the boy was gone, he turned to Desiree, switching back to English. "Don't leave this room. Do not even leave the suite. If you hear anyone trying to break down the door, *hide*."

"What? Karim, what's going—"

"I must go." He ached to hold her, to kiss her. But there would be time enough for that when he defeated these attackers and came back to her.

"Karim—"

"Do not leave this place." He ignored her protests as he walked out the door, locking it behind him for good measure.

As he walked toward the balcony, he pushed all thoughts of the morning's disastrous events behind him. For now, he was the Crown Prince Karim, bearer of The Great One, and his people needed him.

CHAPTER FIFTEEN

IT TOOK A WHILE FOR THE NUMBNESS TO LEAVE Deedee's body. Her mind was still trying to process what happened. His words ... well, *hurt* didn't even begin to describe it.

But she knew they wouldn't have hurt this bad if she didn't allow herself to care for him.

And she thought Cross was bad. At least he had let her down quick and easy. Karim ... he wanted to keep her by his side, like some pet. Never giving her more than his body.

He was cruel and heartless, and she'd seen the extent of it today. Those cutting words ... insinuating that she wanted *his title*, of all things. That she would even think of exchanging her body for his protection and money, like some ... whore that he could—no, he *would* toss her away once he got tired of her. What about when he found a suitable woman to be queen? Was she just supposed to step aside and let him produce heirs? Or did she expect her to be available, waiting in the wings?

Tears pricked at her eyes. Heavens, she had been

tempted for *just* a moment, dazzled by his promise. But it wasn't the wealth or even the chance to do her research in Zhobghadi that made her almost say yes. It was the thought of being with him all the time. Because her heart, her damned foolish heart, had fallen for him. And he didn't feel the same way.

Her wolf growled, as if contradicting her.

"It's true." She wiped the tears at the corner of her eyes. "You think he cares for me? Why would he even say those awful things to me?" Her wolf didn't seem to understand, so she kept on. "I don't know what was worse, that he thought I would even consider being a mistress or that he thinks I wanted to be queen? Or that I wouldn't be happy—"

A realization struck her like a bolt of lightning. His mother. He was talking about his mother. She had killed herself when—

"No, no, no!" She was *not* going to sympathize with him or excuse him. For one thing, she was *not* his mother. If he wanted to explain and apologize, then he could damn well say it himself when he came back.

Her inner wolf whined and howled, reminding her of something. But what?

"Oh no." Before he stormed out, he said to stay inside and not let anyone in. And to hide if anyone broke down the door.

Did she forget that someone tried to take him down the other night? *That net.* The fall that could have killed him.

Fear gripped her heart. As she cleared the haze of heartbreak from her mind, she realized how worried and tense he had been when he left. And for Ramin to have just burst through the door without invitation or permission, there must be something going on. But what?

She crossed the room and yanked on the door, but it didn't budge. "He locked me in, that bastard!" She didn't even realize the door could be secured from the other side. "Help!" She screamed as she jiggled the handle. "Let me out!"

Well, then, she was going to have to break it down. She stepped back a few feet, prepared to hit the door with all her Lycan strength. She could injure herself, but she would heal. And if the door didn't budge, she could shift and use her claws to shred the wood to pieces.

She took a deep breath, crouched down and—

A loud shriek made her freeze. It was followed by another. And another ear-piercing screech. Then two distinct roars sounded at the same time, making the earth shake.

Oh no.

One of the roars sounded very familiar.

Dad?

"No, no, no!" Her heart pounded in a crazy rhythm, banging against her ribs. It couldn't be. But how did her father find her? She had to get out of there now before he and Karim killed each other.

Turning her attention to the door, she braced herself. "Here we go."

She came at the door at a dead run and ... sailed straight through, landing on her chest with a great big thump, the air squeezing out of her lungs. "What the—"

A pair of hands slipped under her armpits and lifted her up effortlessly. As she shook her hair off her face, she looked up. Straight into a pair of ocean-colored eyes.

For a fleeting moment, her heart fluttered at the thought that Cross had come to rescue her. But when her vision focused on the crow's-feet around his eyes and the wrinkles on his forehead, she knew it wasn't him.

"U-Uncle Daric?" It was not Cross, but rather, his father.

The warlock gave her a warm, calm smile. "Hello, Deedee."

"But how—" Another loud shriek and a ground-shaking roar cut her off. She disentangled herself from him and dashed out onto the balcony. "Please, no."

Just as she'd thought. It was her father's roar she'd heard. High above in the sky, the humungous, frightening gold dragon spread its wings as it opened its mouth and spewed out fire. The silver dragon in its path quickly dodged away, then swung around to swipe a claw at its rival.

"Stop!" But it wasn't like they would hear her. But they had to stop fighting, stop hurting each other.

Running back into the suite, she made a beeline for her rescuer. "Uncle Daric, please tell Dad to stop!" She clawed at his arms. "They didn't hurt me or kidnap me! Please!"

"I know," Daric said solemnly. "I tried to tell him but ... you know how he is. When his men said you'd been lost—"

"His men? What men?"

"You didn't know this, but your father had a security team on you the entire time you were away. Your university thought they were hiring freelance drivers and assistants, but really, they were your father's men." His lips pursed together. "Not that that did any good. They didn't even realize you had been gone when the sand storm hit your camp."

"What?" No, she couldn't believe it ... but then again, this was Sebastian Creed they were talking about. "How could he do that?"

"You know he only wanted—"

A light cough made them both stop. "I hate to interrupt this reunion, but maybe we could continue and get this rescue moving along, *oui?*"

Deedee turned her head toward the third person she didn't realize had been in the room. *Where in the world had he come from?* "Who are you?"

The handsome, dark-haired man's smile lit up his face. "Marc Delacroix, at your service. Now, grab onto the warlock so he can use his magic powers and *voila*, we'll be New York in no time, *mon petite.*"

Petite? She was almost six feet tall. No one would mistake her for a *petite* anything. Ignoring him, she turned to Daric. "Wait, how did you get in here? I thought you needed to have been in a place or seen it on a map before you could transport?"

Daric cocked his head at Delacroix. "That's where our Cajun friend came in," he began. "Mr. Delacroix has a special set of skills."

She whipped her head back to the other man. Lycan, definitely. Compact, built like a brick wall and with tattoos running down his arms, he certainly stood out, but he didn't seem special to her.

He gave her another brilliant smile. "Like what you see, *mon petite?*"

"Mr. Delacroix can move anywhere undetected and break into any locked door," Daric said. "Which how I was able to come in here."

"And just in time, too," Delacroix tugged at the collar of his shirt. "I could hear those guards at our heels." He glanced around nervously. "So? Are we going or not, *mon ami?*"

"I don't understand." Deedee rubbed her arms with her hands. "What the heck is going on?"

"When he found out you were gone, Sebastian went into a rage," Daric began. "And then your guards told him you had disappeared in the sandstorms by the border of Zhobghadi, well ... he went insane. I don't know how much he had told you about what happened to him, but it was here that he had been transformed into a beast."

"The accident happened here?"

"It was no accident." Daric's eyes turned stormy. "But anyway, we exhausted our search around the area. Interviewed all your colleagues. No one would tell us where you were."

"Wait a minute, *no one*?" Hanford didn't say anything? Just left her for dead? Or perhaps he was gone too?

"Yes. However, I detected magic nearby. A tremendous amount. And then I saw the veil of magic surrounding the area where Zhobghadi should be."

"The Easifat." She had felt it too, from the inside. "It's the reason I couldn't leave or send word out that I was okay. It blocks electronic signals."

"Magic as well. I prodded at it with my own magic, but I could not pierce it. So, I waited. And finally, when I felt the barriers weaken last night, I went inside. I saw you, on the balcony."

"You saw me ..." *Oh dear, what had he seen?*

"Only briefly," Daric added. "Just long enough to confirm your presence as you were having dinner with the prince last night."

She surely hoped that was Daric's way of saying he didn't stick around for what happened *after*. "And then ..."

"*Mon Dieu!*" Delacroix scrubbed a hand down his face. "Can we not do this back in New York? Before we—"

A loud crash from the outside drowned out the Cajun's words. Deedee's spine went rigid, then she dashed out onto the balcony. "Oh no." A large, dragon-sized crater dented the middle of the enormous terrace, and right in the middle was a pillar of fire. The question was who was it?

As the fire subsided, Deedee's question was answered. Sebastian Creed dusted himself off and got to his feet. When he turned his dark gray eyes toward her, his expression changed.

"Deedee." He limped toward her, clutching the large, bloody gash at his side.

"Dad," she cried as she rushed to him. As her father's strong arms wrapped around her, tears pricked at her eyes. She had never been so glad to see him or smell his wonderful paper and leather scent.

"Baby, are you okay? Did they hurt you?" He let go of her and ran his fingers over her cheeks. "Goddammit, if they harmed even one hair on your head, they're fucking dead. Daric, I told you to get her out of here the moment you get to her."

Turning her head, she realized that Daric and Marc had followed her. "She is unharmed," Daric said. "And she didn't tell me she wanted to leave."

"Didn't tell you?" Sebastian growled. "Baby, you've been gone for days! When I heard where you were, I thought ..." He gritted his teeth.

"What's going on, Dad?" she asked. "I know I've been gone for a while, but I can explain. I got lost and—"

"Baby, it was *here*. This is where ..." Sebastian's eyes

turned into shards of hard flint. "These Zhobghadi bastards ... they captured me and turned me into ... this."

Her stomach dropped. "W-w-what?"

There it was, in his eyes. The thousand-yard stare. "They tortured me for a month. I thought I was going to die in this hellhole and then when my squad finally rescued me—"

The roar that came from above was deafening, and when she looked up, she saw the silver dragon headed straight for them in a nosedive. She braced herself for the impact, but the massive creature angled its body upwards just in time for a foot-first landing. The ground shook as gigantic claws dug into the concrete, and a pillar of fire engulfed the creature as it grew smaller, and finally, Karim walked from the flames.

"How dare you!" The prince strode toward them with a menacing gait. A cut on his temple made blood gush down a cheek, but he didn't seem to care. His eyes burned with rage as he stared at Sebastian. "Abomination! Blasphemer! How dare you take the form of The Great One and challenge me? Did my enemies—" He stopped short when his gaze landed on her. "Desiree, I told you to stay inside!" He fixed an ominous stare on Sebastian. "If you harm her, I will tear you to pieces and spread whatever is left over the desert so no one will find you!"

Sebastian's jaw dropped. "Are you fucking kidding me? Who the fuck are you?" He put his body between Deedee and Karim. "Daric, take her away!"

"You cannot leave here." Karim's tone held a hint of smugness. "The Almoravid are blocking your only means of escape." He cocked his head toward the doorway leading back to the suite, "And I will take you down if you try to fly away with her."

"You think I need doors or wings to take *my daughter* away from this fucking hellhole?"

Karim's expression changed from anger to surprise to disbelief, before he turned back to Deedee. "Daughter? *Daughter?*"

"Karim," she began. "I can explain—"

"No more talking, no more fucking explanations!" Sebastian shouted.

A heavy hand landed on Deedee's shoulder. When she turned her head, she looked up into stormy turquoise eyes.

"Do you want to go, Deedee?" Daric asked in a soft voice.

"Stop fucking around and take her away," Sebastian yelled. "*Now.*"

"It must be her choice." The warlock ignored the string of expletives coming out from her father's mouth. "*Do you want to go?*"

She couldn't breathe. Couldn't think. Couldn't speak. "I—"

Karim made a move toward her. "Let her go—"

"Shut up, asshole!" Sebastian pointed a finger at him. "Or I'm going to put my foot so far up your ass that you'll feel it when you're fifty. *If* I let you live that long."

"Deedee," Daric gripped her shoulder tighter. "You must make the decision."

Karim's voice was dead serious as he said, "You are not going anywhere, Desiree."

And in that moment, something snapped inside her. Karim's hurtful words from earlier rang in her head. The way he'd been so cruel and believed the worst of her.

Surely you don't think you could be queen?

Well, if Karim didn't want her, then there was no reason to stay. She deserved better.

"Yes," Deedee said in a soft voice. "Take me home."

"No!" Karim roared at Sebastian. "I swear to all the gods above and below, if you take her now, I will make you pay!"

"You and what army, fucker?"

"There is no place on earth you can hide her." Karim's eyes were filled with hate and rage. "I will come for her, and even if you have an army of a thousand men, you will not stop me."

Sebastian grabbed onto Daric's arm. "Go now!"

Right before the coldness gripped her and Zhobghadi disappeared from her vision, the last thing Deedee saw was Karim hurtling toward her, his arms stretched wide, and those fiery dragon eyes ablaze with fury.

A coldness wrapped around her entire body, then her feet landed on something solid. She opened her eyes, not even realizing that she had shut them. "Where—Oh!" She was standing in the living room of her parents' loft in Tribeca, her childhood home.

"Deedee!" came her mother's familiar cry. "Oh God, Deedee!" Her arms wrapped around her in a comforting hug as Jade Creed sobbed. Wetness stung her own eyes.

"Mom." She went limp in her mother's arms. "Oh, Mom."

"I thought we had lost you." Her mother cradled her face with her hands. "My baby. I'm so glad to see you. When we heard you were lost—"

Her spine went ramrod stiff. "When you heard I was lost." Pulling away from her mother, she pivoted and turned to face her father. "When you heard it from those men *you* hired to watch me."

"Deedee, baby." Sebastian cautiously walked toward her, palms up. "It was for your own good." His dark blond brows snapped together. "And see? If I hadn't had those guys on you—"

"You need to stop treating me like a child! I'm thirty years old, Dad, not three! You can't keep doing this."

"Well if I hadn't you still would be ... you'd be there with ..." His eyes flashed with the gold of his dragon, and the air grew cold and heavy. "I can't believe it. Another dragon."

"What?" Jade asked. "What do you mean another dragon?"

Sebastian ignored her, and instead focused his stare on his daughter. "Did he touch you?"

"My God, Dad!" She buried her face in her hands, mostly because she didn't want them to see how red her face had gotten.

Karim. Oh Lord. If her dad didn't have those guys watch her, what would have happened?

No, stop thinking that. In a way, she should be glad she got out of there quick. Wasn't it better to rip her heart out in a quick pull, like a Band-Aid, rather than have to suffer any longer. If she had, she might have done something rash.

"Deedee—"

"No!" She put her hand up, cutting off her father. "This ends now. You need to stop meddling in my life."

"You were taken hostage!" Sebastian said through gritted teeth. "What was I supposed to do?"

"You don't—argh!" She threw her hands up and then looked to the fourth occupant of the room—Uncle Daric—

who had remained quiet the entire time. "Take me home, please?"

"Dee—"

"For the last time, leave me alone! Uncle Daric," she pleaded and grabbed his arm. "Now."

Sebastian pointed a finger at the warlock. "Don't you dare—"

The coldness gripped her body again, and relief washed through her as her parents and the living room shimmered away.

CHAPTER SIXTEEN

As she sat in front of her couch inside her brownstone, Deedee ignored the incessant ringing of her cellphone where it sat on the well-worn, comfy couch beside her. She didn't even have to look at the screen to know she didn't want to talk to whoever it was. It didn't matter if it was her mother, her father, or either of her brothers. She just wanted to be alone and eat her gallon of Ben and Jerry's Everything But The Kitchen Sink ice cream.

"Ughh!" She put the spoon and half-empty tub down on the coffee table, grabbed a throw pillow, then slammed it on top of her cellphone. "Just leave me alone," she cried to no one in particular. "I asked you to give me time, can't you just respect that?" Taking the tub back on her lap, she began to shovel the sticky sweet ice cream in her mouth.

It had only been forty-eight hours since she'd returned to New York. In that time, she ignored all the calls and messages from her parents and proceeded to stress clean her entire house, as well as order exorbitant amounts of pizza and Chinese takeout.

When she calmed down enough, the first thing she did was contact work, assuring them she was fine and that she had just been lost in the sandstorm, but thankfully she was able to find a way to get to the nearest city and ask for help, and then her father had sent his private jet to pick her up. With what had happened, they had been sympathetic, but needless to say, the fate of her research trip was now up in the air.

She had also discovered what happened right after she got lost. It seemed Hanford was able to make it back to camp, but didn't say anything or tell anyone that she might have been lost. In fact, he hastily left the camp the next day without speaking to anyone. When she didn't come for breakfast, they had assumed she had slept in. Then a sandstorm had blown through, and everyone had stayed inside their tents overnight. It wasn't until the sandstorm had died down and they were cleaning up the destroyed camp that anyone had realized she was gone. The nearest communications towers were down as well, so it took another day for someone to head out to the nearest town to find a working phone and tell her family that she was gone.

It still seemed like a dream, her time in the palace. A dream that had become a nightmare. One would think now that she was halfway around the world, the power of Karim's words wouldn't hurt her as bad.

But, damn her stupid, stupid heart, because being away from him hurt even more. She didn't know what was worse: the slow simmering emotions she'd kept for Cross for years or the bright burning ones that fizzled out. However, even now, what she felt for Karim didn't seem to be fizzling out any time soon.

Her wolf made a pathetic whine. That was the only thing it could do these days, it seemed. Whine and complain at her. *Stupid wolf.*

The sound of the doorbell made her start. It didn't stop after the first ring, but keep going. "Fine!". As she stood up, ice cream carton in hand, the ringing continued and grew insistent. Except for her parents and people at work, no one knew she was back in New York. *Who could it be?* She told her family to—

Her heart fluttered wildly in her chest. *Oh.* For a second, she imagined who it could be. That he had changed his mind and—

She raced to the door, flinging it open. "I—Astrid?"

Her best friend, Astrid Jonasson-Vrost, stood in the doorway. "I was afraid you weren't going to answer."

"Was that going to stop you?" Astrid, like Cross, was a hybrid—part Lycan, part witch, inherited from her father Daric—and had the ability to teleport short distances. She could teleport herself into Deedee's house from the front door if she wanted to—and did so sometimes.

"No." Her shoulders dropped. "But I'm so damn exhausted and cranky, and I figured you wouldn't turn away a pregnant woman." Her hands went to her protruding belly, and Deedee knew she was ready to give birth very soon. "Let me in please? And—" her eyes dropped to the nearly empty container in her hand, "tell me you have more of those."

"Tons." Deedee laughed for the first time in what seemed like days, and she realized the sight of her best friend was all she needed for that cloud looming over her to go away. "Come in, Astrid, and put your feet up. Goodness, are you sure you only have one in there?"

The blonde winced. "Some days it feels like I have a basketball team inside my belly. And this game has definitely gone on overtime."

When she stood aside to let Astrid in, that's when she realized her friend wasn't alone. Two men—both of them familiar—stood at the bottom of the stoop. "What are they doing here? Did my father send you to check on me?"

Her friend poked a finger at her sternum. "If you'd left your house at all, you'd have realized these two," she cocked her head at the two men behind her, "have been guarding your place for the last two days."

"Nice to see you again, *mon petite*," Marc Delacroix greeted, a big grin on his face. "Seems you're so glad to be home, you never want to leave. I hope you've been tipping your pizza delivery guy generously, seeing as he's made so many trips here."

Deedee rolled her eyes and fixed her attention on her second guard. "Hello, Jacob, haven't seen you in a while. Why didn't you come up and say hello?"

The young Lycan man smirked at her, his green eyes twinkling. "Hey, Dee, how's it going?" Jacob Martin worked at Lone Wolves Security, an agency her father ran that employed Lycans and sent them out on special missions around the world. He was also a family friend, as his father was an adopted brother of Meredith Jonasson, Astrid and Cross's mom.

She crossed her arms over her chest. "What are you two doing here?"

"Seems Sebastian Creed was mighty impressed at how I helped save his only daughter, and Lucas—I mean, the Alpha —was happy I could help prevent Sebastian from razing an entire country," Delacroix said. "So I thought I'd ingratiate myself further by offering to keep you safe. I've learned that favors from powerful men can come in handy."

"Keep me safe? From—" When she turned back to Jacob Martin and remembered who—and what—he was, it dawned on her. That is, the reason why her father would send *him* of all people.

I will come for her, and even if you have an army of a thousand men, you will not stop me.

Karim's words gave her an involuntary shiver. But surely, he didn't mean to just pluck her from her home and take her back. For one thing, that was kidnapping. And even if he did manage to come for her and bring her to Zhobghadi, her family and clan could just take her back.

"Dee?" Astrid cocked her head to the side. "Are you okay?"

"Huh? Yeah, I'm fine. Just ... come in." She glared at the two men. "You guys can stay out here." *Really!* Did her father think that the best way to make amends for sending his people to watch over her was to send *more* people? With a great big huff, she slammed the door.

As they walked into the living room, Astrid waddled over to the couch. She waved off Deedee's offer of assistance as she eased herself down with a long sigh. "How are you doing, Dee?"

She considered clamming up and not saying anything. This was her best friend, after all, and she would understand if Deedee was not ready to talk. When Astrid herself had been brokenhearted, she'd come here and Deedee allowed her to just mope and cry as she needed. But really, what good would it do? "I'm ... doing as well as I can. What do you know about what happened?"

"Only bits and pieces. I wanted to give you time, but it's been two days." Astrid reached out and placed a hand over hers. "When I heard that you were lost, I panicked, I swear I would have given birth right then and there. Zac kept it from me as long as he could because he didn't want me to panic or try to help in the search, which only made me even more frantic. And then while I was stewing at home, feeling so helpless that I couldn't go and find you, I got mad."

"Mad? At what?"

"At you," she said sheepishly. "Because you ran away so far from us, where we couldn't protect you. And I was mad at Cross, too."

"Cross? Whatever for?"

"Because he drove you away." The look in Astrid's eyes told Deedee she truly believed this. "If only he didn't reject you, and if only he declared his love for you, then you wouldn't have left New York. And then maybe you'd be dating by now or maybe we'd even be pregnant at the same time." She rubbed her belly. "You guys always looked so good together, and I know I was always that third wheel—"

"Astrid, no." She shook her head as she reached over and hugged her friend. "Please, don't think that. I meant what I said before. I love you as a sister, a real sister, okay?"

"Damn hormones," Astrid wiped her tears with the back of her hand. "And that stupid brother of mine ... he doesn't even know that you were lost. No one's been able to contact him."

"He's doing important work." Deedee knew all about his work, of course, trying to obtain the two remaining artifacts of

Magus Aurelius before their enemies, the mages, did. Her mother kept her up to date. That didn't mean she wasn't disappointed that Cross hadn't come for her. "Your dad came to get me."

"I know," Astrid said. "It's weird though, huh? How he could have known you'd be in Zhobghadi, even though that veil of magic prevented him from coming inside?"

"I—" She never questioned it at the time, but she realized Astrid was right. How did Daric guess so quickly? "Well, they knew I couldn't have gone far. It was probably a hunch."

"Deedee, what happened while you were there?" Astrid asked, their eyes meeting. "Did they ... hurt you? Is that why you haven't spoken to anyone since you got back?"

She swallowed the lump that had suddenly formed in her throat. "No one hurt me." *Physically*. Astrid was her friend, could she tell her? "I—"

Raised voices coming from the outside caught their attention, followed by a crash and a series of loud thumps.

Astrid's brows squished together. "What the heck was that?"

Her instincts flared, and Deedee didn't bother to wait for Astrid to get up as she rushed to the door and threw it open. "What in heaven's name is going on here?"

Two large men had Delacroix pinned against a dark SUV as he struggled to break free. At the bottom of the stoop, two more guys stood on either side of Jacob, ready to pounce on him.

As Jacob raised his hands, panic seized Deedee. "Jacob, no! We're out in public."

Jacob was distracted by her words for a second, but it was

just enough time for the two men to tackle him and take him down.

"No!" Deedee flew down the steps, and grabbed one of the men. But he didn't budge, didn't even flinch as she used all her Lycan strength to try and pry him off Jacob. However, the man made no move to fling her off or even try to touch her. Who were these men and how were they so strong? She didn't sense any wolves in them, so they couldn't be Lycans.

She heard the sound of the SUV door opening, but she ignored it, focusing on her task of freeing Jacob before they did something drastic. "Get off him!"

"Desiree, stop."

Her blood froze like an arctic storm in her veins. No, it couldn't be ...

"Desiree."

Slowly, she looked up. And cerulean blue eyes stared back at her.

What felt like a lifetime passed as they stared at each other. It must have only been seconds, but everything around her seemed to slow down. Someone was calling her name, but it sounded like they were far away. And she couldn't focus on anything else except Karim's tall, dark frame as it unfolded from the SUV, the two steps he took toward her, and the warm, musky scent of his that transported her back to his desert palace.

She opened her mouth, but nothing came out. He didn't say anything either.

"Deedee, get back inside!" Jacob growled as he struggled against the men pinning him down. "Motherfuckers, how the fuck are you this strong?"

She came back to her senses and realized who these guys were. The royal bodyguards. "Karim, call off your men."

"They were defending themselves and me," Karim said. "I was trying to go up to your door—"

"No one gets in," Delacroix growled, his eyes glowing wolf. "Dragon's orders."

"I *am* the dragon," Karim growled back. "So, these two men are meant to keep me away? They cannot even take on the Almoravid."

"Four against two doesn't seem fair," the Cajun wolf shot back.

"I'm fucking tired of this shit." Jacob went still, then said in a low voice, "Get. Off. Me!"

The two men holding him down suddenly let go, shouting in pain as they waved their arms, flames licking at the sleeves of their matching black suits. The guys pinning Delacroix rushed to their aid, forcing their companions to the ground to get them to roll around in an attempt to smother the fire.

"What's the matter *dragon*? Finally found your match?" Jacob shot to his feet, his eyes glowing with an unearthly light. He lifted his hands, which were both lit up with flames. "Go ahead, light me up. I don't burn easily." He blew at his hands, extinguishing the flames with a dramatic flair. "Maybe you'd like to give it a try? I haven't been tickled in a while."

And that's why Sebastian Creed chose Jacob to be her bodyguard. The hybrid could not only produce and control fire, but was completely immune to it.

"Are you crazy, Jacob?" Deedee railed. "We're out in public! Anyone could have seen you!"

"I have my orders from Sebastian, Dee," he said. "No one comes near you, especially not *this* prick."

For the first time ever, Deedee saw genuine shock on Karim's face. Of course, he quickly recovered. "You cannot stop me—"

"What the fuck is going on here?"

All eyes turned toward the front door, where Astrid stood, hands on her hips. "Jacob," she thrust her chin at the two men nursing burns on their arms. "Did you use your magic in public? You know that's forbidden."

"Aww, Astrid," Jacob blustered. "Those guys were all over me!"

"Oh, my Lord, Karim, your men!" Deedee looked over at them. "They need to go to the hospital—"

"They will be fine." He nodded at the two men, who immediately stood up and bowed, their fists pounding on their chest.

"But—"

"They are Almoravid and they will heal quickly."

"Those aren't just—"

"Just who the hell are you?" Though it took her a while, Astrid eventually made it down the stoop and now stood nose-to-nose—or rather, nose-to-chest—with Karim.

"I am the Crown Prince Karim Idris Salamuddin of Zhobghadi, heir to the throne and bearer of The Great One."

"Well, I'm Astrid Jonasson-Vrost, Future Beta of the New York clan and take-no-shit from anyone fucking bad ass." Despite her advanced pregnancy, Astrid clearly wasn't intimidated by Karim's title or his looming stance over her. "What the hell are you doing here?"

"That is no way to address a prince."

"This is my territory, *prince*." She stared him down, and they stood there, just waiting for the other to flinch.

Desiree slapped a hand over her head. "Karim, just go, okay? We're causing a scene here. Go and never come back." She turned her back on him and marched up the steps.

"Desiree!" Footsteps followed her up to her front door. "Stop!"

She whirled to face him. "I'm not going back to you so I can be your fucking mistress!" Goodness, she never ever cursed. While her father was a former marine and cursed like it was going out of style, her mother hated it, so she tried to avoid it. But that damned man just drove her to the brink.

"Desiree, I told you there was nowhere on earth you could hide from me," he said in a deadly voice.

"How did get my address?"

He snorted. "You told me your name; it was easy enough to find you. And information on your father, if you know the right people."

Of course. Creed Securities provided services to all kinds of high-level individuals all over the world, from billionaires to celebrities to politicians. Karim would have had the right connections to get the information he needed.

Her heart sank. Because for a moment, she thought he was here for *her*. But it was obvious, he wanted to know more about her father and his dragon. Would he use her to get to him?

"If you want my father then you already know where his office is and where to find him. Go fly up to his building and have at it, maybe it'll do you both some good and then you can both stop hounding me."

"Desiree, I didn't come here for him, I came here for you."

"Me?" Oh, she was tired of this. Tired of getting her hopes up and then being disappointed again and again. "What do you want with me?"

"I—" He faltered for a moment. "Desiree, I do not like how things ended between us. And that you just left without hearing me out."

"What, never had a woman leave you? You always do the leaving, right? Or sending away?"

"I suppose I deserve that." His nostrils flared. "Invite me inside so we can talk now and iron things out."

"Absolutely not, Your Highness. We're done talking."

"Desiree," he said in a warning voice. "I've come here to make you an offer."

"An offer?" Her voice pitched higher. "Oh pray, do tell. Are you going to offer me the world on a *diamond* platter?"

"No, I've come to ask you to be my queen."

Deedee waited for the punchline. Or the hidden cameras to come out and tell her this was a prank of some sort. But no, nothing happened. And from the dead-serious expression on his face, she knew that he wasn't joking. "Are you kidding me? After all you said that morning? You think I *want* to be your queen?"

He didn't seem surprised at her refusal. "Desiree, listen to me. The things I said before you left were said in the heat of the moment. The Easifat was waning and I was desperate." He raked his fingers through his hair. "I didn't want to let you go, but there was no other way. Not without putting the burden of the throne on you."

"Oh, so when you thought I was some poor, broke

university scholar, I couldn't hack it." Was he really trying to make this all better or did he fly halfway around the world to insult her more? "But now that you know my family is richer than Midas and I'm the daughter of a dragon, I'm worthy to be queen and bear your heirs?"

"It was you who brought up heirs," he spat back. "Why would you remind me of my duty if you didn't desire it yourself?"

"Oh, for God's sake ..." She raised her hands in frustration. "You really don't know why I brought that up?"

He said nothing, but his jaw tensed, and his eyes hardened into chips of blue ice.

"Tell me, Karim, when you gave me your first offer to stay with you, did it ever occur to you how I would feel once you did find someone to be your queen and have your children? What was I supposed to do when that time came? Just step aside? Or watch some other woman get pregnant with your baby and—" She choked, unable to say more because her heart was twisting in knots imagining it. Some beautiful Zhobghadian woman standing beside him, her stomach round with his child, looking up at him in adoration. "You can't have thought I would stand for that." *I deserve better than to be cast off when it was time to do his duty.*

Karim stared at her, his entire body going taut. "Desiree ... I didn't think—"

"That's right, you didn't think." *And neither did I when I fell for you, and I'm paying for it.* "Just go. Please."

"This isn't over."

"Yes, it is. If you care for me even a little bit, you'll leave me be." She turned away and walked back into her house. When the door shut behind her, she leaned back and let out a long sigh, the adrenaline draining from her body. Frankly, she was glad for the physical and mental exhaustion, because she just didn't have the strength to do anything, even cry.

Her wolf whined again, scratching at her, trying to get her attention. She could feel its desperation and heartache. *I know*, she told her animal. *I feel it too.*

Seconds passed as she heard the sounds of murmuring voices, the closing of a car door, and the roar of an engine. A knock on the door made her spin around to open it.

Astrid stood there, arms crossed over her chest, head cocked to the side as her amber eyes searched Deedee's. "Anything you care to tell me?"

What else could she do? "I'll get the Ben and Jerry's."

CHAPTER SEVENTEEN

KARIM IGNORED THE LOOKS AND GLANCES HE COULD feel on him as he entered The Plaza Hotel, two each of the Almoravid flanking him on either side. He had only arrived in New York this morning, so the paparazzi hadn't been tipped off to his presence, but he knew soon they would descend on him like vultures to carrion.

The sea of people milling about in the lobby parted as they strode toward the elevators. His lead guard, Gakurh, pressed the call button, as the rest of the Almoravid blocked him from curious onlookers. No one even dared to come near him when the elevator doors opened, even those who had been waiting before him, and he entered first, followed by his guards.

This was a mistake, Karim thought as he watched the numbers on top of the doors begin to ascend. His ministers told him it was a mistake leaving Zhobghadi so soon after the Easifat had ended and without setting a coronation date. Arvin had warned him it was a mistake to go after Desiree once he found out where she was. Captain Fariba insisted it was a mistake to go to New York without any preparations. Only Aunt Zafirah and Amaya had wished him luck on his mission to win back Desiree. And he was prepared to get her back at any cost. He had been so confident that once she had calmed down, she would listen to him and see reason, and he would prove his detractors wrong.

But now, after seeing her, witnessing her anger, and being so thoroughly dismissed, he realized he should have listened to them.

The elevator dinged, signaling that it had reached the penthouse suite. He didn't bother to wait for any of the guards to alight first into the small foyer or open the door for him, instead yanking it open and striding inside before letting the door slam loudly. Shrugging his coat off, he tossed it onto a nearby couch, then headed straight to the fully-stocked bar to pour himself some scotch.

The triple shot he took only made his throat burn, and he slammed the glass down on the marble countertop so hard, it broke into pieces. "Godsdamnit all to hell!"

And godsdamn her father, that charlatan, for taking Desiree away before he had a chance to explain to her. As soon as the Easifat lifted and he was able to communicate with the outside world, he sought out the information he needed. In his position, he had amassed many contacts over the years, some who were able to procure any type of information he wanted, for the right price.

Yet, despite paying through the nose, he didn't get much information on Sebastian Creed, except for those publicly available and redacted military files and reports. The man's security, both offline and online, were top-notch. Even in the darkest corners of the web, the man did not exist.

Desiree's information was easy enough to obtain, however, since his contacts were able to break into her university's computers. As soon as he got her address, he flew to New York.

It was the last piece of information he needed that couldn't be found at all, at least, not yet. While there were public records on Creed, Desiree, and their family, there was no information to be found about humans who could transform into wolves. No news stories, police reports, or even crazy conspiracy theory blogs. Only folk tales and fictional stories.

What was she? He thought that maybe there was no one else like her, but she did mention "her kind." And apparently, now, there were also people who could make fire appear from their hands. The world truly was much simpler before he'd met Professor Desiree Desmond Creed.

The sound of the doorbell jolted him out of his reverie. *Who in An's name could that be?* His guards wouldn't just let anyone even get past the elevator. And no one outside Zhobghadi knew where he was. Hopefully, it wasn't one of those damned photographers, sneaking up on him again.

"What do you want?" he snarled as he opened the door.

"That's no way to greet someone you consider a brother, now is it?"

Karim let his guard down. "I thought I was a 'royal pain in your ass.'"

Duncan MacDougal smirked at him. "Most of the time."

"Hello, my friend." He took the arm the Scotsman offered him and clasped it, as they always did. "It's not that I'm not happy to see you, Duncan, but what are you doing in New York?"

"Well ..." Duncan stepped aside, revealing the woman behind him.

"Julianna Anderson of New York." Karim folded his arms over his chest as he regarded the female.

"Hello, Your Highness." She didn't bow, nod, or curtsey to him, but instead, met his gaze head on.

He would never admit it, but her mismatched eyes—one blue, one green—unnerved him. There was an intelligence and sharpness in them, and something that said this woman was not easily won over with shallow charm. In short, she saw right through him.

"Looks like she led you on a merry chase," Karim said to his friend.

Duncan put an arm around Juliann. "Worth every mile." She rolled her eyes, but her mouth was tugging up at the corners.

He motioned for them to enter his suite. "So, what do I owe this visit? Anything I can do for you?"

Duncan and Julianna stepped inside. "Actually, perhaps it's something we can assist you with," the Scot said.

"Assist me? With what?"

The couple looked at each other, nodded, then turned to him. "With this, perhaps?" Their eyes suddenly took on an eerie glow. A familiar sight he'd only seen one other time.

Karim had to double blink, to make sure he wasn't hallucinating. "Mother of *Enki*, you too? And you *two*?" He marched toward the bar and poured himself another drink. Taking a deep breath, he turned around. "Close the door behind you." He motioned for them sit on the couch as he settled himself on the armchair, glass in hand. This conversation needed to be done sitting down, with alcohol. "It makes sense, I suppose, my friend."

"That we were alike in this way too?" Duncan had that boyish grin on his face that many women seemed to fall for.

"I suppose." The information wasn't absorbing in his mind quite yet. Julianna, Duncan, and Deedee were all the same. But wait ... "How did you know I was here?"

"Sebastian Creed," Julianna said. "He's an ... associate of ours. Knew the moment your plane touched down. Apparently, he was about to come here, but luckily, Duncan and I were around. We convinced him to back down and let us come instead."

"*Ishtar's tits*, I have never wanted to scream my bloody head off more when I hear that name." He gulped down the contents of his glass.

"We were there when her father got the news she was missing," Duncan explained. "And I had no idea he'd be coming to Zhobghadi."

"None of us did," Julianna added. "He, Daric, and a small team went to her site to try and find her. When Daric discovered she was in Zhobghadi with you, he went ballistic and came up with this plan to rescue her without anyone's knowledge. Before we knew it, they came back with Deedee, and Creed told us there was another dragon in the world."

"It had to be you," Duncan said. "I just knew it. Somewhere, deep inside, I knew you were different."

And perhaps, The Great One knew, too, that Duncan was like him. That's why they had orbited to each other. "I'm sorry for the deception, my friend. It was necessary."

"I understand, believe me."

"And Creed? I suppose he's spinning some tale that I

took his daughter? And how is it that you're associated with him?"

Julianna shifted in her seat and didn't meet his gaze, but Duncan met his eyes. "What happened, Karim? Because I don't believe you would take a woman captive. Not against her will anyway."

The burden he didn't realize he was carrying seemed to be lifted off his shoulders. Duncan didn't believe any of it. He really was like the brother he never had. "I swear to you, I did it for her protection, and there was no way to send out word to her family." And so, he told his friend the entire story of how he came to be the bearer of The Great One, and how Desiree arrived at the palace, leaving out the part of them becoming lovers of course, and continuing up until her father came to take her away. "And so, you know what I am now, too."

Julianna's mouth slackened. "All these years, we thought there was only one."

"You are not the only one who thought this." And his people, too, were shaken by the appearance of a second Great One. For a millennium, they believed there could only be one, and now, they not only saw two, but witnessed them battle in the skies. That was another reason Arvin had begged him not to go—he believed the people might begin to question their beliefs, which could in turn cause unrest. But he couldn't stay, not when Desiree was out there. "And now, you will tell me about your people."

"We're—"

"Duncan," Julianna grabbed his hand. "No. You know we can't."

"I think the cat's out of the bag with this one, darlin'." He raised her hand to his lips and kissed it. "He knows about us; we know about him. What's the harm in letting him know? That's why we came here, right?"

"The council forbids this." She yanked her hand away and crossed her arms over her chest. "And I thought we were here because you wanted to protect him? If you did, then you wouldn't reveal anything else about Ly—us."

"Karim is my friend—no, he's my brother." Duncan's bright green eyes bore into him. "He wouldn't do anything to risk my life or that of my family."

"All of you?" Karim said incredulously. "Even little Roslyn?"

"Aye. Except for Mum, but that's a special case." He looked to Julianna.

After what seemed like an intense, silent stare-down, she shrugged. "Fine. Go ahead."

Duncan turned to him. "We're called Lycans. We live and share our bodies with our animals—our wolves. Like with your dragon, we can call on our wolves and shift into their physical forms. And before you ask, no, we don't turn with the moon, though there is one exception. Other than that, we can pass ourselves as normal human beings. The bigger world doesn't know about our existence."

"Deedee is a part of my clan," Julianna said. "Her mother is a Lycan, and she was born here and is pledged to New York. My brother is the Alpha, and I was sent to Scotland to forge an alliance with Duncan's clan."

Ah, it was a coincidence then. Or perhaps fate. "And what about the ones who have special powers? I saw a man who disappeared before my very eyes, and another one who could make flames appear from his hands."

"Warlocks and witches exist too," Julianna added. "And when they mate with us, their offspring can be born as hybrids. Part Lycan, part magical being."

"And there are more of them? And of you?"

Julianna's keen eyes narrowed at him. "What are you doing here, Your Highness? Why come here, knowing that Sebastian Creed is out to get you? Is there some sort of Zhobghadi code that states that there must only be one dragon? Are you planning to kill him?" Her gaze sharpened. "Because I can assure you: that's not going to happen. He is pledged to us, and any threat to him is a threat to all of us. My clan will do everything to protect him, especially now that we need him."

"Need him? For what?" Karim searched her face, but found no answer. So, he continued. "I am not here for him. Yes, I want to know more about him, but he is not my main purpose for coming here."

"Then what is?" Julianna prodded. "Tell me, and maybe I can convince my clan that you mean us no harm."

He sighed. "I am here for her."

"Her?" Duncan echoed.

"Her. Desiree Creed. The daughter of the dragon. I came to her this morning, but I was unsuccessful. Her father put guards on her to keep me away, but I intend to have her—."

"I beg your *fucking* pardon?" Julianna shot up to her feet.

"Julianna, that's no way to talk to royalty." Duncan seemed amused though. "What would the dowager say?"

The she-wolf bared her teeth at Karim. "I beg your fucking pardon, *Your Highness*?"

"Julianna—" Duncan began.

"You can't be going around snatching people because you want them. That's called kidnapping."

"What do you think I am, a barbarian?" He stood up, too, and towered over her with his hands raised high, a move that Duncan didn't seem to appreciate as the Scot shoved his way between them.

"Brother or no, I'm going to kill you if you harm my mate and the mother of my child." Duncan's words held a deadly edge, and his eyes began to glow.

Karim took a step back and lowered his arms. "Your child? My friend—brother—that is joyous news." He clapped him on the shoulder.

Duncan's hand went down to Julianna's middle. "Isn't it?" The lethal expression on his face disappeared and was replaced by one of ... bliss?

"Can we get back on task here?" Julianna frowned. "So, if you're not here to kidnap Deedee, what do you want with her?"

"She is mine. I want her to be my queen."

Duncan slapped his hand on his knee. "*Och*, so you're in love with her."

"I'm not—" His friend's words sunk into him like a stone tossed into a pond. He had never been in love with a woman before. Never thought it would ever happen to him. But this feeling, this pain ... it could only be this. The realization hit him like a bag of rocks to the face.

"You look like that time in Year Twelve when Leslie Abberforth got you with a bag of rocks to the face." Duncan chuckled and slapped him on the shoulder. "Knocked some sense into you too, if I recall. So, what're you gonna do now?"

"I must go to her and tell her." He rolled his shoulders back. "She will listen to me and—"

Julianna raised her hand. "Whoa, hold your horses, cowboy. That's not something you just blurt outright. Besides, you said you already went to see her this morning?"

"Right before you got here. I obtained her address and went to see her, but her father put guards on her. One who controls and is immune to flames, and the one who walks in shadow." That was what the Almoravid had called the dark-haired one, when he demanded an explanation as to how the palace had been infiltrated. They had looked at all the security footage around the palace and saw no one come in. Captain Fariba said he must have walked in the shadows because no one saw him come in, and the only place he could hide were in the dark corners.

"And then what happened? Did they stop you from talking to her?"

"Not quite." Heat crept up his collar. "Well...." He relayed the disastrous events of that morning.

"Oh no." Julianna shook her head violently. "If you turn around and tell her you love her now, then she'll think you're insincere. Believe me, that's not what she needs right now."

"That makes no sense."

"Women's logic," Duncan explained. When Julianna glowered at him, he kissed her cheek. "I mean, it makes perfect sense. You should listen to my mate, she's beautiful and smart. Please, continue, darlin'."

Julianna's lips pursed. "Tell me again, if what happened between you and her was consensual, then why did she have Daric take her away? Why not explain to her father that she wasn't kidnapped or held against her will?"

"It was her choice to leave. Because she was angry at me," he groused. "We had a fight just before Creed arrived. I asked her to stay, gave her an offer, and she accused me of trying to make her my mistress."

"And what exactly did you *offer* her?" Julianna asked.

"Anything she wanted. A position in the palace. Money to fund her expeditions. Or she didn't have to do anything at all and I'd take care—"

"*Och*, mon, that sounds pretty much like a mistress," Duncan interjected.

"So, you insulted her." Julianna's sharp eyes sliced into him. "And then what?"

"I thought she was angling for something bigger. To be my queen. I did not want to raise her hopes, so I told her that was the one thing I cannot do. You don't understand." Godsdamn, what was it about this woman that he just spilled his guts when she asked a question? "But I would give her everything else except that."

"You fucking bastard." But Julianna's voice wasn't excited or agitated. It was low and deadly. "And what about when you did take a queen and you had kids? Was she just supposed to hang around and see all that or were you going to send her to a harem retirement home with all your other castoffs?"

Gods above and below, did women have a hive mind of sorts? "She made that clear to me this morning that's what she thought I meant. But it is not. Having anyone else but her was the furthest thing from my mind."

"Then why did you offer her that? Couldn't you ... I don't know, date her first or something? Get to know each other?"

"I ..." He didn't know what to say. At the time, he thought

he already knew everything he needed to know about her. She was beautiful, passionate, but also so kind and intelligent. Perhaps his heart had already known what his mind did not, but he had been desperate to keep her, but also protect her from—

"It's not about her." Duncan's bright green eyes lit up with understanding. "It's about your mum."

Karim had never told anyone outside his family about his mum except Duncan and Desiree. They had been friends for a few months at Eton when one of those snotty uptight kids dug up the old gossip about his mother's suicide and began taunting him with it. He didn't want to go back to Zhobghadi, and he'd been trained not to act on his impulses, so he didn't try to fight them. So Duncan had beat those bastards to a bloody pulp and was gated for a month. After that, Karim had confided in him what really happened.

"It's all right," Duncan said in a soft voice. "You don't have to say anything." He looked at Julianna, as if pleading to her not to ask anything else and trust him. She nodded and then sat down, seemingly mollified for now.

"Thank you my fr—brother." He sank back on the armchair and placed his face in his hands. "I don't know what I'm supposed to do now."

"Grovel," Julianna offered.

"Grovel *a lot*," Duncan added cheerfully. "I've heard girls really like it. Get down on your knees."

"A future king does not—" When he saw the dead serious look on Julianna's face, he thought better. "All right, I will ... do my own form of groveling. But first, I must find a way to see her. I don't know how I'll manage that though. She hates me and doesn't want anything to do with me."

"Better she hates you than be indifferent," Duncan pointed out. "At least she feels something for you. You just have to woo her."

Grovel and woo her? "I must see her." The ache in his chest at being away from her was too much. His dragon roared in his head.

Mine. Ours. Mate.

The voice was so loud and ringing, he was deafened for a moment. *Mate?* He rubbed his temple with his fingers. "Duncan ... you called Julianna ..." Did he imagine it? "You called her your ...."

"Mate?" Duncan cocked his head at him. "Aye? And?"

"Is that just between two Lycans?"

"Usually, but not all the time. What're you saying, Karim?"

"Oh. My. God." Julianna's eyes widened to the size of dinner plates. "Karim. Does your dragon call Deedee your mate?"

"I ... yes."

Mine. Ours. Mate, The Great One repeated, as if to prove a point.

They looked at each other. "My brother, there's something else you should know."

There was more? "You're not going to tell me unicorns or Santa Clause is real, too, are you?"

"No, not at all." Duncan drummed his fingers on the arm of the sofa. "Er, well, Lycans can call their significant other mates as a general term, but more often than not, we are referring to our True Mate."

"It's the one we're destined to be with." Julianna's gaze slid to Duncan, a warm smile creeping on her lips. "We don't recognize them right away, not all of us anyway, but there are obvious signs."

"What signs?"

"Well, your wolf—er, animal will feel possessive and connected to the other person," she added. "And er," her hands went down to her belly. "You get pregnant the first time you're together, as long as you're not using condoms."

Karim stared at her, dumbfounded.

"And that look on your face tells me you didn't wrap your willy, didja?" Duncan guffawed. "Oh dear."

"But how ... she said it wasn't easy ... and her—your kind didn't—" Karim's brain scrambled for the right words. Desiree could be pregnant. With his child. At this very moment. His head was spinning.

"Here." Duncan shoved something at him—a silver flask. "From the distillery."

"Thank you." He took it and threw his head back, taking three big gulps before giving it back.

"So, congratulations?"

"This changes everything. No—" He stood up. "This changes nothing. It is always as I have known, my heart has known. She is mine, and she must be my queen."

"Wow, I'm a little turned on," Julianna stage-whispered to Duncan.

"Oi!" Duncan growled.

"I'm joking, you oaf. Besides you should be glad that, since I got pregnant, I'm only turned on all the time and not freaking out or crying at the drop of a hat." She kissed him on the mouth. "All right, my clan and I will back off for now," she said when she turned to Karim. "Let's win you a queen."

"I must go and see her." Not even her two guards could keep him away now, not if she was carrying his child.

"But take a day or two and get some groveling lessons from Duncan," Julianna said, making Duncan chuckle. "He's pretty good at it."

"And you need to bring some big guns," Duncan said. "More than just your declaration of love. A grand gesture, if you will. Something she can't ignore."

"Hmmm ..." Karim thought for a moment. "I may have an idea." It was underhanded, but he was a man in love, and he was desperate.

CHAPTER EIGHTEEN

DEEDEE CLENCHED HER TEETH AND BALLED HER HANDS into fists as she exited the New York University Archeology Department, tears pricking at her eyes. *Don't,* she scolded herself as she walked out of the austere, red-bricked building that was decades older than her, where dozens of the world's most prominent archeologists had passed through. No, no, no, she was not going to break down here, where any of her colleagues could walk by at any moment and see her bawling in defeat.

"That wasn't fair of them to do that, *mon petite.*"

"*Mother almighty!*" Deedee jumped back, and clutched her chest. "How is it you do that?"

"Do what?" Delacroix asked, a grin on his face.

"Just ... show up like that?" She didn't even hear him following her, and her enhanced senses could pick up a pin drop a mile away.

"I dunno." He shrugged. "I just do it."

"I told you guys to stay outside," she said. "You weren't supposed to follow me in. How did you get past the guards?"

"You done yet?" Jacob was leaning against the outside wall. He ran a hand through his longish, golden-red hair. "What happened?"

"They're taking back her funding," Delacroix said. "After she got lost in the desert, they didn't have confidence that she could continue with her research."

"Were you inside the boardroom too?" He had basically repeated what the board of trustees had told her verbatim. "How come no one saw you?"

"I—"

"Those assholes," Jacob cracked his knuckles. "They know how important this is to you, right? I knew it was bad when they asked you to come in."

"Don't worry, *mon petite*, there must be some way to appeal."

Deedee slapped her hand over her eyes. How was this her life now? Two days ago, these guys were virtual strangers to her, and now, they knew all her business.

She shouldn't have invited them to come into her house, but she felt bad they had to stay outside her place all day and night. They weren't going to leave her alone, since they were so determined to guard her, so she thought they might as well stay inside. However, they seemed to have taken that as an open invitation and made themselves at home on her couch, eating her food, and watching movies on her TV.

"It seems strange, *non*? It was a freak sandstorm, anyone could have been lost. What could have swayed their minds so?"

It wasn't a what. It was a *who*.

She knew it had to be Hanford, that slime ball. First, he left her to die out in the desert because he didn't want to be outed as a predator. And now, he probably found out that she survived and was using this to show her how powerful he was and that she better shut up about his assault.

This was really frustrating—no, it was enraging. But frankly, she was just too tired right now to even think of fighting back. However, now that she knew to what extent Hanford would go to punish anyone who said no to him, she knew she couldn't just stay quiet. Because if he did it to her, then who knows how many more women had he done it to or would do it to in the future? The next thing she needed to do was call the police in London, where she knew Hanford was based. Or should she have called the NYPD? But did she need to go get a lawyer first? How did it work if they were from different countries, and the assault happened in another?

"How about we go to a diner?" Jacob asked. The man ate almost as much as ... well, she did these days. "Drown ourselves in French fries smothered in gravy and cheese. Isn't that what you guys eat, Delacroix?"

"I'm Cajun, not Quebecois."

"Yeah, yeah. Whaddaya say, Deedee?"

The two of them looked at her hopefully. "Fine. I guess I am kind of hungry too." Maybe food would help. She couldn't think on an empty stomach after all. Maybe after a meal, she could regroup and figure out what to do. About her career going down in flames and that asshole Hanford. "Let's go get some lunch."

They made their way back to the parking lot, and as usual, the two Lycans were joking with each other and trying to make her smile. She hated to admit it, but it was kind of nice to not be alone with her thoughts all the time.

Because whenever she was by herself, all she could think about was—

"Halt." Delacroix stopped and raised a hand. He glanced around, then nodded at the black SUV blocking their car.

"Not again." Jacob rubbed his hands together, his eyes glowing. "That bastard doesn't know when to quit, does he."

"Calm down, *mon ami*. We are in public."

Deedee felt her heart race in anticipation, and her wolf raised its head, waiting. The passenger door of the SUV opened, and sure enough, Karim stepped out.

"I'm not here to harm anyone." He raised his hands, palms out. "I came to talk. Just talk. As you can see, my bodyguards are inside," he nodded back to the SUV behind him, "and they will stay until I say they can come out."

Oh, she wanted to tell him to leave her alone. She'd done it already, right? But now, here he was back again, and her traitorous heart did a little flip-flop as soon as she saw him. Whether he was wearing his traditional garb, his military uniform, or in his dark suit as he was now, Karim just had the presence that made everyone stop to attention. And goodness, it hit her just how handsome he was. Had it only been a few days ago they were wrapped up together on that balcony?

"Say the word, Dee." Jacob was already raising his hands. "Say the word, and he's gone." Delacroix nodded in agreement.

"Let's talk, Desiree. Just talk."

Her wolf begged and whined, and she knew there would be no peace. She would have to harden her heart against him if they were alone for even a second. She had to, otherwise, she didn't think she could survive another disappointment. "I don't understand why you're still here. I thought I made myself clear the other day. Not even if you have an army would I come back with you. So I suggest you leave now."

"I didn't bring an army." He cocked his head back at the SUV. "I brought someone else."

"Someone—"

The car door flew open, and an excited squeal pierced the air. "Deedee!" Amaya flew out of the car and straight into her. Small arms squeezed her tight. "Surprise! Are you surprised? I was so excited when Karim sent for me and told me I was coming to see you. You left so suddenly after the Easifat that I thought—"

"Slow down, Amaya." She put the little girl down with a short chuckle. "Breathe. That's it."

"Oh Deedee! I cannot believe I am here. In New York. And with you.

"Yes, I can't believe it either." She slid a dirty look toward Karim, who suddenly found a stone on the ground interesting.

"Karim said that if I asked you nicely, you might show me around?" Big doe eyes looked up at her. "Please, Deedee? I want to see New York with you."

"I ..." What was she supposed to do? It's not that she was busy or had to go to work. And if she were honest, she had felt guilty at leaving Zhobghadi without saying goodbye to the girl. "Sure. Why not?"

"Hooray!" She hugged Deedee then turned to Karim. "How was that, Karim?"

"You did well, little one." He held a hand up and Amaya rushed to him to slap her palm to his. "Go on ahead into the car, we will be along soon."

As soon as Amaya was inside the SUV, she poked a finger at Karim's chest. "That's not fair. You play dirty."

"I play to *win, habibti.*" He brushed a knuckle on her jaw, making her shiver. "Surely you know that about me by now."

She groaned inwardly. Really, did she expect any less?

———

Deedee had to admit, she was having fun. Although she'd lived in the city most of her life, she had avoided most of the touristy places, as all New Yorkers did. And now it seemed in a single afternoon, she had visited them all—Times Square, The Empire State Building, Central Park, The Natural Science Museum, and of course, The Met, where Amaya had been thrilled to see the Ancient Egyptian exhibition.

She rode in the SUV with Karim and Amaya, while Jacob and Delacroix followed behind in their vehicle, along with two of the Almoravid. She tried to discreetly check on the two guards that Jacob had burned, and although their arms were covered up, they didn't seem to be in pain or uncomfortable. That was something she had been meaning to ask Karim. Were they wearing fireproof clothes? Perhaps it was a requirement when protecting a dragon shifter.

"This is amazing." Amaya's eyes widened as their server placed a large dish of ice cream on their table. After having some New York-style pizza for dinner, Deedee brought them to a famous dessert place on the Upper East Side, where they specialized in gigantic chocolate ice cream sundaes. The three of them sat in one table, under one of the restaurant's iconic Tiffany lamps.

"Try it." She motioned to the three straws sticking out

from the monstrosity of a dessert.

Amaya didn't need a second urging as she happily sipped from her pink straw. "*Mmmm!*" Her eyes lit up, in that way only a child who was about to get a sugar rush could.

Karim looked suspiciously at his own straw and then took a sip. "It is ... very sweet."

"That's the point." As she took her own sip, she closed her eyes. "My brothers and I used to have to get one each of our own. Neither of them would share with me." When she opened her eyes, she saw Karim staring back at her—or rather, her lips, as she licked a bit of chocolate from the corner of her mouth. The heat in his gaze was unmistakable.

A bright flash blinded her, and all carnal thoughts evaporated out of her mind. When her eyes focused, she saw what had caused it—a man was outside on the other side of the window, a large professional camera in his hand.

"Damn paparazzi." Karim barked at his bodyguards, who were already halfway toward the door.

"Let me take care of this, *mes amis*." Delacroix stood up slowly and made his way toward the exit. "He won't bother us again."

"Don't kill him!"Deedee exclaimed.

"What?" He seemed taken aback. "Kill him? That wasn't my plan."

"You said he wasn't going to bother us again," Deedeee pointed out. "What was I supposed to think?"

He waved a hand at her. "Don't you worry your little head, *mon petite*. Just enjoy your dessert, okay?" With a dramatic flair of his hands, he marched out of the door.

"I hate him and like him at the same time," Karim muttered under his breath.

"I get that." Marc Delacroix, indeed, was both easy to read and an enigma. And she still hadn't figured out how a Cajun from Louisiana came to New York and somehow ingratiated himself to the Alpha and her father.

"I'm afraid that one photographer is just a sampling of what we'll have to endure." Karim lowered his voice so only she could hear it. "Soon there will be more of them. They will descend on us and ..." His eyes flickered toward Amaya, who was happily scooping whipped cream into her mouth. "This is not how I wanted her introduced to the world. I have sheltered her all these years, and now I've exposed her."

She wanted to reach over and smooth the lines of worry from his face. But that would mean touching him, so instead, she rubbed her hands down her skirt. "Karim, you can't protect her forever. Surely you don't mean for her to stay in Zhobghadi her entire life? Unfortunately, the media has gotten worse when it comes to gossip and celebrity worship. She is a princess, and unless you plan to keep her inside the palace forever, she will have to get used to this. Better to teach her how to deal with it now, than later when she's less resilient."

"I never thought of that." A hand reached out to cover hers. His palm was rough and warm, and memories flooded into her brain. Memories of the palace and his bed. "Thank you for that reminder, Desiree."

Despite her brain telling her arm to move her hand away, she didn't budge. "It'll be all right. She's a bright child. But she won't be one forever."

Amaya let out a loud burp. "Excuse me," she said with a giggle. "That was good, can I have another?"

Karim checked his watch. "I don't think so. It's time to go

back to the hotel and go to bed."

"But Kariiiiiim!"

He gave her a warning look. "If you behave and go straight to bed, maybe Desiree would be inclined to spend more time with you tomorrow."

How could she say no? Especially when both of them were looking at her expectantly. "What would you like to do, Amaya?"

"Whatever you want to do, Desiree." She yawned loudly. "We can go back to the museum again, and you can tell me about the mummies."

"I think I've had enough mummies," Karim grumbled.

An idea popped into her head. "Okay, let me take care of tomorrow. I have an idea, but I have to see if I can pull it off."

"Hooray!"

By the time their plates had been cleared and Karim paid the check, Amaya was heavily drowsy. She was nestled in Karim's arms as they exited and headed toward the SUV. Jacob, Delacroix, and the rest of the Almoravid were already there, and thankfully, there were no photographers around.

Karim placed Amaya into the SUV and then said a few words to the driver and guard in the front.

"Well, I guess this is goodnight—"

"But our evening isn't over," he said.

"It's not?" He knocked on the roof and then the vehicle began to pull away. "Karim? What's going on? Amaya—"

"Will be fine. She has her nanny with her who will put her to bed." He motioned behind her. "I want to show you something."

Turning around, she saw a sleek black limousine that hadn't been there earlier. "Karim, I—"

"Please."

The single word seemed to knock down all her objections. When had Karim ever said please? She couldn't remember. He commanded, not pleaded.

Oh yes, she did. Only once did those words pass from his lips. When he pleaded for his mother. "All right," she found herself saying. "But where are we going?"

"It's a surprise." A hand on the small of her back led her to the waiting limo, where one of the Almoravid had already opened the door. Before they came in, he turned to Delacroix. "Thank you for your assistance."

"Anytime, *Your Highness.*"

Jacob flashed a suspicious look at Karim. "We'll follow you in the car."

Deedee knew there was no use arguing, so she allowed him to assist her inside. The brush of his fingers on hers made her heat shoot across her body. How was it that he could affect her with a simple touch? The entire day, he had been on his best behavior, which she assumed was for Amaya's benefit. But now they were alone, would he try anything? And would she let him?

The limo door closed, and soon the vehicle began to move. They headed downtown, then west toward SoHo, until they reached one of the more quiet side streets off Lafayette Street. They slowed down in front of a classic cast-iron building the district was known for.

The door opened and Karim went out first, then offered his hand to help her out. "What is this place?" She peered through the large windows, into the vast, brightly-lit space inside. "Are we at an art gallery?"

"Indeed." He guided her to the front entrance, opening

the heavy door for her so she could go inside first. "But this is a special art gallery."

Glancing around, she thought it looked like many of the art galleries in New York. "What's special about it?"

"The owner of this particular place is an expat from Zhobghadi. Despite the fact that he lives here, we have kept in touch. I make it a point to visit when I'm in New York."

"Oh." Although the place was lit up, there was no one else around them. "Where is everyone?"

"They're normally closed at this time, but he's kept it open just for us."

"Your Highness!" An older man with white hair appeared in the doorway on the left, his face all lit up as he approached them. He placed his fist over his heart and bent his head low. "Prince Karim, welcome, it's wonderful to see you again. How was your trip?" His accent definitely placed him as a Zhobghadian. For a moment, she felt a pang of longing for that palace in the desert.

Karim acknowledged him with a curt nod. "Good evening, Bashir. Thank you so much for allowing us to come. This," he gestured to Deedee, "is Professor Desiree Desmond Creed. Desiree, this is Mr. Bashir Dana."

"How do you do, Mr. Dana?" She offered her hand which Bashir took graciously.

"I'm glad to meet you as well, professor. But please call me Bashir."

"Then you can call me Deedee." She looked around. "His Highness tells me that you're formerly from Zhobghadi. What made you move to New York?"

"Well, art was my passion," he said. "While Zhobghadi is a wonderful country and I am missing it every day, I'm afraid my interests were a bit ... stifled. I was part of the trade mission here in New York, when I met my now-husband. He's an artist, too, you see. We fell in love, opened this gallery, and the rest is history." His eyes narrowed at them and he opened his mouth as if he wanted to say something, but shut it again.

Bashir's knowing look made her feel like she was under a microscope, so she changed the subject. "Do you feature Zhobghadian artists here?"

"We feature artists from everywhere," Bashir said, his chest puffing up. "But, yes, we do devote space to Zhobghadian artists. I select the pieces myself. Come," he motioned toward the next room. "I have some amazing etchings done by a girl from the southern cities...."

Bashir proudly showed off his artists, giving them tidbits and insights about each one and their work. Deedee appreciated art as much as the next person, so her eyes glassed over when he went into the minute details of every picture or sculpture, but she did love listening to Bashir talk in his Zhobghadian accent, as well as his enthusiasm for his clients.

They finished about three-fourths of the room before Bashir stopped short, his palm going to his forehead. "Oh, excuse my rudeness, I didn't even offer you any refreshments. I have bread and tea in the back; I'll bring them along shortly. Please feel free to view any piece you want." He bowed and scuttled away, disappearing through a doorway in the far-right corner.

"Interesting man," she commented. "How did you know about him and his gallery?"

Karim shook his head. "He's one of the few expats we

have, so we keep tabs on him."

"Ah, I see." To make sure he didn't say anything about The Great One.

"He still travels back and forth for business, always trying to find new artists to display here."

"He seems like a nice enough man. I—hmmm ..." Something on the far side of the gallery, on the last wall whose paintings they hadn't yet seen, seemed to call to her.

She walked over to the wall, her eyes narrowing at the painting that caught her eye. As she drew closer, she gasped.

"Desiree?" Karim touched her on the shoulder lightly. "Are you all right? You look like you've seen a ghost."

Not a ghost.

Painted eyes the color of the ocean looked out at her and made gooseflesh rise on her arms.

She squinted at the painting, her vision blurring temporarily. And when they refocused, she knew she hadn't been hallucinating.

This painting, it was unmistakable. Unmistakably *Cross*.

It captured him from the waist up, wearing a loose white shirt, his face turned to the viewer. He was standing on top of a cliff of some sort, and behind him was a long, narrow inlet framed by steep cliffs. The painting was done with such detail that she could practically see his long blond hair whipping in the wind. It was uncanny, really.

"Desiree, are you all right?" Karim's tone was more forceful.

"I'm fine," she said. *But how?*

"Your Highness." Bashir came over to them, tray in hand. "I made these myself. I'm sure Deedee would love to try some of our Zhobghadian bread?"

"Bashir, what can you tell me about this artist?" Her eyes tracked down to the signature scrawled on the lower left-hand corner. "S. Strohen?"

The older man's brows knitted together. "My assistant was supposed to take it down today as we just finished the show. Sold out every piece actually, except this one. It's an exhibition piece, not meant for sale, and we were to return it tomorrow."

"Is the artist from Zhobghadi?"

"No, from New York actually. Very eccentric." He shrugged. "I deal mostly with the agent. Strohen's a recluse, you see. Never does any interviews, media appearances, or promotions of any sort. No presence online. But extremely talented and highly-sought after." He nodded at the painting. "I mean, just look at it." He pointed to the figure. "It's like the entire painting is alive. You can almost smell the freshness of the air or touch the linen on his shirt. And those eyes ..."

She swallowed. The artist had captured the blue-green of his eyes perfectly. How could anyone do that, unless they spent a lot of time staring into them? Deedee had done so herself, and if she had any artistic talent, she was sure she could paint that exact color too. "Is there any way to meet Strohen? I'd like to know more about this painting."

Bashir eyes darted around mysteriously. "Um, apologies, I'm afraid the artist is very reclusive and refuses to speak to anyone. I can put you in touch with the agent."

"Oh." The agent probably wouldn't know anything about how Cross appeared in this painting. Maybe it was just a coincidence. "It's fine."

"I would consider it a personal favor and owe you a debt if you found a way to contact this artist for us," Karim said.

The old man looked stunned, but quickly composed himself. "I shall endeavor to do my best, Your Highness. Now," he lifted the tray in his hands, "let's have some of these refreshments, shall we?"

The smell of fresh-baked bread tickled her nostrils, and once again, she was reminded of Zhobghadi. She snuck a peek up at Karim, wondering if this was his plan.

They sat down at the cafe table set up in the corner, nibbling on bread and drinking tea. She found Bashir utterly charming, and his stories about his life in Zhobghadi and New York were entertaining. Still, her mind kept going back to the painting. And then to Cross. It seemed like forever since she'd thought of him, longer still since she'd seen him.

When they were done, Bashir walked them back to their limo, thanking them for a lovely visit and telling them to come back any time. After the car pulled away and Deedee waved one last goodbye, she settled into the plush leather seats, her mind going back to Cross once again.

"Everything all right?" Karim asked in a soft voice. "Is something bothering you? Is it that artist?"

It was at that moment she realized that Karim was still blissfully unaware of Cross. Of who he was and that he was, inadvertently, the reason she had left New York. She should tell him, right? He should at least know that much.

But the thought of opening those wounds up again made her hesitate. And seeing that painting, she thought that it would make her long for him again, but surprisingly, she didn't feel anything more than a slight fondness. She missed Cross, yes, but as her friend. Someone she could always talk to and rely on for support.

And what was Karim to her? Before everything had

turned sour in Zhobghadi, she thought she had fallen for him. Could she trust her confused heart?

"Desiree?"

"It's nothing," she said. "Nothing at all."

The ride continued in silence all the way to her house. When the limo stopped in front of her brownstone, she cleared her throat. "I had a nice time today. Thank you for bringing Amaya out."

"I'm glad you enjoyed her company. I did it for her, too," he said sheepishly. "Forgive me for being underhanded."

"It was a good kind of underhanded. I'm glad she was able to leave the palace and come out here. I might be able to snag some tickets to the hottest Broadway show for you and Amaya tomorrow. I'll have them sent to your hotel." She reached for the door. "I'll see myself inside, no need to come out."

As she exited the limo and climbed out, she couldn't help feel a small pang of disappointment as Karim just let her walk away. A cold rush of air chilled her, so she picked up her pace as she climbed the stoop steps, fishing her keys from her purse.

"Desiree."

The set of keys in her hand dropped to the ground with an echoing clink. Turning around slowly, she held her breath. Cerulean blue eyes stared at her with such intensity that she wanted to melt into a puddle. "Karim?"

He took a step forward, crowding her against the door. "I cannot hold this in any longer. They said I shouldn't say it right away, but I must."

"They?"

"It doesn't matter. All that matters is that you listen to what I have to say." Then he added, "Please."

"I ..." She nodded anyway, despite the protests of her brain. This close, she could smell his desert-tinged scent.

"You misunderstood me that morning—" He shook his head. "There was a misunderstanding, and I did not state myself clearly, so it was only logical you came to your conclusions. I was so afraid of ..." He stopped again, seemingly to compose himself. "When the Easifat died down, I knew it was time to let you go. But I just couldn't. At the same time, I couldn't let the same thing that happened to her happen to you."

She heard the hitch in his voice and knew who he was talking about.

"I was afraid. I'm still afraid now. It's not easy, this life." His jaw tensed. "There are duties and consequences. I grew up alone in a palace, surrounded by tutors and servants and guards. It was only until I went to school in England that I'd even spent an extended amount of time with others my age. But that was all right, because all my life, I only knew duty. But my mother she ..." He swallowed audibly. "She was not used to it. And it made her bitter and unhappy, until she couldn't take it anymore. My father loved her, but it was not enough. And he loved another, too, after her. In his own way."

Deedee bit her lip. "Do you think ... he made Amaya's mother consort to protect her?"

He nodded. "I believe that he would do such a thing. He just didn't realize that he was hurting her, too. She died because she didn't think she had anything to live for, because her husband thought her unworthy."

"That poor woman. And Amaya." So much unnecessary loss and tragedy.

"You are an archeologist. You study the past. And we are supposed to learn from the past, right? So we do not commit the same mistakes as those before us. But then I realized I was doing the exact same thing as my father did. Making you feel unworthy. You think I thought you unworthy of the position of queen? No, Desiree. It is the position which isn't worthy of you. It is *I* who am not worthy."

She gasped when he stepped even closer, placing a palm behind her on the door. Their bodies were barely touching, but the heat emanating from him warmed her.

"I can't take back what I said, but know that I will do everything to earn your forgiveness, and do what it takes to make you mine."

Her mind was spinning, making her dizzy. "Why are you doing this?"

"Because I love you, my *habibti*. My beloved."

It was like the entire globe came to a halt. He ... loved her?

They stood there in silence for what seemed like a lifetime, and she saw his face falter for a moment. "If you do not feel—"

The world began to spin again, and a wave of dizziness made her lean back against the door. "I don't *know* how I feel, Karim. It's just all going so fast." Days ago, she would have given anything to hear those words from his mouth. Her time in the palace had been like a fairy tale, and she had been caught up in the romance of being in a handsome prince's arms. But then reality had hit her like a bucket of cold water to the face. Being with him would mean sacrificing a lot, possibly her career, and maybe even her family and her clan. Fairy tales were not real, after all.

And then, as she'd been reminded tonight, there was Cross. Should she tell Karim about him, the reason she'd been out in the desert in the first place? Did it matter now?

"I suppose so," he answered in a quiet voice. "I know I am heaping all this on you so soon. And you don't have to say anything." He leaned down and pressed a kiss to her forehead. "Should you ever return my affections, I know it will be when I am worthy of them." His velvety voice made her temperature spike. "Goodnight, *habibti*, I will see you tomorrow."

Unable to speak, she watched him in silence as he walked away from her. She wanted to say it back. Her heart cried out. Her wolf was desperately scratching at her. But the words wouldn't come out. It felt disingenuous to say it to him, when she wasn't all in. When she was still reminded of her feelings for Cross. Or what her feelings had been, because even now, she couldn't even recall feeling so deeply for her friend.

She touched the spot on her forehead where he pressed his lips, an ache inside her growing. *Oh, Karim.* It was Karim, it was always him.

As his limo pulled away, her gut clenched. "No!" She trotted down the steps, but came to a halt at the end of the sidewalk as she watched the vehicle grow smaller in the distance. *Too late.* Her inner wolf howled in disappointment, and for once, she felt the same.

As she walked back toward her house, she realized she should have said it back. Oh, why did she hesitate? Hopefully tomorrow won't be too late.

CHAPTER NINETEEN

DEEDEE CHEWED HER LIP AS SHE WAITED IN THE LIMO outside The Plaza Hotel. For most of the day, all she wanted to do was rush here and see Karim, but unfortunately, she had other things to take care of, like trying to salvage her career and snagging tickets to the most sought-after show on Broadway for her, Karim, and Amaya. Sadly, the latter was the easier of those tasks to accomplish. She had called up the front desk of his hotel, and surprisingly, they patched her through when she identified herself. But Karim was out, so she spoke with his personal secretary, Vahid, and told him what she had planned for tonight. The polite young man assured her he would take care of arrangements, and they settled on a time for the limo to pick her up.

And now, here she was, waiting nervously for Karim and Amaya to come. The limo went directly to the rear entrance so as to avoid any paparazzi. When the door opened, her heart jumped.

"Good evening, Desiree." That smoky, velvety voice caressed her skin like mink fur.

"Good evening," she managed to croak back. She scooted over to the other end of the seat to give Karim enough room. "Where's Amaya?"

"She forgot something upstairs, but she'll be along."

They would have a few minutes alone before Amaya joined them. Would this be the time to talk? Lord, he was so distractingly handsome in his dark suit, and she noticed that his beard was now trimmed neatly. It made her want to reach out and touch his face.

"Apologies that we have to use this entrance." His nose wrinkled at the dumpsters just outside the window. "We're lucky tonight that there aren't many photographers camped outside. It's probably because that singer and Australian actor split up, and she's supposedly hiding out at The Mercer Hotel with her new beau."

"I didn't know you kept up with the gossip rags," she teased.

"Only to use them to my advantage." He frowned. "And I know there's already been talk of Amaya. They will probably think she is my love child or something even more salacious."

"We don't have to go out, you know. We could just stay—"

"No." His hand covered hers, the warmth sending an aching desire straight to her core. "You are right. I cannot shelter her forever and keep her a prisoner. Princesses are usually not allowed to study abroad and have normal lives, but I would like her to have that choice someday. But I must also prepare her."

"Prepare her?" She echoed. "How?"

"I was out today, meeting with a PR firm here in New York. In the past, I have let the press do and say as they want, but no longer. I have retained their services so that we can control the story. An official press release will be out tomorrow which introduces Amaya to the world so that there will be no questions as to who she is."

"That's a wonderful idea."

"I'm also mulling the idea of having an embassy here." His tone was quiet, almost … hopeful?

"I—"

The door opened again, and Amaya bounding into the limo made her start and Karim move away. "Hello, Amaya."

"Deedee!" The young girl scrambled into the empty spot in the middle of the seat. She opened up her small pink handbag which matched the dress she was wearing. "Here." She handed her an envelope.

"Thank you, Amaya." On the front of the envelope was her name.

"It's a thank you card, I made it myself," she said proudly. "Karim said it would be a good idea."

"Thank you, it's lovely. I'll open it later." She tucked it away in her purse.

"Where are we going?" Amaya asked. "Karim said you had a surprise."

"Yes," she said. "You'll see when we get there."

The limo drove south toward the theater district, weaving its way through the traffic as it approached Times Square. When they got to Fifty-fifth and Broadway, they stopped outside one of the many theaters in the area. The marquee was lit up and the posters plastered around showed a young woman on horseback, a crown on her head as she stretched a bow in her hand.

"*The Last Princess?*" Amaya's brows furrowed together. "What's that?"

"This is a Broadway show based on a movie about Princess Arya."

Her nose wrinkled. "And who is this princess?"

"She's only the most amazing girl ever." Amaya must *really* have been sheltered because *The Last Princess* was a classic animated movie that came out almost three decades ago. It was only last year that it came to Broadway and became a smashing success, so much so that it was booked out months in advance. However, with the right connections, getting the tickets hadn't taken much effort.

"What makes this princess so amazing?" Amaya sniffed. Obviously, she was not impressed. Deedee wondered if she miscalculated. Maybe real princesses weren't fans of fictional ones.

"I'm sure it is a good story," Karim interjected. "Tell us more about this Princess Arya."

"She can do anything," Deedee declared. "She can shoot bows, fight with a sword, ride horses, outwit bridge trolls, and she even rescues a prince."

"Rescues the prince from what?"

"An evil ... er," she shot Karim an apologetic look. "A dragon."

Karim looked amused. "Sounds like an interesting show."

"But dragons aren't evil!" Amaya shook her head. "Why would a dragon kidnap anyone?"

"It's just a story, little one," Karim assured her. "You will enjoy it."

"I probably should have picked another show." Deedee rubbed her palm on her forehead. "Sorry, I didn't think—"

"It's a wonderful surprise." Karim reached over and pulled her hand from her face. "Thank you. I'm sure the tickets must have cost you a lot, and I should—"

"No, they were free," she said. "Don't worry, I know the right people."

The limo door opened, and one of the Almoravid peeked inside to let them know it was okay to get out. Karim alighted first and helped Amaya out. When it was Deedee's turn, Karim offered his hand, which she took, but instead of letting her go once she was out, he tucked it into the crook of his arm and led her into the theater, and she found she didn't really want him to let go.

As soon as they entered and she pulled out their tickets, the ushers led them upstairs to one of the private boxes on the balcony. When the curtain parted, an older woman was already there, waiting for them.

"Good evening, Your Highness." The woman bowed her head. "Welcome to our show. I'm Evie King, one of the executive producers of *The Last Princess*."

"Good evening, Ms. King. Thank you for this wonderful opportunity to watch your show." Karim gave her a curt nod. "This is my sister, Her Royal Highness, Princess Amaya of Zhobghadi."

"How do you do, Your Highness?" Evie bowed to Amaya. "I hope you enjoy the show."

"She's not too fond of the idea of evil dragons, Evie," Deedee said with a chuckle. "And to be honest, neither am I."

"I suppose not. Deedee, I'm glad to see you home." Evie came over to her and enfolded her in an embrace. "We were so worried about you."

"Uh, thanks."

"How do you know each other?" Karim asked.

"Close family friend," Evie explained. "My husband works for her father. And my family is pledged to New York."

"Ah." A gleam of understanding crossed his face. "Thank you for the tickets."

"You're very welcome," she said. "We are honored by your presence. And I assure you, this box is very private."

"Evie was the original voice of Princess Arya," Deedee explained.

"That was thirty years ago," Evie said with a chuckle.

"She's a great singer, actor, and composer. She's an EGOT, you know?"

"A what?"

"Hey, what's shaking, Aunt Evie?" The curtain had opened behind them and Jacob walked in, Delacroix following behind. Though Deedee had ridden in Karim's limo, her two shadows followed behind in their car as usual. Seeing as she wasn't really in any danger, she wasn't sure why they still insisted on guarding her, but she was already used to their presence. Also, it wasn't like she could keep them away at this point. Last night, she had forgotten about them and locked her door before they could come in, but this morning she found them on her couch, Jacob eating the last of her cereal and Delacroix flipping through the channels on her TV.

"Hello, Jacob. I'm doing well. I had dinner with your mother the other night." Evie kissed him on the cheek. "You should call her."

"Awww ..." Jacob scratched his head.

"Aunt?" Karim asked.

"My husband and Jacob's dad are brothers," Evie explained.

"Jacob was the one who got the tickets," Deedee added. "Thanks, by the way."

"Meh." Jacob waved her away and then sank down in one of the chairs in the box. "What time does this thing end?"

Evie laughed. "The boys never did like Princess Arya. Not even my son was impressed, and he hated it when his classmates asked him for my autograph."

"I for one, am happy to be here." Delacroix sat down beside Jacob. "Thank you for the opportunity, Ms. King. I have never been to a Broadway show before."

"Oh, you'll love it," Evie said. "All right, curtains up in ten, I should get backstage. Enjoy the show!" With a final wave, she walked out of the box.

"This really is wonderful." Karim motioned for them to sit on the three front seats. "Thank you."

"I hope you enjoy it," she told Amaya. "It's one of my favorite stories from when I was a kid."

They sat down, making small talk until the house lights dimmed. Finally, the orchestra began to play the overture, and Deedee found herself humming to the familiar melody of the *Princess Arya* soundtrack. She smiled to herself, remembering how she would drive her father and brothers crazy, as she always wanted to play it all the time.

A sudden pang of guilt hit her—it had been days since she'd talked to her father and mother. By now, they should know Karim was here; after all, Jacob would have to report back to him. But they didn't do or say anything. Were they giving her time, or did they simply not care anymore?

She felt as if someone was looking at her, and when she

turned her head to the left, saw blue eyes staring into hers. Even in the dim light, there was no mistaking his gaze. She wanted to tell him now, in the intimacy of the theater, how she felt, but Amaya sat between them. So, she settled on giving him a shy smile before turning back to the action on stage.

Once again, she found herself enjoying spending time with Karim and Amaya. After the intermission, Karim convinced Amaya to switch seats with him since he was closer to the stage and she would be able to see better. When the second half began, Karim slyly slipped his hand over hers when they shared the armrest, then threaded his fingers through hers. It was a good thing Deedee had seen the show once before and the movie countless of times, because she could hardly concentrate when all she could think about was how warm his palm was and how good his hand felt. Her she-wolf heartily agreed.

When the finale came and the cast came out for their curtain call, everyone in the audience got to their feet for an extended standing ovation. Finally, the house lights came on again.

"Did you enjoy the show?"

"That was wonderful!" Amaya's cheeks were flushed with excitement. "Did you see her fight the Black Knight? And he turned out to be the prince? Then those cyclops tried to eat them, and she shot each one of them in the eye with an arrow!" She jumped up in her chair and waved her hand around. "She's the best sword fighter in all of Galadria! Karim, I want to take up sword fighting when I get back to Zhobghadi. May I, please?"

"Er, we'll talk about it," Karim said.

"I have another surprise for you, Amaya." Deedee grabbed her purse and pointed to the door. "Evie asked us to be her special guest backstage and meet the cast."

The little girl's eyes went wide. "Really? I get to meet Princess Arya?" She shrieked, then hugged her. "Thank you, thank you, thank you!"

They made their way backstage with Jacob and Delacroix leading the way. As they descended the stairs, Karim sidled up to her. "I cannot thank you enough. I have never seen Amaya so happy as she is now." He nodded at his sister, who was chatting with Delacroix and Jacob. The Cajun seemed to indulge her as she tittered on and on about the show while Jacob merely rolled his eyes.

"You're welcome, but feel free to take back your gratitude when she starts singing the songs or plays the soundtrack non-stop," she said with a chuckle.

His hand landed on the small of her back as he guided her away from the crowds going against them trying to exit the theater. "I could never take back anything I told you," he whispered into her ear.

She shivered visibly, and her toes curled thinking of his words last night. Oh, why didn't she plan a different evening? Something private, where she could tell him her thoughts and feelings?

"We're here." Jacob said when they reached the plain black door near the front of the theater. He pushed on the door and nodded at the man standing guard by the entrance.

"Your Highness!" Evie greeted as she ushered them inside. "Our cast is eager to meet you. This way."

Evie led them into the backstage area, and she began to give them an informal tour. When they reached the stage area, the entire cast, still in their costumes, was lined up to greet them. Amaya was over the moon, and she got pictures and selfies with the cast and crew.

"I promise you, we won't publicize the photos, Your Highness," Evie assured Karim. "It's only for my own personal scrapbook."

"It's all right, Ms. King," Karim said. "In fact, if you wouldn't mind, I'll have my people from Glaser and Baskins PR contact you in the morning for a few photos? I'm sure it would be nice to have them for the Zhobghadi Royal Family's first press release."

Evie beamed. "I don't mind at all. I'll be sure to send them what I have right away."

They wrapped up the photos and autographs, then said goodbye to Evie and the cast and crew before heading out to the waiting limo which had been parked in the back alley. Although Deedee was happily nodding to Amaya's excited jabbering, she couldn't help but feel like she would burst any moment if she didn't say anything to Karim. But when would she find the opportunity? Surely, she couldn't do it while Amaya was around. An idea struck her, but she would have to talk to Jacob and Delacroix first.

"Go ahead," she said to Karim and Amaya when they were in front of the limo doors. "I need to ask Jacob something." Turning around, she walked over to the pair who were keeping guard by the backstage door. "I need to talk to you guys."

Delacroix cocked his head. "What is it, *mon petite?*"

"Er, I was wondering if tonight ... you guys wouldn't mind *not* coming into my house?" She felt her face go hot all the way to the tips of her ears. "I wanted to invite Karim in and—"

"What?" Jacob exclaimed. "Are you crazy—"

If it was possible, she got even redder. "I only need to talk—"

Delacroix grabbed his companion by the arm to silence him. "Say no more." He winked at her. "I understand."

"Hey!" Jacob yanked his arm back. "Are you serious?"

"I think if we do not give them some time alone, they will seriously combust with all the sexual tension between them." The Cajun grinned at her. "We will stay away for tonight. It is obvious that the prince would chew off his own arm before he harms you. Come, *mon ami*." He cocked his head back toward the theater. "We can go to Blood Moon, and perhaps we can find some fair and friendly companions, *non*?"

Jacob looked conflicted, but Deedee could see him crumbling, especially at the chance of a night off. "Fine. But we'll be back tomorrow morning," he warned her. "I don't want to hear or see any shit when we come back in the morning, okay?"

"I said we're only going to talk—" She shut her mouth when Jacob narrowed his eyes at her. Oh, who the heck was she kidding? "Fine. I'll see you in the morning." Pivoting on her heel, she went back to the awaiting limo and went inside.

"Everything okay?" Karim asked.

"Yes." She swallowed the nervousness bubbling in her throat. As the limo lurched forward, it was like her stomach was left behind in that alleyway.

"Amaya, your nanny will take you upstairs to our suite," Karim said to his sister as they approached The Plaza. "Say goodnight to Deedee before I take her back home."

"But Karim—"

"No buts, it's getting late," Karim said firmly.

"Fine." Amaya stuck her lower lip out. "But will I see you tomorrow?" she asked Deedee.

"Maybe," she answered. "I mean, it depends on what Karim has planned."

"I do have an idea, but I want to run it by you first."

The limo stopped, but before she could say anything else, the door opened, and a man popped his head in. "Your Highness, apologies for the intrusion."

"What is it, Vahid?" he asked.

"Mr. Glaser is upstairs, and he wanted to personally go over the press release with you before he sends it out in the morning," Vahid said. "He says it shouldn't take too long."

Karim sighed. "That's what he said the last time, but he does tend to get very long-winded." He turned to her. "I'm sorry, I must go upstairs. The limo will take you home."

Her heart sank, but she understood. He was doing this for Amaya. "Of course. How about breakfast tomorrow morning?" She smiled at Amaya. "There's this place I know where we can get these huge pancakes."

"Pancakes?" Amaya's face lit up.

"Yes, they're the size of your head," Deedee said with a laugh. "Third Street Diner. You can't miss it. Let's say eight o'clock?"

"We shall see you there," Karim said. "Goodnight, Desiree."

She bid them goodnight, then the door closed. Settling into the leather seat, she looked out, watching Karim and Amaya as they entered the hotel. Tomorrow then, she would tell him. Yes, the first opportunity she got; she would say it.

She'd been practicing it in her head since last night, so it should be easy, right?

————

The limo dropped her off in front of her townhouse, with one of the Almoravid opening the door for her as she gathered her coat and purse. "Thank you." She waved him away when he attempted to follow her to her door. Surely she wasn't in any danger between the sidewalk and her front door, so there was no need for him to escort her.

Taking her keys out of her purse, she entered the darkened front foyer. As she reached for the light switch on the left side, her hand froze. Her she-wolf's hackles rose, and she knew there was something—no, someone—inside her house.

With a careful, quiet gait, she crept into the living room. Her eyes were just adjusting when she heard a voice call out from the darkness.

"Deedee, it's me."

Her body deflated like a balloon when she recognized who it was. Heading over to the nearest light switch, she flipped it on, bathing the room in light, revealing the figure standing in the middle of her living room.

Yes, there was no mistake. It was Cross.

Her mouth went dry at the sight of him. Oh, he seemed almost larger than life now, in the flesh so to speak. This was definitely Cross, but somehow ... he seemed different. His mouth was pulled back into a grim line, and his entire body was tense, like he was being stretched taut by invisible strings.

Not only that, but he was physically different. The sides of his head were shaved, but the top was left long and pulled back into a ponytail, while his beard was more grizzled. The tank top he wore showed fresh new ink down his arms and hands. When her gaze went north, she was taken aback by the stormy, turquoise depths of his eyes, and for a brief moment, the memory of that painting flashed back in her mind. They were the same, yet not, and she couldn't put her finger on *why* it seemed so.

She wrung her hands together. "What are you doing here?"

He took a step toward her, heavy boots thudding on the hardwood floors. "I came as soon as I heard you were taken."

"Too late, that was days ago." She stepped around the couch to meet him halfway, dropping her purse on the loveseat. "Much too late."

The words made him flinch. *Good.*

"I'm sorry."

You should be. But she kept her lips pursed together.

"I was wrong, Dee."

Hold on. She blinked. This is what she had been dreaming of these past months, right? That Cross would come to her, tell her that he was sorry, and that he was wrong to have rejected her.

"I shouldn't have stayed away from you."

Her entire body felt like jelly, and she sank down onto the loveseat. "Cross, you can't—"

"Hear me out." In an instant he was beside her, taking her hands into his. "I've been on communication blackout for days. Your father's message that you might be in danger arrived a few hours ago, and I came as soon as I could. I've been waiting here for you."

Did he know she'd been out with Karim? "I ... I don't know what to say."

"I should have been there to rescue you, Dee." He scrubbed a hand down his beard. "No, I shouldn't have driven you away."

"You didn't—"

"Of course I did." There was that slight smile, the one she remembered so well. Her heart began to thump in her chest, realizing how close they were and that his hands were wrapped around hers, holding them so intimately. She'd always felt so small and delicate next to him. "You told me how you felt, and I should have tried ... Deedee, I ..."

It was like a thousand butterflies began to flutter in her stomach. His face was coming in closer, his hands gripped hers tighter. This was it ... the moment she'd been waiting for, for what seemed like years. His eyes closed as he moved in and—

She turned her face away, and his lips landed on her cheek. And even that felt *weird*.

A sigh escaped his mouth, and he leaned his forehead against her temple. "I'm sorry, Dee."

"No, don't be sorry," she whispered. "Be anything else but sorry."

And suddenly, it was like the butterflies in her stomach just disappeared. Cross was here because he felt guilty, that he thought he was the reason she had run away and had been taken. The truth was, she did that all by herself, and if she hadn't, she never would have met Karim and fallen in love with him. Oh, she knew it be true now, more than ever.

"You feel different about me now?" Soulful ocean-colored eyes searched hers.

"I don't think I knew how I felt about you." She never loved Cross—or maybe she did, but it was a childhood crush, nothing more. It was time to put it away and grow up. "Do you feel different about me after all these months?"

There was a long pause before he answered. "I could, Dee. I'm sure I could learn to love you back ... that way."

"Oh goodness." She shook her head. This was all so wrong and she wanted to laugh. "Now what? Are we supposed to date, get married, and live happily ever after? No, thank you. I'd rather be alone than to be with someone who was with me because of guilt. I deserve better."

"That's not what I meant, Dee."

"Isn't it?"

"I—" He squeezed her hands tighter. "I keep messing this up. I didn't mean to push you away. If you hadn't gone on that trip, you would have been safe here."

"Don't blame yourself for what happened to me. First of all, I'm an adult, and I make my own decisions." She gave a little laugh. "Second, my father overreacted to this whole thing."

"I thought I could love you the way you love—loved me," he admitted. "But that's wrong. I shouldn't have come here. I would have used you to forget—" His lips clamped together.

She looked up into his face and realized that something *had* changed in him. This Cross in front of her ... he seemed harder and more closed off. Not the carefree young man he'd been in their youth. "What happened, Cross?" His jaw hardened, but she pressed on. "Please, I'm your best friend. You can talk to me. You can tell me anything."

"Dee ..." His voice was raw, like his throat was thick with emotion. "I found—"

The rapping at the door made him stop. Who could that be at this hour?

Cross tensed and placed a hand on her knee. "Don't move. I'll go check who it is."

"What?" Before she knew it, Cross disappeared and then reappeared by her front door, peeking out her peephole. "Who is it?"

"Stay inside," Cross warned. "It's that guy Sebastian warned me about in his message."

"That guy—oh no!" Did her father send Cross to get rid of Karim? Of all the sneaky— "Wait, Cross, you don't understand."

"If he thinks he can just come in here and take you—"

"Desiree? Who's in there?" The knocking became more insistent. "Open this door now!"

Her stomach dropped when Cross grabbed the doorknob and yanked it open. On the other side, Karim had a fist raised, knuckles out. When his eyes landed on Cross, his eyes blazed with the fury of his dragon.

"Who in *An's* name are you, and what are you doing here?"

Cross stretched to full height and his eyes, too, were aglow. "I should ask you the same. You're not taking her from here, I don't care if you're a prince. Or a dragon."

Karim's eyes were an icy river of blue. "What is this man doing here in the middle of the night?"

"Karim, I can explain—"

"Leave now," Cross warned. "Stay away from her."

"Do you have any idea who you're speaking with?"

"Do *you*?" Cross countered. "We've taken her back. You can't just stroll in here and take her away again."

"I don't know what that *blasphemer* has told you, but I did not kidnap her nor am I here to—" Karim stopped short, his expression turning to confusion, realization, then finally back to anger. "You. It's you."

Cross seemed taken aback. "Me?"

Karim's gaze flickered to her. "It's him, isn't it? The man in the painting."

"What painting?" Fury crossed Cross's face as he stepped forward and grabbed Karim by the collar. "If you've taken a painting—"

"You dare touch a prince of Zhobghadi!" Karim wrenched Cross's hands away. "I'll show you—"

"Stop! Please, stop!" Deedee cried as she got between them. "Don't." She was looking at Cross.

"Deedee, I don't understand. Your father—"

"Look, I know you just got here," she began. "But you don't know the whole picture. He's not here to kidnap me. If he was, then I'd be gone by now. Find Jacob, and he'll tell you the truth."

"My cousin?"

"Yes. He should be at Blood Moon."

"Dee, I'm not leaving you alone with him."

"Go," she urged Cross. "If you do care for me, then you'll leave. Now."

The look of hurt on his face made her heart lurch. But if he didn't leave now, Karim was going to go all dragon, she could feel it. Her she-wolf could feel it, and was warning her with loud yips.

"All right." Cross's shoulders sank. "If you want me to go, then I'll leave."

"Yes, just go, Cross."

He leaned down to whisper in her ear, then put something in her hand. "Call me if you need me, and I will find you." And with that, he disappeared.

She blinked, then opened her hand and stared at what he had placed in her palm. It was a small gold disc, stamped with a wolf's head. What was this? And what did Cross mean when he said he would find her? And what about—*Karim!*

She didn't even notice that he had turned around and was walking toward his waiting limo.

"Karim, wait!" She dashed down the stoop steps and grabbed his arm. "Don't go, Karim," she pleaded.

He stopped and turned his head to her. "Don't go? Why, because he's gone now?"

"Don't be like this, Karim."

"I came to you because I could not wait until tomorrow to see you." He grit his teeth. "And then I find another man in your home, in the middle of the night! And not only that, he's the one in that painting you were so fascinated by."

"I wasn't—"

"Don't lie to me, Desiree," he growled. "I deserve the truth."

He was right. Karim had been truthful to her, but she hadn't. "Cross is my friend. My best friend. We grew up together." Tears burned in her throat, but she continued on. "Then a few months ago, we were attacked, and I thought I was going to die, so I confessed my feelings for him. He didn't return them."

"And then what happened?"

"I left New York. I mean, got the grant and went on my dig—"

"So, *he* is the real reason."

His words sounded so final, like a door slamming as it closed. "No, I didn't leave because of him. I mean ... yes, it was too painful to stay here, but I still had to do my research—"

"That's not what I meant, Desiree."

She looked up at him. "What do you mean? I don't understand."

"Don't you?"

The tone of his voice chilled her. "Karim, I—"

"Save it," he sneered. "Save it for the one that is really in your heart."

His words shook her to the core. Did he really believe that? Oh Lord, she should have told him earlier. Should have returned his words as soon as he said it. But the numbing pain made her stay in the spot, watching helplessly as Karim got into his limo, and the vehicle drove away.

When she realized that he was finally gone, her knees buckled. She caught herself before she crumpled to the ground and hobbled over to her stoop. She sat down and buried her face in her hands as the tears began to flow, though she clamped her lips to imprison a sob welling in her chest. Despite her throat aching with defeat, she managed to stand up and drag herself upstairs and back into her home.

When she stumbled inside, a sound from the living room sobered her up. *What in the world?* Rushing toward the sound, she stopped when she saw who was standing next to her couch.

"A-Astrid?"

Dressed in her bathrobe, her stomach still rounded with pregnancy, her best friend stood there, her brows furiously snapping together when she saw Deedee's tear-stricken face. "Cross brought me here, said you might need me. Zac's not happy but he understands." She waddled over to her. "Dee, what happened?"

She collapsed into her best friend's open arms. "Astrid ..."

CHAPTER TWENTY

"WHAT IS IT NOW?" KARIM BARKED AT VAHID WHEN HE came into the suite.

The hapless secretary was practically shaking in his moccasins. "Y-Your Highness. Mr. Glaser is outside and wants to speak with you."

"I am tired of that man's fawning. Will you be useful for once today, and tell him to go away?"

Vahid flinched. "Y-yes, Your Highness." His bow and salute with his fist over his heart was quick, as if he couldn't wait to leave.

Karim did not blame him because he'd been a real beast this morning. Amaya even told him so when she walked out this morning after she threw a tantrum when he told her there would be no pancakes for breakfast and that she should pack because she would be leaving for Zhobghadi that very day. The media, of course, had already received the press release, and now they were camped outside The Plaza. He feared for her safety and wondered if it was a mistake to introduce her to the world. Mistake or no, Amaya had been furious and refused to speak to him, not even before she left for the airport.

Yes, he'd been a total bastard the whole morning. Gods, he'd been in a fury since last night when he left Desiree's home.

It was such a contrast to earlier in the night. He was practically walking on air, having her on his arm, holding her hand in that darkened theater. And he could see it in her eyes. Tenderness. Affection. And maybe even love. It took all his strength not to whip out the black velvet box he'd been carrying in his pocket since he left Zhobghadi and propose to her.

That damned Glaser and his press release! As soon as he was done, he had raced to her home. He thought to surprise, and maybe she would finally say those words he'd been waiting to hear.

Little did he know that *he* would be the one surprised, to find her alone, with another man.

The Great One snorted in displeasure. It wanted to burn this rival to ashes. Sure, Desiree made the other man leave, but then she told him the truth.

Finally, he knew the real reason she couldn't return his feelings. It wasn't because things were going too fast, but rather, it was because she was in love with another man. He should have known, after seeing her face when she saw that portrait of him. She must really love him, for his rejection to drive her far away. Was she thinking of him the entire time they were together? Wishing he'd been the first one to take her, initiate her into lovemaking? The one who's child she could be possibly carrying?

He let out a roar and grabbed the first thing he could—a

vase filled with flowers—and slung it against the wall, sending glass chips, water, and long-stemmed roses, everywhere. "*Nergal*, take it all!" And he would let the God of Plague and War have everything he possessed if it would make this confounding ache in his chest go away.

"Well, did that help, or did you just destroy a perfectly good crystal vase?"

"Who—how did you get in here?"

That fiendish pregnant woman—Astrid, Future Beta of New York—was standing in front of his door, her hands on her hips and face scrunched up in fury. "You're not asking the right questions, buddy. Maybe you should be asking *why* I'm here."

"I've doubled the guards, and we've hired our own extra security to keep people away from this floor. How did you manage—" The door swung open, and Delacroix stepped in, answering his question. "Of course."

"Hey, *cherie*, I showed you my trick, maybe next time, show me yours?"

"Sorry, my back was killing me, and I had to get in here and give this asshole a piece of my mind!" Astrid rubbed a hand on her lower back, then hobbled over to the nearest chair. "Anyway, where was I?" She looked up to Karim. "Oh yeah, I was about to tear you a new one."

"You're mad at *me*?" The nerve of this woman. "Did you not know that it is your *friend* who is in love with another? That she was the one who had him in her house—"

"Hold on!" She raised a hand up. "As much as I want my best friend and my brother to end up together, it's obvious to me that you're the only one she wants."

"Your brother?" Now he was confused.

"Yes, Cross is my brother." She snapped her fingers at him. "Keep up, okay?"

Upon closer inspection, he did see the similarities in their features. The lips and the chin, for sure. "He was the reason she was out there in the desert. She ran away from him."

"And would you blame her? She laid her cards out, and he rejected her. So, she got her heart broken. It happens. *She got over it.* Then you kidnapped—er, 'met' her, and now for some reason, she's in love with you."

"She is not in love with me." The words were like knives cutting across his skin. "I have offered her everything, even my own heart, yet she does not return my feelings. Then last night, I saw him. With her, inside her apartment." Even now, jealousy crept under his skin, coursing through his veins like a vigilant poison.

"Yes, so Cross came back for her. And she had it for a moment, what she thought she wanted all these months, but instead she kicked him out and chose *you*, you bastard! And what, the moment things get tough, you throw a temper tantrum without letting her explain? Are you a fucking toddler who found out Santa Claus wasn't real? Put on your big boy pants, Your Highness, and deal with this like an adult."

Her words made his head spin, like he was riding on a Ferris wheel that suddenly halted. "She's ... in love with me?"

"Yes, you moron!" She shot to her feet. "Ding, ding, ding, give the man a prize!" She marched up to him and poked her finger at him. "And another thing—" Her eyes went wide.

He waited for her to continue, but she stood there, motionless. "Yes? What other thing?"

She sucked in a breath. "My water just broke."

"How is that relevant to Desiree—" He felt the wetness on his slippered feet. "*Mother Inana!*"

"Oh. My. Fucking. God!" Astrid cried. "I'm actually having this baby!"

"We should call a doctor!" He glanced over at Delacroix, who had surprisingly turned pale.

"You don't understand," she moaned. "I'm actually having this baby *now*." An ear-splitting shriek escaped her mouth, one that made him want to run for the sand dunes and never return.

"I can get you to the hospital—"

"No hospital, please." Her talon-like fingers dug into his arm. "I just need to lie down—"

"Are you crazy? You can't give birth here!"

"My doctor's too far away, and I'm not going to make it." Beads of sweat formed on her forehead. "Delacroix!"

"I'm already on the phone," the Cajun hollered back. His cellphone was pressed to his ear as he muttered to himself silently.

"Call my dad, he'll know what to do," she cried. "Where's your bed?"

"I—" He grit his teeth and lifted her up in his arms. She didn't protest at all as he carried her into the master bedroom and then lay her gently on top of the covers.

"Oh God, I'm not birthing this child around you," she moaned.

"Believe me, I am as thrilled as you are at the prospect." He pivoted to walk away from her but her fingers wrapped around his hand and pulled back. "What—oww! *Dagan's* beard, woman, are you trying to break my hand?"

"Don't leave me!" Another shriek left her mouth, and he

resisted the urge to pry her talons away. "I don't want to be alone."

He huffed, then knelt down beside the bed. "All right. I am a prince. I can handle this." His tone was full of confidence. "So, why don't you take a deep breath and—"

"I am fucking breathing," she heaved. "I do it all the fucking time. I don't know how that's supposed to help."

"And I suppose profanity eases your pain?"

"Actually, it does," she snapped. "God, if Deedee ever takes you back, I hope you suffer worse than you are now when it's time to have your baby."

"I can't possibly suffer more than I am now." The prospect of Desiree having their child and being in so much pain made him break out into a nervous sweat.

"Asshole," she bit out, then clenched her teeth as her hand went down to her stomach. "Oh God, take my pants off, this baby's almost here."

Now *that* was the last straw. He got up and extricated her fingers from his. "I am sorry, but there are just some things I cannot—"

"Astrid! Astrid, are you okay?"

When he turned around, he saw the warlock behind him, and a second man he'd never seen before. The unknown man rushed over to Astrid and grabbed her hand. "I'm here. Okay, baby, just breathe. In and out. In and—"

"Why the fuck is everyone telling me to breathe?" Astrid screamed. "I know how to fucking breathe, just get this baby out of me!"

The man turned to the warlock. "Daric—the doctor."

"I'm on it." Daric shimmered away.

Karim cleared his throat. "I should probably leave."

"You probably should," Astrid said through gritted teeth. "This isn't going to be pretty."

"You're gorgeous, baby," the man—Astrid's husband and mate, presumably—said as he brushed her hair out of her face.

"Did I say I wasn't, Zachary?" she spat. "What I meant was, *your* face won't be so pretty once I'm done—"

Zachary leaned down and kissed her. "I love you too, baby."

Astrid sobbed. "Me too. I'm just scared."

"The doctor will be here soon," he soothed. "Hang on just a bit, okay?"

As they whispered to each other, Karim suddenly felt out of place and quietly exited the room. With a deep sigh, he closed the door gently.

"Everything okay in there, Your Highness?" Delacroix asked.

"I think it will be fine." He heard two more voices coming from the inside of his room, and he assumed the warlock had come back with the doctor.

Walking over to the bar, he took out his personal bottle of Three Wolves Whiskey Duncan had sent over the other day and poured out two glasses, offering one to the Cajun.

"Thank you." He took the offered glass and raised it. "To the new parents, eh?"

"I will drink to that." He clinked his glass to the other man's and then they both downed their drinks. "Do you think they will be long?"

"Probably not too long." The scream from the other room, followed by a string of profanities, made them both wince. Delacroix sank down on the couch. "At least, I hope not."

Karim joined him, taking the bottle with him and refilling both their glasses. They sat there without saying a word, sipping their whiskey and cringing in unison whenever Astrid bellowed and yelled.

Finally, after what seemed like an eternity, a different scream pierced the air—that of a healthy baby. Both men rose from the couch as the door opened.

"It's a girl." Daric's smile was as wide as the Sahara, and he approached Karim. "Your Highness, thank you for staying with my daughter while I went to fetch her husband. And for lending us your room."

"Daughter?" *Of course.* He was a carbon copy of that man—Cross. Was everyone around here related?

"If there is anything I can do for you, let me know. I am in your debt." He bowed his head. "Though perhaps I may be able to return the favor in the future."

He doubted it, but nodded anyway. "Congratulations. Now, if you will excuse me, I need to call the front desk and arrange for them to move me to another suite."

———

Karim settled into his new suite sometime later, just one floor below his old one, since his previous one was now occupied. He'd called Vahid and explained to him what happened so that the man didn't accidentally enter the wrong suite. Also, after hearing what Astrid had to say, he instructed him to cancel their trip back to Zhobghadi.

The woman's words stung, but she was right. He told Desiree that he was going to do what it took to make himself worthy of her, and the moment things went wrong, he ran away without allowing her to explain.

He had hated it when she did that to him back in Zhobghadi, so he knew she must really be hurting right now. Yes, he was jealous of that other man, and he doubted that he would ever feel all right when any man hovered around her, but he should have trusted her and listened to her explanation.

If Duncan were here, he would probably say that he was shite at this groveling and wooing thing. But how could he possibly win her back now?

I should go to her.

The Great One snorted in agreement.

Yes, that's it. Get down on his knees, beg her to take him back. With a determined stride, he walked to the door and yanked it open. What he saw on the other side made him stop.

"Hello, is—Karim?" Desiree's light green eyes lit up in surprise. "What are you doing here?" She swung her head around. "Where did he go?"

"Me?" He was surprised his voice even worked right now. "This is my room."

"But Daric brought me here. He said Astrid had her baby and she needed me." She scratched her head. "But he just disappeared."

"The warlock brought you here?"

"He must have made a mistake." She glanced around. "I thought we'd be at the Medical Wing of The Enclave."

"Wait!" He reached out and took her hand before she could try to get away. If the warlock had brought her here, it must have been for a reason. "Don't go."

"Astrid—"

"Astrid is upstairs."

She looked even more confused. "Upstairs? Here?"

"In my old suite. She was there when her water broke. It was too late to bring her to the hospital, so her father brought her husband and the doctor, who delivered the baby in my room."

"So, she *is* here ... but why did she come?"

"She, uh, came to see me this morning to 'tear me a new one' as she put it."

Recognition lit up her eyes. "Oh. Sorry about that. She really shouldn't have—"

"Yes, she should have. I deserved it." Silence hung between them like a thick fog. Finally, he said, "Can we talk, Desiree? Please?"

"I—" Hesitation was evident on her face. "I don't know if there's anything to talk about."

"I beg you. Please."

Her expression faltered. "Fine, but I can't stay too long." She stepped inside his room when he motioned for her to come in. Crossing her arms over her chest, she turned to him, not saying anything. And so, he spoke first.

"I shouldn't have accused you of those things last night."

"No, you shouldn't have." Her tone was so chilly it could have frozen the desert sun.

"I didn't know the whole story until Astrid came to me this morning."

"No, you didn't."

He raked his fingers through his hair. "But I was so jealous, seeing that man in your house. I assumed the worst because ... because I was hurt that you didn't return my feelings."

"Karim ..." Her voice shook as she said his name, and her arms dropped to her sides. "Y-y-you just left last night."

"I'm sorry."

Her lower lip trembled. "Y-y-you didn't let me make things right. I was going to fix it."

Hope bloomed in his chest. "Fix what?"

"What was between us. B-but you walked away before I had the chance to make things right. To tell you."

He took a step forward, crowding her personal space. "Tell me what, *habibti*?"

"That I love you too," she sobbed. "And now you don't believe—Karim, what are you doing?"

He was getting down on one knee when he paused. "Groveling, apparently." He gave her a small smile. "They say a future king kneels for no one, but I will do so for you."

"Stop, please." She grabbed his forearms and pulled him up. "Don't. You shouldn't have to—"

"But I do. It's part of groveling, you know." But he allowed her to pull him up, then leaned down toward her. "I feel like I've waited so long for you to say those words."

"I love you, I do," she whispered. "I don't think I ever stopped. Not when—" She hooked a finger inside her blouse and fished something out. Something gold and shiny. "I couldn't bear to take it off."

His heart nearly burst out of his chest at the sight of the necklace around her neck. "Do you remember when I gave this to you, *habibti*?"

She nodded. "The first night."

"The first night we made love, yes." He caressed the

necklace where it lay on her collarbone. "It belonged to my mother." She gasped, but remained silent, though she looked up at him, her eyes shiny with unshed tears. "It was the only thing I had left of her. I crept into her room that night she ... she ... and I took it."

"Karim ..."

He brushed away the tear that fell down her cheek. "I couldn't bear it. I wasn't enough for her to stay. I'm never enough. And now I've proven it again, by not trusting you."

"Shh ... Karim. You're enough. More than enough for me." She got on her tiptoes and pressed a kiss to his throat. "And you have to believe I'm strong. Strong enough for you."

"Yes, that was my mistake. You are strong, my Desiree. Stronger than I or anyone can see." He dug his fingers into her hair and pulled her head back to capture her mouth in a kiss. He felt like he'd been parched for days—no, years—and she was his only salvation. He would have continued to kiss her, but they were both out of breath.

"Karim, please. I need you."

And so, he swept her up into his arms and carried her back to his room. He lay her down on the bed and stepped back so he could take his tunic and pants off. She too, made quick work of her skirt and blouse, but he stopped her when she reached for her bra.

"Allow me." He unhooked the front of her bra, freeing her breasts. The white gold chain lying between them made his instincts stir, and he moved over her and took her sweet mouth once more. "I'm sorry, I can't wait. It's been too long. This might be quick," he said against her lips.

"We can do slow later." She moaned and lifted her hips

when he reached for her panties and took them off. "I need you now, inside me."

He pressed a finger to her entrance. Gods, she was already soaked. The air was bursting with her scent and arousal mixed together. His cock was already hard and it twitched with pain. He wanted to wait and savor her.

Her hips pushed up against him. "Now, Karim. Please."

"A queen doesn't beg," he rasped. He pressed the tip of his cock against her core. "My *habibti*. My beloved. My queen." *Mother of my children.*

Her hands raked down his arms as he pushed inside her. It was still a tight fit, despite her arousal, so he had to move in inch by excruciating inch at a time. Finally, when he was fully inside her, she let out a breath and relaxed.

He made love to her slowly, but it was too much. Her heat grasped around him, her scent, and the way she moaned and gasped was too exciting. He moved quicker, picking up the tempo as her movements and sounds encouraged him. When she cried out and tightened around him, her beautiful face twisting as she reached her peak, he couldn't hold on.

She continued to wring out every ounce of pleasure from him, and he let out a roar as he emptied himself inside her. He thought she moaned his name, or screamed I love you, but the white noise from his orgasm made his ears ring. His spent body collapsed on top of hers, and he held her close, as if she was going to disappear any moment and he would wake up from this wonderful dream.

When feeling returned to his body, he rolled over and withdrew from her, then wrapped himself around her. Unable to help himself, he moved a hand down to her stomach. It had been driving him crazy, the last few days, thinking about what Julianna and Duncan had told him. Were they really True Mates?

Mine. Ours. Mate.

The Great One seemed to think so, but never in the thousand-year history of their people had they ever recorded such a phenomena. What if it wasn't the case and she had some other man waiting for her? What if it was that other man, Cross? He shook his head. No, he had to believe they were meant to be together.

She sighed against him and turned to face him. "What are you thinking of?"

"That you are beautiful." He leaned down to kiss her forehead. "I'm glad you showed up at my door."

"I can't believe Daric made a mistake and brought me here instead of upstairs," she said. "He said Astrid was asking for me."

"Hmmm."

She raised a brow at him. "Hmmm? What do you mean, hmmm?"

"Well ... I wonder if the warlock—Daric, brought you here on purpose?" The man's words came back to him. About being able to return the favor. Did the warlock deliberately bring her to his door?

"Huh." Her brows furrowed. "It's not like him to make such a miscalculation. I wonder ..."

"You wonder what?"

"Well, I've heard some things ... no one has confirmed or denied it, but I've overheard that Daric can see the future."

"The future?" That wasn't what he had been thinking of. Was such a thing even possible?

"He doesn't speak about it. No one does. It makes sense.

Plus, how he knew where to find me in Zhobghadi and—" A ringing sound made her jolt and sit up. "Sorry, that's my phone."

He groaned. "Must you answer it?" He rather liked having her complete attention, just like when they were back in the palace.

"It might be Astrid. I mean, for real this time." She scrambled off the bed.

Leaning back on the headboard, he watched her naked body with delight as she stalked to the corner where she had chucked her purse. When she bent down to retrieve it, his cock twitched at the sight of her rounded bottom, and he stifled a groan.

"I still can't believe Astrid gave birth in your suite." She fished her phone out of her purse and answered it. "Hello?" She frowned. "Hey, Bastian ... no, um ... I was busy. Right ..." She chewed at her lip. "Yes, I'm with him. I'm guessing Dad knows since he's the one who sent Jacob and Delacroix ... is that so? Tonight?" Her mouth formed into an *O*, then she quickly glanced at Karim. "I'll ask him. I can't guarantee ... yes, I'll do my best. All right, bye." With a deep sigh, she put the phone down.

"What's the matter, *habibti*? Who was that?"

"My brother, Bastian."

"Is everything all right? You look worried."

She sighed, then crawled back into bed with him. He had already pulled the covers away and they cuddled underneath. "It seems he's playing peacemaker between me and my parents."

"Wait ... you are quarreling with your mother and father?"

She nodded, then told him what happened when she returned from Zhobghadi. "I just ... I can't believe they did that, you know? Then Dad went all super protective and took me away. And now they ask my baby brother—who they know I could never say no to— to invite us to dinner tonight."

His mind flashed back to the events of that day, when they came to take her away. And then he thought about his child—the one who could at this very moment be in her womb. Though he hadn't yet met him or her, he was very sure he would kill anyone to protect them. "I think we should go."

"What? Really?"

He sighed and ran his hand down her back. "You cannot be fighting with them forever. Besides, they are your only parents, and you should be happy they are still here."

"I—oh, Karim, I'm sorry." She looked up at him, those light eyes so full of love and tenderness. "I suppose I need to face them at some point."

"*We* need to face them." He caught the hand lying on his chest and squeezed it. "Together."

"Yes." She pressed a kiss to his side. "We will."

"But not until tonight." He rolled her over and covered her body with his, his cock already hard as a rock. "We still have time."

"Won't Amaya be back soon?"

"I've sent her home."

"Home?"

"Yes. The press release was sent, and despite our pleas for privacy, they found out we were staying here. I can handle them. I've been doing it for years. But what if one of them got into our suite? Or popped out of the trunk of the limo? She was distraught, of course, and was furious that I sent her away."

"I'm sorry, Karim," she said. "I didn't think about that."

"It's not your fault, *habibti*. It is the world we live in and the greedy people who run it. But I promise you; I will make things right with her." At least Amaya would not be angry at him anymore, not if he brought Desiree back to Zhobghadi.

His thoughts went to the black velvet box he'd been carrying around since he arrived in America. The jeweler back home had fashioned one of the remaining yellow-green diamonds into the most stunning engagement ring he'd ever seen. The final jewel would grace her crown as queen, though he saved that for her to decide on the design. Once things were settled with her family, he would ask her properly, maybe even tonight. And then bringing her back to Zhobghadi would not only be a possibility, but a reality.

CHAPTER TWENTY-ONE

"ARE YOU SURE YOU WANT TO DO THIS?" DEEDEE ASKED Karim as they stepped into the elevator that took them up to her parents' loft in Tribeca. She'd lived here most of her childhood and young adult life, but somehow, the thought of entering this place made her nervous. She loved Karim with all her heart, but if she had to make a choice between him and her family, it would only end in sorrow.

"I am sure." He squeezed her hand. "They are your parents. You cannot stay mad at them forever. Think of our own child." He cleared his throat. "I mean, in the future. You would want our children to know their grandparents, right?"

"Of course I do." Why did the thought of having children with Karim not make her nervous or wary? She always thought she'd have kids one day, if she were ever so lucky, but not so soon. Besides, she and Karim hadn't even had the chance to talk about what they were, at the moment. He talked of having her as queen, but never as his wife. Couldn't they date for a bit before going through all that?

The elevator stopped, and they stepped out. There were

two doors in the main foyer, and she led them to the one on the right.

"This is an interesting space," he said, looking around. "Your parents have the entire building to themselves?

"Oh, right, er, they share the loft space with Daric and his wife. Same building, different apartments."

He raised a brow. "Ah, so you grew up here. And Astrid lived next door?"

"Yes." *And Cross.*

"You were lucky to have your best friends so near."

When he placed a hand around her shoulder, she smiled and leaned against him. "Okay, show time." She pressed the doorbell and waited. It didn't take too long for the door to swing open, revealing her mother.

"You're here." Jade Creed's eyes lit up. "Darling." She stepped forward and embraced her, and she nearly wept. Her mother's face when they fought the other day nearly broke her heart. And while she felt betrayed that Jade didn't say anything about those men following her, she was still her mother, and she would forgive her for almost anything. "I missed you."

"Me too, Mom." She pulled away reluctantly. "Mom, this is Prince Karim."

"Mrs. Creed." Karim nodded in acknowledgement.

"Your Highness, lovely to meet you." Jade curtseyed, being half-English herself. "I was told your sister, the Princess Amaya, was in New York too? Did you bring her to dinner?"

"Yes, she was, but she is on her way home now. She did enjoy New York every much, especially The Met Museum."

"Oh, Deedee was the same with the mummies." Jade winked at her.

Deedee craned her neck above her mother's head. "Is everyone here for dinner?"

"Oh dear, forgive my rudeness!" Jade stepped aside and motioned for them to come inside. "Yes, dinner's almost ready. I don't cook but Gio was nice enough to send all of Deedee's favorites from *Muccino's*."

They stepped inside to the familiar loft apartment, and Deedee couldn't help but feel nostalgic, as she did each time she came here. It had gone through a few changes and upgrades over the years, especially with three Lycan children around. The corner by the entrance could never stay clean and organized, especially during the winter when they would pile all their boots in the corner. The space opened up to a large living room, and the TV in front of the couch was tuned to a football game. She recalled that the sectional couch had to be replaced twice when, as a teen, Bastian threw several wild parties over the course of a summer. Of course, Jade and Sebastian were only aware of that *first* time the couch had been replaced.

As soon as they stepped into the living area, two nearly identical figures stood up from the couch and walked over to them.

"Your Highness," Jade began. "These are my sons, Wyatt and Bastian."

"What's up?" Bastian said with a raise of his chin, his slate-colored eyes surprisingly friendly as he and Karim exchanged handshakes. Of course, despite their age difference, she and him were always close growing up, and it was nice to see her brother had her back.

"Your Highness." Wyatt bowed his head low. "It's nice to meet you finally. I was a few years behind you at Eton, though I'd never had the pleasure."

"I didn't realize," Karim said, then turned to Bastian. "Were you at Eton as well?"

Bastian guffawed. "Hell no. Spent a year there and told my folks to get me out. Grandma Fiona insisted, even though I told her I wouldn't fit in."

"He tried to get expelled," Deedee said, with a wink at Bastian. "And that last prank nearly did it."

Wyatt, that pretentious ass, looked mortified. "I'll never live that down."

"Well, look what the cat dragged in."

All eyes turned toward the kitchen door where Sebastian Creed stood, feet planted shoulder's width apart and tattooed arms crossed over his chest. His stare could have frozen any man, and the air in the loft suddenly felt thick as molasses.

"Dad, be *nice*," Deedee warned.

"This is my home." He walked toward them with deliberate, heavy steps. "I can be nice," he glared at Karim, "and not so nice to anyone I want."

"Why don't we sit down to dinner?" Jade wound her arm around Sebastian's. "Before it gets cold."

Deedee threaded her fingers through Karim's and led him toward the dining table, which had been set up elegantly with their finest china and linens.

"This looks lovely, Mrs. Creed," Karim said as he pulled out a chair for Deedee.

"Thank you, Your Highness. It's an honor to have you here." When her husband snorted, she gave him a death glare. "I'll grab the salad and appetizers."

"I'll help, Mom." Bastian followed her into the kitchen.

As they settled into their chairs, it seemed neither Karim nor Sebastian was going to back down on their staring contest, and so Wyatt spoke up first. "Your Highness, are you enjoying New York?"

"Yes, I am," he answered. "It's an exciting place. I've been before, of course, but there's something about it that's different from anywhere else I've been."

"And when will you be leaving?" Sebastian asked.

Karim looked down at her and smiled. "Not any time soon. I hope to establish an embassy here."

Sebastian huffed. "Not soon enough, then."

"Dad," Deedee hissed.

It was a good thing Jade and Bastian came back with the food at that moment. "What did I miss?" Bastian asked cheekily as he put a plate in front of Deedee.

She slapped her head. *Oh brother.* This was going to be a long night.

"Aren't you going to be king or something, Your Highness?" Bastian took a swig of wine. "How's that going?"

"Preparations will be made as soon as I return," Karim said, his gaze sliding over to Deedee's. "I have business to take care of beforehand."

"The embassy, right?" Wyatt offered.

"Yes, among other things."

Sebastian stabbed his fork into his salad bowl. "Maybe with some kind of presence abroad, your country and people can finally answer for its crimes."

If it were possible, the air grew thicker and colder in the room. Jade went pale, as it was obvious her hope for a peaceful dinner had been thrown out the window.

Karim politely wiped his mouth with his napkin and set it on his lap. "I think perhaps it would be best to put the pleasantries aside and speak plainly."

Sebastian leaned forward. "I can't agree more."

"I love your daughter," Karim declared. "And she loves me." That seemed to shock the entire table into silence. "I would do anything to make her happy, and you must feel the same. But it is not our relationship that you object to, but something else entirely that irks you."

"'Irks' me?" Sebastian's voice grew deadly. "Your people did this to me."

"Did what?" Karim straightened in his chair. "Give you the gift of The Great One?"

"Gift?" Sebastian bellowed. "You call taking me against my will, locking me up, and torturing me for weeks a gift?"

"Sebastian," Jade gasped. "I thought you didn't want the kids—"

"They're not kids anymore, Jade," Sebastian said. "They should know what happened to me."

Nerves rippled through Deedee's stomach as she watched her father's eyes go blank. Beside her, Karim went still.

"I was separated from my squad while on the way to a mission. Someone came at me and I blacked out. The next thing I remember was that I was in a dark room. I yelled and called, but no one came. They would only give me food and water through a slot in the door." His jaw tensed. "A few days passed. Finally, someone came in. They drugged me and then took me out of that dark room and strapped me to a table. Then they started the torture. Over and over again for days."

The entire table was silent. Her mother's eyes were shiny,

while both Wyatt and Bastian were visibly pale. As for Deedee, her throat burned with unshed tears. Oh Lord, she didn't know. None of them knew. They always said it was an accident, whatever it was that turned him into a dragon. Her dad obviously did his best to make sure they were shielded from the awful truth.

"What did they do?" Karim asked in an uncharacteristically soft voice.

"This." Sebastian lay his hand, palm up, on the table. Tattoos covered his entire left arm from the wrist, disappearing into the sleeves at the elbow. But Deedee knew they extended all the way to his chest. She'd also seen the scars the ink was meant to hide. Long, thin crisscrossing strips up and down, like he'd been cut with a knife over and over again.

Karim's eyes grew wide as he saw them. "You've been through the bloodening ceremony?"

"Is that what you call this fucking torture?"

Everyone looked to Karim, so he continued. "The Almoravid—the personal bodyguards of the Zhobghadi Royal Family—undergo the bloodening ceremony." He paused. "I'm not supposed to reveal this to you but ... it's a ritual where the chosen ones are infused with the blood of The Great One. It makes them stronger and faster than normal people."

Deedee gasped. "When I tried to pry them off Jacob—that's why they were so strong and why they didn't need to go to the hospital. So, they take your dragon's blood and bond it to your guard?"

"Yes. Though the blood is actually a mixture of all the previous bearers' blood, kept in a sacred vessel in the high priest's temple. Every year, the current bearer adds to the mixture to keep it full."

Sebastian slammed his fist on the table. "You mean to tell me, your people tried to turn me into one of your bodyguards?"

Karim gave a slight shake of his head. "That many scars is unnecessary. It only takes three days and nights. Three scars at the most. I know, I've seen it myself. Why anyone would do that to you, I do not know. Besides, only a citizen of Zhobghadi and someone hand-selected after years of training with the army would be eligible."

Why was this all so familiar? Her thoughts went back to when she had heard about this ritual before. Or rather, *where.* "The mural!"

"Mural?" Jade asked. "What mural?"

Her fingers clutched at Karim's arm. "The mural in the dining room. The panel where Prince Hammam was strapped down while the high priest infused his blood and soul with The Great One."

Cerulean blue eyes lit up with recognition. "Yes. That's ... that could be an explanation."

"It has to be."

"Will one of you explain what's going on?" Sebastian said.

"Dad, how long ... how many days did they do that to you?"

"I don't know ... maybe a month?"

She and Karim locked eyes. "Thirty days and nights," they said in unison. The time it took for Prince Hammam to turn into The Great One.

"Deedee?" Jade asked. "What's wrong?"

She took a deep breath and quickly explained to them the tale of how The Great One came to be. "See, it's a folktale. A myth, but not really. Many civilizations used stories to explain things they couldn't understand because they had no knowledge of science. But in this case, it was probably *literally* what happened."

"But why me?" Sebastian asked. "I didn't do anything to those people."

"Perhaps it was because you were in the wrong place at the wrong time," Karim said. "I was not even born when that happened to you, so I do not know who did it." Karim's hands curled into fists, and he lay them on the table. "But I will find out. This is a great immoral act, a crime against our traditions." His eyes narrowed. "Will you answer a few questions for me, Mr. Creed?"

"What questions?"

"I was a born with The Great One in my soul and my mind. Growing up, I have always known what I will become someday. But you ... you were made. Tell me, what was it like when you transformed? Is that how you escaped your captors?"

Sebastian's teeth bared. "I don't know what you're talkin' about. I had this beast inside my head for years, but it never came out. I thought I was going crazy. Got discharged because of it. I couldn't shift or do anything, not until," he looked at Jade, and his expression softened, "not until I met her. My True Mate. She was in danger, and my dragon just took over."

She'd heard it many times before, of course, the story of how her father's dragon had been latent until that moment.

When she glanced over at Karim, she saw him tense. "Karim?"

He looked back at her, his gaze intense. "*Habibti*, about that—"

The door burst open with a loud crash, and everyone got to their feet.

"What the fuck is going on?" Her father's eyes flashed gold. "Who the fuck are you?"

Two members of the Almoravid stood in the doorway, the metal door at their feet. A third man made his way to the front from behind the burly guards.

"Vahid?" Karim said. "What are you doing here?"

"Most sincere apologies, Your Highness." Vahid bowed low and saluted to Karim with a fist to his chest. "You must come quick."

"What is wrong?"

"There is news from back home and ..." His eyes darted to the other occupants of the room.

"Speak, Vahid. Whatever you need to say, you can say in front of them. You've already interrupted our dinner."

"Highness." Vahid's voice was almost a squeak. "Zhobghadi. There is a coup back home."

This time, it was Karim's eyes that flashed a different color. "A coup?"

"Yes, Your Highness. Parliament has been dissolved, and your ministers have all been arrested. The palace is locked up, and there is a total communications blackout."

"What?" Karim roared. "How did you find out about this?"

"My wife, Your Highness," Vahid began. "You know my family has been loyal to yours for generations. She was able to send out word to me just before all communication was cut off."

"Have there any been demands?"

"I don't know, Your Highness. But perhaps we should head back home?"

"The jet—" Karim's face went pale and then his eyes burned again. "Amaya."

Fear gripped Deedee's heart. "Oh no. Is she back there already?"

He shook his head. "No, but she should be landing any moment." He let out an anguished growl. "I swear, if they have hurt her, I will burn them to ashes."

"Karim." She stepped into his arms, embraced him, trying to comfort him. "What are we going to do?"

He stroked a hand down her back. "I will find a way to get back as soon as possible. Those usurpers, whoever they are, will pay for what they've done."

She turned to her father. "Dad, we need to help Karim. His sister, she's only eleven years old. Anything could happen to her."

Sebastian's face darkened. "As much as I'd like to tell you to go pound sand, I know my daughter. If I don't help, then she might do something stupid like follow you back and get herself killed trying to save your sorry ass."

Karim snorted. "I do not need saving, and she will not be coming with me."

"At least we agree on that."

"What?" Deedee shouted. "I need to help them. Amaya ... Zafirah ... they could be in danger."

"Baby, you've got a dragon"—her father looked over at Karim—"two dragons, plus I have a band of Lycans at my disposal. You forget, this is what I do for a living." Her father almost looked excited at the thought of staging an attack on Zhobghadi. "Besides, the answers I've been searching for, for decades, might be there."

"We can take my jet," Bastian offered. "I can have it ready in an hour."

"A jet might be too late," Karim said. "Your warlock friend; is he around?"

"He's with his daughter and granddaughter, but I'm sure Daric wouldn't mind giving us a ride." Sebastian pulled out his phone.

Deedee clenched her hands into fists. "You're not going without me."

"Yes we are, and you are not coming!" Karim said.

Sebastian looked up from his phone. "Finally, you're talking sense."

Deedee wanted to pull her hair out. "And I thought *one* of you was overbearing. I'm coming with you, and you can't stop me."

"You cannot, I will not put you in danger."

"I'm a Lycan, remember?" She raised her hands, curling her fingers. "Fangs. Claws. Remember that?"

"You still cannot go," Karim roared.

"And why the heck not?"

"Because you are carrying my child!"

Deedee felt the world stop spinning under her feet. Heat crept up her cheeks, and she didn't even dare look at her father, though she could certainly feel the anger off him in waves. "Karim, I told you, it's not possible—"

"Unless we were True Mates."

Her knees felt like jelly. "H-how do you know about that?"

"One of your kind—Julianna Anderson—told me." Karim's hands gripped her arms. "Search your heart ... your soul ... you know it is true."

Air was trapped in her chest, making it hard to breathe. She and Karim ... True Mates?

Her she-wolf howled and she knew it. "Karim, I ..." The breath expelled from her lungs. "Oh, my Lord." Her hands went down to her belly.

"Are you sure?" Jade asked. "Darling, are you pregnant?"

"I don't know for sure." She swallowed hard. "But my wolf, she knows it."

"The Great One has been telling me, from the moment I first laid eyes on you, that you were our mate."

"Motherfucker!" Sebastian lunged at Karim, but was pulled back by his sons. "You got her pregnant? You better be marrying her—"

"Dad, stop!" Deedee rubbed a hand down her face. "Please, can we get back to the subject of how we're going to rescue Amaya and take back control of Zhobghadi?"

"You mean how I'm going to do it," Karim said. "You will stay here until I am done."

"No—"

"I will not put you and my child in danger."

"If I *am* pregnant then that means I can't be harmed." She looked at her mother. "Isn't that right, Mom?"

Jade nodded. "It's true. A woman pregnant with her True Mate's child is indestructible."

Karim looked taken aback. "What?"

"Didn't Julianna tell you—and, by the way, how do you know Julianna Anderson?"

"It's a long story." He squared his shoulders. "It doesn't matter, you are not coming with me." He turned to Sebastian. "The warlock?"

"On the way."

"Karim, please." She gripped his collar. "I can't let you leave without me." Desperation clawed at her. What if something happened to him and she wasn't there? "Can't we figure this out?"

"There is no time, *habibti*." He carefully pried her hands off his jacket. "You must stay here where you are safe and my enemies cannot get to you. You know the lengths they will go."

"How can I forget? I was there, in the desert. I was the one who knew you were in trouble, and I was the one who took that net off of you. I'm not helpless, you know."

"I know, Desiree."

"I'm strong. You said it yourself."

He took her hands and kissed each one. "I know. But I am not. If anything were to happen to you and our child, I wouldn't be able to bear it. There would be no force strong enough to keep me here in this mortal world."

"Karim—"

"I am here," Daric said as he shimmered into the room. "What can I do?"

"I'll explain on the way." Sebastian grabbed his arm with one hand and planted the other on Karim's shoulder, pulling him away from Deedee. "We need to go to Lone Wolf. Now."

Karim pushed her away. "I will see you soon, habibti. Remember that I love you."

"No!" Deedee reached out, but it was too late. Daric, her father, and Karim disappeared, her hands clutching only air. "No!"

Slim arms embraced her, and her mother crushed her against her body. "Deedee, darling, it's all right. They'll be back."

A cold knot formed in her stomach. Her mind was telling her that her mother was right. Her father was a dragon, a trained soldier, and ran one of the top security firms in the world. His Lone Wolves were a force to be reckoned with, an elite group of Lycans who always completed their missions. Daric would be with them and could take them back in a second. And Karim, well, he was the bearer of The Great One.

But there was something about this whole thing that didn't sit right with her. And she feared that there was more to this than meets the eye.

———

Deedee didn't get a wink of sleep, nor did anyone else in the Creed household. She and her mother curled up on the couch while Wyatt and Bastian were busy coordinating with the Lone Wolves office, waiting for word. But the only thing they could tell them was that Sebastian had taken a few of the Lone Wolves with him to Zhobghadi and that anything else was on a strict need-to-know only basis.

It was dawn, and they had already gone through what seemed like a gallon of coffee—and Deedee ate most of what had been dinner because she was pregnant, after all—and still no word.

"Something's wrong." She jumped to her feet. "I know it." Her she-wolf wouldn't lie still. It was pacing, snarling, and scratching at her. "Bastian, is your jet on standby?"

"Yeah." Her brother rubbed a hand down his face. "We can leave in an hour. But ... does Zhobghadi even have an airport? And if there's a coup and communications blackout, then we probably won't get permission to land. I could find an alternative airport ..."

"Do it," she said. But leaving in an hour would be too late. She just knew it. If only there was a way she could just transport herself to Zhobghadi in an instant.

Oh, my Lord. I'm an idiot.

Jade yawned. "Darling, what is it?"

Her heart thumping in excitement, Deedee fished something out of her pocket. The coin Cross had given her. *Call me if you need me, and I will find you.* She rubbed the surface with her thumb and said, "Cross."

"Cross?" Wyatt said. "What about—Cross?"

Sure enough, the hybrid appeared in the middle of their living room. He glanced around, frantic. "Deedee? Are you okay? Did he hurt—*oomph!*"

"Oh, Cross!" Relief poured over her as she threw herself toward him, embracing him tight. "I'm so happy to see you!"

He soothed a hand down her back. "I'm happy to see you too." He pulled back. "What's the matter?"

She straightened her shoulders. "You said to call you when I need your help, right? Well, do I ever need it."

CHAPTER TWENTY-TWO

THEY'D BEEN AMBUSHED.

Karim didn't know how his enemies knew, but they had been prepared for their arrival. He let out a frustrated groan, trying not to move too much, lest the chains wrapped around his body burned any more of his exposed skin. Beside him, Creed was in a similar position, restrained against the wall of the cell they shared in the palace dungeon.

When the warlock took them away, they first stopped by the headquarters of Lone Wolf Security, an elite team Creed ran under his security firm, employing only Lycans trained to do the most dangerous missions. They came up with a plan to take six of his men to initially infiltrate the palace and first rescue Amaya, Zafirah, Arvin, Ramin, and anyone else being held against their will, while figuring out who the leaders of the coup were and take them down.

They would take the *azdaha* passage into the palace and spread out in teams of two to search for the hostages. Karim would take Daric to the places where they could likely be—in the residential wing or perhaps the dungeons, so that the warlock could whisk them to safety back in New York. If any of the other teams found them first, they could radio Daric through their wireless comms devices.

But their enemies had been waiting, and as soon as they entered the secret passage, it filled with smoke, confusing them. It was chaos, and the Lycans went down one by one, while he and Creed had been chained up immediately. As for the warlock, he was easily knocked out, as, aside from his powers, he was completely human.

Once they were all secured, they had been separated from the others, and he and Creed were taken to the dungeon underneath the palace, and gods only knew where the others were. He didn't recognize any of their captors as they all wore dark masks over their faces and spoke very little as they worked on securing them with the silver chains to the wall.

"I swear to all the gods above and below, when I get out of here ..." He hissed as the silver chain slapped at his forearm, leaving a burning, itching sensation on his skin.

"You and me both," Creed gritted. "Goddamn, what the fuck is this thing?"

"Zhobghadi silver," he explained. "Non-toxic to humans and Lycans, but deadly to us. It is the one thing that can restrain The Great One. Makes it difficult to call on it."

"Motherfucker. They've used this on me before."

"They? Who?"

Creed gnashed his teeth together. "We—the New York clan and other Lycans—have enemies. Nasty motherfuckers called mages. They're kinda like witches and warlocks, but evil. They've been trying to get rid of the Lycans for generations. Caught me one time and tried to control me."

"I did not realize." So, there really were more strange

things out there in the world. "I wonder how they knew to use the silver?"

"The only thing that matters is we get outta here. If only we can get to Daric, he can free us. How the hell did these fuckers know we were coming?"

A dark, foreboding thought entered his mind. "Only the members of the royal family know about the *azdaha* passage. Myself, my sister, my aunt Zafirah, and my cousin Arvin. Oh, and my ward Ramin knows as well."

"Hmm." Creed's silver eyes narrowed. "Your cousin ... he'd be king if you were gone, right?"

"Yes, but—No." He shook his head vehemently. "Arvin is loyal. He was the one trying to find out who attacked me in the desert and was trying to unseat me."

"Sounds like he's also in the best position to betray you."

"Stop talking nonsense!" A large pit formed in his stomach. *No, it couldn't be.* He couldn't believe it.

"I'm just trying to help you narrow down the suspects. And—" Creed tensed and his brows snapped together.

Karim knew why; he could feel it too. The prickling sensation along his neck. The feeling that there was someone else in the room. The dungeon was dark and the only light came from torches lit in the hallway outside the cell.

"What the fuck—"

There was an awful creaking sound as metal grated against metal. The door swung open and an eerie feeling crawled over Karim's skin as something came out from the shadows.

"My, you both look like you're in big trouble," Delacroix grinned. "Looks like we came just in time, *mon petite.*" He reached into the darkness behind him, and pulled someone into the light.

"Holy moly!" Desiree took a deep breath as she staggered in from the shadows. "That was—" She looked at Delacroix. "*What* are you?"

"Deedee!" Creed bellowed. "What the hell are you doing here?" He turned his razor-sharp gaze to the Cajun. "You! I told you to look after her and protect her, not bring her right into the middle of this shit."

"*Pardon, mon ami*, but she was insistent and would have gone with or without me," Delacroix said with a shrug. "It would have been better I was by her side, *non*?"

"You should not have come, Desiree," Karim said with a shake of his head. "I did everything I could to protect you."

She walked over to him and captured his face between her palms. "I knew it. Felt it in my heart that something was wrong." As she touched her mouth to his, he savored her taste and scent before she pulled away.

"How do we get you out of here?" Delacroix rattled the chains around Creed, making the other man moan in pain.

"Ow! Goddammit, stop! That shit hurts!"

"Zhobghadi silver?" Desiree checked the chains carefully. "Where're the locks?"

"I'm afraid they've been soldered in."

The Cajun grabbed Karim's chain where it was stuck to the wall and gave a strong tug. While it did budge slightly under his enhanced strength, the silver rubbing on Karim's skin burned like the fires of Gibil. "Stop!" He commanded through gritted teeth.

Desiree winced. "We could try to rip it out, but we'd have to do it slowly so as not to hurt you both."

"Unless you got a blowtorch on you, only Daric can get us out of here quickly." Creed blew out an impatient breath. "But they knocked him out and took him away. If you get him, he can change the silver into something else. You'll have to find him though."

"The palace is huge. You may not have enough time. Go, Desiree. Save yourself and our—"

"We don't need Daric." She put a finger to his lips, then took something out of her pocket. It was a gold coin. "Cross came with us. He's waiting outside the city with backup, and he can use this to track us and transport in here, even though he's never seen the palace. He has the same powers as his dad, so he can free you."

"Cross?" Karim's mood darkened.

"Oh, come on," Desiree rolled her eyes. "I chose you, remember?" She kissed him again, slow and sensual.

"For fuck's sake," Creed spat. "Can you lovebirds cut that out so we get out of here, now?"

"*Mes amis.*" Delacroix held up a hand. "I hear people coming."

Deedee held the coin up to the light. "Let's get you out—"

"Wait. Those might be the guards." Karim took a deep breath. "If they do not find us here, they might sound the alarm. And we have yet to find Amaya or the others. You have the advantage as they do not know you are here."

"*Oh, poop.*" Desiree bit her lip. "Delacroix, can you—"

"No worries." He grabbed her and pulled her into the shadows.

Dagan's beard, how did he do that? It was like he completely melted into the darkness, disappearing from sight.

The footsteps came closer, until finally, he could hear

them just outside the cell. Someone stepped forward into the light, someone he didn't expect.

"Aunt Zafirah!" He struggled against the chains, ignoring the way they stung at his skin. "Are you all right? Did they hurt you? If they have, I will make them pay."

"Hurt me?" Zafirah's tone sounded mocking. She didn't look like she'd been hurt or tortured. In fact, she was dressed well in an elaborate kaftan that looked out of place in the dingy dungeon. "And why would anyone hurt me?" She walked closer to him, cocking her head to the side. "How are those chains, Karim? Keeping you secure?"

Something was definitely not right here. "What in An's name is going on?"

She laughed and then flicked a finger at his chin. "You're not so smart, are you, Karim?" Her eyes gleamed with malice. "Didn't think your old aunt would be capable of staging a coup?"

"You!" He struggled again, biting his lips until they bled so as not to scream in pain. "I don't understand. Why, Zafirah? We are family."

"Yes, that we are, my dear boy." Cold eyes bored into him as her mouth curled into a cruel smile. "I'm of royal blood, I married a nobleman my father had chosen and did everything he asked! And yet, because I was unlucky enough to be born second *and* a woman, I wasn't fit to rule. But my brother, the one born with The Great One's spirit, he was given everything. Even when he married that horrible English woman and further humiliated our family by making her queen, no one batted an eyelash. Not even when I spread rumors of her 'supposed' infidelity." Her eyes narrowed to slits. "But now, the tables have turned. Decades of planning have finally come to fruition."

He could not believe it. His loving, gentle Aunt Zafirah ... she was behind all this? "So, you concocted this plan with Arvin to install him as king? And what of The Great One?"

"My darling boy knows nothing of this plan. Even now, he's upstairs, locked up with Amaya in her room, thinking that they've taken his poor, poor mother to be tortured." She grinned. "And as for The Great One, well ... we already know it is possible to transfer its spirit to *any* vessel." Her gaze flickered to Creed. "As proven by our experiments."

"What the fuck are you talking about?" Creed's voice shook with anger.

She sauntered over to him. "Mr. Creed, it's lovely to see you again. I see you've come back for another taste of Zhobghadian hospitality. The last time you were here, I didn't get to formally make your acquaintance, but that was probably for the best. I must admit, it was a great coincidence that your dear daughter was stuck here, is it not?" A dark brow rose. "Or perhaps it was fate."

The older man's eyes turned blank. "You ... who the hell are you? And how do you know what happened to me?"

"It was *I* who had you captured," she said. "That nobleman who my father made me marry? Turns out we had many things in common—including the desire to take down my brother and his government and become true, pure-blood rulers of Zhobghadi. And so, we researched all the ancient texts, trying to find a way so our son could have The Great One's spirit transferred into his body. Despite the fact that all bearers have been born dragons, our research has shown it was not always so. The story of Prince Hammam had some basis, after all. And so, we dug deep into the archives and found that it took at least ten generations before The Great One's spirit was fully infused in our bloodline and started birthing dragons."

"This is blasphemy, Zafirah!" Karim bit out. "How could you?"

"Blasphemy? Is knowledge blasphemy? Our forefathers thought it best to keep our people in the dark and locked up in our borders, in the guise of protection. All it's ever done is keep us ignorant." Her lips thinned. "After years of searching, we found our answer. The exact ritual that could infuse the blood and spirit of The Great One to any human. All we needed was a test subject, someone no one would miss." She looked at Creed again. "You were the perfect specimen. So strong and courageous, just like Prince Hammam. Survived each bloodening, growing stronger as you bonded with the spirit of The Great One. It was too bad that your compatriots came and killed my husband before the ritual was completed. Shot him between the eyes and then rescued you." Her voice was flat and emotionless. "Still, I'm glad that despite the incomplete ritual, you were still able to transform. It gives me hope that my own son will be able to survive and become the bearer, just as my husband and I planned."

"You're insane," Sebastian said. "You would let your own son go through that torture?"

"Torture?" Zafirah shot back. "It would be a great honor! Besides, he will have no choice." She turned back to Karim. "Once the 'insurgents' kill our dear, beloved Prince Karim, my son will be next in line since there are no other heirs. Of course, parliament and the ministers will try to fight it since Arvin is not the bearer of The Great One, but when he shows them that he can transform, then they will have no choice but to crown him as King of Zhobghadi."

"You've planned this entire thing just so your son could be king? Does he even want to be king?" Karim spat.

She shook his chains, making him hiss in pain. "He deserves the crown! All you've ever done was flitter your life away. You haven't even taken the throne yet. *Hmph*. Weak, just like your English mother. Queen Grace was an insult to the throne and our people."

"You are not fit to breathe her name," Karim raged.

Zafirah laughed. "Before you die, I think it would be best you should know the truth."

"The truth?"

"Yes. Well, I couldn't just take the risk of her producing a spare, could I?" She sneered. "I had to get rid of her."

Karim felt the blood drain from his face. "No ... you ... I saw her."

Her dress whipping in the wind.

Falling ...

Zafirah's cruel laugh cut into his chest. "You saw her jump. But you did not see who *made* her jump."

"You forced her to kill herself?" Rage burned in him like the heat of a thousand suns.

"In a way." Her smile was mysterious. "Of course, your father was harder to kill. He was always surrounded by the Almoravid. But, oh, I found a way. I tested the method on his little consort first."

Amaya's mother? Gods, did he even know this woman? "You are a monster, and I will kill you with my bare hands."

"Will you now?" Zafirah sniffed. "And what of Amaya? If you try to escape, I'll kill her."

"You'll kill her anyway," Creed said. "And besides, you don't have the manpower."

His aunt's jaw hardened, but she remained silent.

"You had, what, three or four guys take us down?" Creed huffed. "You had the element of surprise, that's for sure, but you put us together, and probably all my men together because you don't have enough people to guard us all. Same with the sister and your son. Hmmm ... let me guess. You got your ragtag bunch—probably hired mercenaries with big guns, and locked up all the ministers and members of parliament, threatening their lives and families if they don't obey. What happens when they realized you don't have as many goons as they think? I bet this little coup of yours wouldn't last a day against us."

"Ah, but there's your mistake. I don't need men." Zafirah cackled. "What was that saying? The enemy of my enemy is my friend?"

"What are you—" Creed growled when more people came inside the cell, just behind Zafirah. "Motherfucker!"

The three men wore red robes that covered their faces. One of them pulled his hood down, revealing a pale, bald head, and red eyes. "Excellent work, Zafirah," he said. "I see you've kept up your part of the bargain."

"Of course, old *friend*. You've been so helpful all these years. The magic potion you gave me mimicked heart attacks so well, not even the royal doctors could uncover foul play."

His mouth widened into a sickening smile. "We are glad to be of service."

Zafirah cocked her head at Creed. "And now that I have the prince, you can have Creed."

"Fuck you!" Creed cursed. "You're not taking me."

"On the contrary," the pale man said. "We are taking you with us, and you will obey."

"Over my dead body."

"No need for that." His hand reached under his robe and took out a pendant on a long chain. "With the necklace of Magus Aurelius, you will do everything we say."

"What is going on?" Karim looked from the mage to Creed. "Who are these men?"

"Mages," Creed answered. "And that nasty little piece of jewelry around his neck allows him to control humans."

Realization hit him. "You. *You* made my mother jump."

The mage said nothing, but merely smiled.

"I always thought were not very smart, but my, my you do surprise me," Zafirah said. "Years ago, the mages approached me. They figured out what I had done to Creed, and they proposed an alliance. They helped me get rid of everyone standing in my way. In exchange, I was going to give them a dragon of their own and an army of the Almoravid. But seeing as we already have a dragon to spare, I'm happy to hand over Mr. Creed."

"You fucking bitch!"

"Shush," Zafirah said. "Please, it is really pathetic."

"The citizens of Zhobghadi will not stand for this," Karim said. "I have many people loyal to me. They will not simply accept Arvin."

"They will when he saves Zhobghadi." Her nostrils flared. "Oh, don't you look dumb right now?" She let out an exasperated sigh. "Don't you know we share so much more with the mages?"

"Family or not, I will kill you," Karim vowed. "You deserve no less than a long, painful death."

"Ha, you are delusional. I've been brewing this plan for decades. Sewn up every loose thread so there's nothing but victory for me." She turned to the mage. "You will have them ready in a month? Once my son has been bonded to The Great One?"

"At our orders."

"Take your dragon then, as payment."

"Goddammit!" Creed bellowed. "When I get my hands on you—"

"Save it." The mage raised the necklace. "You will soon be ours."

A loud growl echoed through the cell.

"What in *Inana's* name—" Zafirah sucked in a breath.

A humungous black wolf emerged from the shadows, silent as a cat. Its dark eyes glowed briefly, then it jumped, sailing right into the mage who held the necklace. However, another of the mages threw himself forward, and they fell in a fury of claws and fangs.

"Guards!" Zafirah cried. "Get him!"

Footsteps thundered as several masked men dressed in black rushed into the cell. The black wolf, its muzzle covered in blood, snapped its teeth at the men. Two lunged at the wolf, but instead of attacking, the animal backed away and melted into the shadow. Before the attackers could figure out what was happening, the wolf emerged again—from behind them and took the two men down.

"Now, Cross!"

Karim turned his head toward the achingly familiar voice. Desiree stood in the dark corner where Delacroix had first emerged, fists clenched at her sides. In an instant, several more people shimmered into the room. He recognized Cross, of course, as well as Wyatt, Bastian, and Jacob.

"The necklace! Don't let him get away!" Cross shouted.

"Think you can get this?" The mage slipped the necklace back into his robe. "I don't think so." The remaining men and mages converged around him. "Before I go, I'm going to leave you all a sample of power we have amassed. Sorry, my dear," he said to Zafirah. "Since I'm not getting my dragon, it looks like my monsters won't be able to wait that month." He laughed cruelly as he pivoted and headed for the door.

"No!" Wyatt gave an inhuman growl as the muscles under his face crawled. "Get him!"

It was chaos in the small space. Fang, fur, and fists flew everywhere, and even a fireball or two. "Cross!" Creed screamed over the din. "Get us out of here."

Cross tore through the mayhem to get through them. His eyes glowed like twin turquoise fires as he waved a hand. Instantly, the chains around them turned into rope, then fell to their feet.

Creed cracked his neck. "Thanks. The necklace?"

A muscle ticked in the other man's jaw. "Got away, damn him."

"Karim!" Arms wrapped around his middle. "You're safe," Desiree whispered, then she looked up at Cross. "Thank you."

"My sister," Karim suddenly remembered. He saw Zafirah, trapped in the corner, unable to get through the fighting and lunged toward her, locking his arms around her. "Where is she? Where is Amaya?"

"It doesn't matter. She'll be dead. We all will be." She

fought against him, gnashing her teeth and thrashing around. "It's too late, Karim. You heard what the mage said."

He only held her tighter. "What in An's name are you talking about?"

"The power he talked about ... the mages, we share a history with them. Who do you think sent the *oubour* a thousand years ago?"

His grip slackened. "No."

"Yes." She staggered away from him. "It's too late, Karim. They are coming. Argh!" An ear-piercing howl escaped her lips as Desiree wrapped her up in the discarded rope.

"You vile bitch." Desiree yanked tight. "How could you! And you made me believe we were friends. Pushing me and Karim together."

Zafirah lifted her head. "I had hoped ... if he chose you, then maybe he would be forced to abdicate, since he wouldn't want you to have the same fate as his mother. Then I wouldn't have had to kill him."

Karim saw a hint of sadness in his aunt's eyes. Did Zafirah still have some remorse in her?

"I feel it." Cross's face went slack. "The magic. It's coming for us. Closing in."

He could too. A great, dark energy coming for them. "The *oubour*. Monsters my ancestor faced a thousand years ago. They will consume Zhobghadi until there is nothing left." His skin crawled. "And then who knows what next. We must stop them."

"That's the last of them," Jacob said triumphantly, blowing the flames from his hands with a flourish. Behind him, Wyatt, Bastian, and Delacroix stood in their Lycan forms, the bodies littered at their feet.

"How do we stop these monsters?" Creed asked.

"Only one thing can destroy them. Dragon fire."

"Well then." Creed cracked his knuckles. "Looks like it's time to fly."

Karim turned to Desiree. "Amaya, Arvin, and Ramin ... they're upstairs in Amaya's room. And the warlock and the other Lycans are somewhere here as well." He bit out a curse. "And the people. My people—"

"We will take care of them and everyone else."

Her voice was so confident and self-assured that he couldn't help the pride growing in his chest. "Bring them into the palace walls, it's the safest place. Find Captain Fariba. He will know what to do." They had many safeguards in place, of course; evacuation and emergency procedures every citizen of Zhobghadi would know by heart. While it seemed excessive, he was glad for them now. "Stay safe and save everyone you can."

"I will." A loud, earth-shattering screech made her wince. "Go now."

He knew in his heart that his mate would succeed. Her strength and will was as strong as his own, and she would do her best to protect those who needed her most. "I will see you soon, *habibti*." He kissed her sweet lips quickly, knowing it would not be long before they were together again.

"Let's get outta here." Creed's eyes flashed gold. "Somewhere with more space."

He grinned. "Now you are talking."

Karim led Creed out of the cell, navigating the maze-like dungeon with ease. The moment he could smell the fresh outside air, he called on The Great One. *Protect us now again from our enemies, oh Great One.*

Flames engulfed his body as he felt the beast inside him start to grow and stretch. His hands elongated into claws, and scales covered his body. Once he was fully transformed, it let out a deafening roar. Beside him, the gold beast gave its own thundering war cry.

The two beasts lifted off the ground, their mighty wings flapping heavily to assist in the vertical takeoff. Once the silver dragon had gained enough height, it darted forward, toward the sounds of bone-chilling shrieks.

Karim could feel Creed's dragon in their wake. They were almost identical, though the gold dragon had more horns and spikes along its back and on its head. Indeed, The Great One looked almost elegant and refined next to the terrifying creature.

The gold dragon snapped its jaw, and Karim focused his vision forward, toward the large black shapes ahead of them.

There, Karim pointed out.

The oubour.

Massive black blobs, growing and heaving as they approached. At first, Karim thought there were only about a dozen large creatures about the size of soccer stadiums, but upon closer inspection, he saw that each one was composed of thousands of smaller, shadow-like creatures. And they were all headed toward the capital city. The fastest one was already climbing the section of the city wall. Hopefully, the citizens there had already evacuated.

The Great One let out a roar and flew faster.

Now or never.

The Great One opened its mouth, releasing a torrent of fire and lava over the creatures. As the fire hit its target, shrieks of agony and pain rang in the air, and the creatures burst into flame.

Karim whooped in triumph, and they veered around again, going for a second pass at the ones they missed. Glancing over at the gold dragon, it too, seemed to be making short work of the oubour in its way.

They worked in tandem, swooping and swinging around to hit their targets. Even without words or means of communications, they knew which section to cover and where to go to maximize damage. When one dragon finished a line and had to make a U-turn, the other charged forward, making sure the vile monsters didn't have a chance to rest, breathe, or regroup.

Finally, it seemed that there was only ash underneath them. Creed was still chasing a few stray ones, but when they were gone, he flew back around. Gold eyes met silver ones, and as if in agreement, they both headed toward the palace.

When the great balcony was in their sights, The Great One slowed down, then landed on the tile with a graceful thud. Flames swirled around the massive dragon, growing smaller and smaller as Karim returned to his human body. Looking up, he saw the gold dragon flying overhead, making a final sweep before landing beside him, clawing up the tile as it too, was consumed by fire.

When Creed was fully transformed back, Karim narrowed his eyes at the other man. "You still owe me for the other time." He cocked his head toward the east side of the balcony where another dragon-sized crater still lay unrepaired from when the gold dragon crash-landed.

"Send me a bill." Creed was scowling, but then he did

something that utterly surprised Karim. He held out his hand. "Nice work, son."

"You too." He took the offered hand and shook it. They each squeezed, and held on tight, as if trying to break the other's hand or dare them to pull back first.

"Dad! Karim!"

They let go as they heard the sound of the female who occupied a space in both their hearts. Desiree was running toward them, and right behind her was Amaya. Others also began to file out onto the balcony to greet them—Ramin, Captain Fariba, several members of the Almoravid, as well as the Lycans. Daric and Cross, meanwhile, appeared right beside them.

"A little help?" Creed said to Daric as he motioned to his naked body.

With a wave of a hand, the two men were dressed in loose pants and shirts. And just in time too as Desiree and Amaya skidded to a halt. His beloved embraced her father first, as Amaya let out a whoop of happiness when Karim lifted her up.

"Are you all right, little one?" He asked. "Are you hurt? Did they—"

"I am good, Karim." However, her voice still trembled. "I was scared. But I knew you would come for me. And that you would rescue me and defeat the oubour."

"You know I will always come for you, Amaya. You are my family." He embraced her as her arms encircled his neck, his chest tightening. Someday, he would tell her the truth about her mother. It would hurt him because it would, in turn, cause her pain. However, he believed his sister was resilient enough to weather through it. She was a princess of

Zhobghadi, after all, and the blood of their ancestors and The Great One ran through hers as much as it did through his.

Setting down Amaya, he turned back to Desiree, who was still in her father's arms. Though he longed to hold her, he wanted them to have their moment. He waited patiently as they disentangled from each other, and as he predicted, she immediately looked to him. Walking up to her, he engulfed her with his arms and held her to his chest.

"You scare the ever-living daylights out of me, you know." She pushed against his chest "Not just what you did now, but pulling that stunt with Daric."

"Forgive me, Desiree. *Habibti.* My one and only."

"Promise you won't ever do that again."

"I cannot promise that I will not put your safety above all else," he said. "But I will promise that I will treat you with respect and as an equal. I—" He bit out a soft curse when he remembered what he had left when his clothes burned away when he transformed. The ring would be somewhere among the ashes of his clothes, but he had been so distracted, he forgot to go back for it.

Her brows knitted together. "What's wrong?"

"It's just ..." He blew out a frustrated breath. "Now would have been the right moment."

"Right moment for what?"

"To give you the ring I've been carrying around with me."

Her mouth formed into a perfect O.

"Would you say yes?"

"Even without a ring."

He cleared his throat, then got down on one knee. "Desiree—excuse me—Professor Desiree Desmond Creed—"

She let out a chuckle, then nodded at him to continue. "Will you do me the honor of being my wife?"

"Yes, Karim." Her eyes filled with tears. "I will."

He got to his feet, lifted her in his arms and spun her around. "I have never been happier in my entire life."

"Me too." She cradled his face in her hands and planted her lips on his for a kiss that melted his insides and made his knees weak. When they were both out of breath, he pulled back and set her down on her feet.

"I am very glad for you both."

Turning his head, he saw the warlock grinning at them, happiness gleaming in his ocean-colored eyes.

"Uncle Daric, did you see ..." Desiree shook her head. "Never mind."

"I'm happy for you too, Dee."

Karim stiffened as his rival stepped forward. However, for the sake of his new fiancée, he would control the urge to punch that man's face in.

"T-thank you, Cross." The smile she gave her friend was warm, but nothing like any smile she had given Karim. "Thank you for everything."

"Yes, thank you for bringing my mate and future child into the middle of a dangerous coup that also nearly turned into the apocalypse," Karim bit out. He couldn't help it.

"Karim!" Desiree slapped him playfully on the arm. "Behave, please."

"All right." If his future father-in-law could do it, he supposed he could too. So, he held out his hand. "Thank you for your assistance."

Cross shook it, and squeezed his hand in a genuine gesture of friendship. "You're welcome, Your Highness."

"Now," Karim said. "There is one last thing."

"What's that?" she asked.

He took her hand and then pulled her along, toward the edge of the balcony. She gasped when she looked down and saw the hundreds of people in the courtyard below them.

Karim addressed them in Zhobghadian, his voice booming. "My people, once again, the gods have saved us!"

A cheer rang out from the crowd.

"They have sent not only The Great One, but a second protector to raze our enemies to ashes! We will live and thrive for another thousand years." He raised his fist high and then hit it over his chest. Below, the people followed suit, thudding sounds rippling across the courtyard.

"We have the gods to thank, but also our new allies. We owe our lives to these people who have put their safety at risk for our sake. And for that, we give them our heartfelt gratitude."

Another raucous cheer burst from the crowd, this time lasting much longer, up until Karim held his hand up.

"And now, we have been given another gift. It was her people who came to our aid, and because of her presence here, we are still standing. My people, I present to you, Desiree Desmond Creed. Daughter of the dragon. And your future queen and mother of my heir."

This time, the crowd's noise was deafening. Happy cries, shouts, and praise rang up to the heavens. The people saluted them and began to chant her name.

"What are they ..." Recognition and awe lit up her face. "Are they calling my name?"

"Yes, *habibti*." He planted a kiss on her cheek, then stepped back. "I have told them that it is because of you and your people we are saved and that you will be their queen."

The Great One was roaring in his head, and he couldn't ignore it. So, for now, he allowed the beast to take over. He transformed into his dragon form, then jumped off the balcony as his wings sprouted. The crowd cheered when The Great One appeared, veering upwards just in time. As it soared overhead, the chants of his mate's name grew even louder.

It let out a roar as a burst of fire exploded in the sky. Over and over again, the words repeated in Karim's mind.

Mine. Ours. Mate.

And then it added. *Heir.*

EPILOGUE

ONE YEAR LATER ...

COFFEE CUP IN HAND, DEEDEE STRODE OUT ONTO THE balcony, taking in a deep breath. With the Easifat behind them, the air smelled fresh and light, while the rising desert sun felt warm and comforting on her skin. It was days like this that made her want to just laze around in bed, especially when she knew her husband was waiting for her.

Her she-wolf mewled, not liking the fact that it was away from their mate.

He needs his sleep, she told her animal. *Both of them do. They've been flying all night, remember?*

It let out a whine.

Yes, I miss them too when they're gone, but it's all done now.

A familiar voice interrupted her conversation with her inner animal. "Good morning, my Queen."

Swiveling around, she returned the greeting. "It's certainly a beautiful one, Arvin, especially now that the sandstorms are gone."

"The gods are good." He bowed his head. "Should we

have our morning meeting now that we are once again able to communicate with the outside world?"

She gestured toward the table set up behind her. "How about just an informal chat over breakfast, to give us some time to get back into the swing of things. It's been a nice holiday, and so we should ease ourselves into work."

"As you wish, Majesty."

As they sat down to breakfast, Deedee contemplated on how much she had relied on Arvin in the past year. As Zafirah had said, he really did know nothing about the plot to overthrow Karim and install him as king. He had been shocked, of course, and anguished by the turn of events. Karim accepted his resignation from his position as Vizier, and Arvin made an official proclamation renouncing any claim to the throne. He even offered to go into exile abroad, but with Zafirah in prison for the rest of her life, that would mean he would never see her again.

Desiree had seen the sincerity and true remorse in Arvin, and since she knew he was innocent in all this, offered him a position on her staff instead—as her personal adviser, to help her with her duties as queen and navigate the tricky ins and outs of Zhobghadian culture and royal protocol. And what a godsend he was. She was sure she would have committed dozens of faux pas without him.

Arvin poured her some more coffee. "Who would you like to speak with first once the communications towers are running?"

"Oxford, definitely. I know they're waiting for my answer about the dates for the dig."

Though as Queen of Zhobghadi, she didn't need to work another day of her life, she couldn't bear to just completely put her beloved career behind her. And so, she established the first ever Department of Archeology at Zhobghadi University, with the help of her alma mater. Her former colleagues and professors at Oxford had been excited at the prospect of being the first ever team to be invited into the country, and they were eager to begin.

"And you still want them here in a month?"

"Yes, definitely."

Of course, Deedee would have invited them sooner, but the whole Hanford affair had shaken the academic world to its core, and for months, it was the only thing anyone would talk about.

About a few weeks after her wedding and coronation, a group of women had come out accusing Hanford of sexual misconduct. And after that, even more women came forward, and it seemed that he'd been preying on women since he was a graduate student. There was a lot of mud-slinging and intimidation throughout the whole affair, especially against those poor girls who had found the courage to blow the whistle on him.

It was then that she decided she could no longer keep quiet, and she too spoke up and even became a witness in the trial. Karim, her family, her clan, and the people of Zhobghadi supported her throughout the whole ordeal. The press had a field day, of course, but Deedee had used them to her advantage to bring light to the scandal and what women had gone through.

When Hanford was given a prison sentence that basically ensured he'd be put away for life, many legal analysts concluded that it was the queen of Zhobghadi's testimony of how Hanford had assaulted her and left her for dead that had turned the case around. The whole time, Karim and her father had been plotting about a million long, painful, and tortuous ways to kill him. Hanford was probably lucky he ended up in prison instead.

By the time they finished their meeting and breakfast, the sun was already above the mountains in the distance. "I should go check on my son." Deedee got up, and Arvin followed suit. "He's probably hungry again."

"My regards to the prince."

Deedee bit her lip. "Arvin. How is ... your mother?" She knew that he visited her almost every day in the Zhobghadian prison just on the outskirts of the capital city.

His face fell. "The same as always. She doesn't speak much about what happened. Prefers to ask about my day. I don't tell her any details about you of course, I swear—"

"Thank you." She placed a hand on his arm. "I appreciate it. I just want to know that she's ... well."

"Thank you, Majesty." He saluted her. "If you'll excuse me ..."

"Of course." She watched him go, sadness creeping into her. It really wasn't fair that he'd been caught up in this ugliness. His relationship with Karim had been fractured, and even now, she could feel the strain between them. Hopefully, time would heal their wounds.

Heading back into their suite, she made a beeline for the nursery. The door was ajar, but she wasn't surprised. This early, there could only be two people sneaking in to see Caspar.

"... and The Great One turned all the oubour into ashes," Amaya said in a quiet voice as she stood over the crib on top of a stool, waving a stuffed silver dragon in her hand.

"Telling your nephew about the legend of The Great One and Prince Hammam?" Deedee asked as she approached them.

"No." Amaya shook her head and then showed her what was in her other hand—a *gold* stuffed dragon. "I was telling Caspar about how Karim and Mr. Sebastian saved us all."

She couldn't stop the smile forming on her lips. "And when will you be telling him about mummies?"

"Not until he's older, of course," she said matter-of-factly. "Much older, if he's anything like Ramin. He gets squeamish when I get to the part where they put the organs in the jars."

Her gaze turned to the young man, who was standing beside Amaya, rolling his eyes. "I do not get squeamish, Highness." He saluted Deedee. "Good morning, my Queen. How was your morning? What did you have for breakfast today?"

Deedee was determined to become fluent in the local language as quickly as possible, so she instructed Ramin and Amaya to only speak with her in Zhobghadian. "It was a good morning, Ramin. Thank you for asking." The monophthongs still tripped her, so she had to speak slowly. "I had bread, honey, and coffee. How about you? What are your plans for today?"

"I have a sparring session with Jacob and Delacroix, then I will study for my exams." Having recently turned eighteen, Ramin was now eligible for the Zhobghadian Royal Army. It seemed that he truly was resolved to join the ranks of the Almoravid someday, and Deedee had every faith he would pass his exams with flying colors and achieve his dreams.

A creaking sound of a door opening made them all freeze

and turn toward the newcomer in the room. "Your Majesty." Ramin got to his knee as he bowed.

"Good morning, Ramin. Amaya." He gave them a curt nod. "Good morning, Desiree." Karim's velvety, rough voice caressed her skin, and he looked so deliciously rumpled from sleep. When he turned those cerulean blue eyes to hers, she just about melted. "*Habibti*, you left our bed before I could greet you good morning properly."

"You're here now and you just greeted her." Amaya looked up with her dark, doe eyes, her brows furrowing in confusion.

Ramin coughed and then turned to Amaya. "Your Highness, perhaps we should head out to the balcony? Jacob and Delacroix should be waiting for us."

"All right." Amaya took one last look at Caspar, then placed the stuffed dragons inside the crib. "They will keep you company until I return. Goodbye, Caspar, I will see you later." She hopped off the stool, then happily skipped toward the door. "Let us go, Ramin. Maybe Jacob will show me that trick again with his fire." The young man followed her as she disappeared out the door.

Karim crossed the distance between them. "Finally, I have you alone." His hands slipped around her waist and pulled her to him. His warm scent and the feel of his body against hers never failed to make her knees weak.

"We were *alone* just two hours ago. Of course, you fell asleep right after," she said wryly. "You didn't even cuddle me."

"You know these flights are tiring, *habibti*. But I keep you satisfied all the other nights of the year." He wiggled an eyebrow at her.

"Well ..." She traced her fingers down his chest. "If you get so tired, maybe we should invite my dad next year. He can tag team with you."

Karim couldn't hide his grimace. "We will talk about it."

She chuckled. While Karim and her father weren't exactly the best of friends, they had certainly put a lot of their differences behind them, for both Deedee and Caspar's sake. "I was kidding. You know visiting here makes him uncomfortable. He finds it creepy that the people here worship him like he's some kind of god."

It had been a surprise to all of them that the people of Zhobghadi had accepted the existence of a second dragon. Though it did make sense seeing as half the city had seen the battle of the two dragons against the oubour.

"Thank An for small miracles. He is—"

A sharp cry interrupted him, and Karim turned to the crib. "What's the matter, my son?"

"Probably hungry." She reached in and cradled Caspar in her arms. "There, there now. Mommy's here." Walking over to the rocking chair, she untied her top and began to nurse him. Lord, he was so beautiful, her son. She never thought she would feel this way about a person, but it was like her heart would burst whenever she looked at him.

Karim knelt beside her, and began to stroke his small head. "You must eat, my boy, so you can grow strong like your father. And some day, you too will be able to call on The Great One."

Since she was a Lycan, they knew there was a possibility that their son would be just like her. It would certainly be unprecedented, but they decided to just let things happen as it was meant to. However, when Caspar was born, Karim said that he could sense the soul of The Great One in him.

They sat in comfortable silence, waiting for their son to finish. When he did detach from her, Karim took him in his arms. "Allow me," he said as he put him over his shoulder and burped him.

She stood up and re-tied her top. "How about some breakfast, my love? It's still set up for you. Amaya's probably on the balcony with Ramin, Jacob, and Delacroix."

"Ah." His dark brows furrowed. "Yes, we should probably go." He changed Caspar's position so he was nestled in his arms, and they walked out of the nursery together. "By the way, I have some news for you."

"What news?"

"Nick Vrost sent me a message this morning. He wants the Cajun back in New York."

"Oh."

When Deedee moved to Zhobghadi, her father had insisted she take her two bodyguards with her as added protection. Karim didn't object, seeing as the two men had certainly proved their mettle and their loyalty. However, Delacroix technically was a trainee for the New York Lycan security team, and was under the Beta's command. As a personal favor to her father and husband, Vrost allowed Delacroix to go with her to Zhobghadi, with the condition that he could be recalled back any time.

"He says he's ready to finally retire," Karim continued. "And as his last act as Beta, he wants Delacroix back on the Guardian Initiative team."

She chewed her lip. "I'm going to miss him, but I know they could use his help." Since they had attacked Zhobghadi before, she and Karim made it a point to keep up with what was happening with the mages.

It seemed like they had grown stronger and bolder in the last year, as they attempted to steal the dagger several times and attacked many of the weaker Lycan clans over the world. The Guardian Initiative, a team that the Alpha and her father had set up to defeat the mages, were being run ragged, trying to pin down and stop the mages. Cross and his father had been crisscrossing the globe, trying to find the mages, the last artifact of Magus Aurelius, as well as keep the dagger safe.

Speaking of Cross, she hadn't seen him at all since he came to help them free Zhobghadi. He didn't even show up for her wedding and coronation, or to visit Caspar, but she understood he was busy. She kept his coin with her, though she hadn't been tempted to use it. She knew that he would come and visit her, when he was ready.

"Ah, here they are." Karim cocked his head toward the other end of the balcony. Sure enough, the three men were already in the heat of their sparring session. Ramin was in the middle in a defensive position, Jacob on his left, and Delacroix on his right. The hybrid threw a fireball at the young man, which he dodged easily. However, he left his right side open and Delacroix came in and tackled him to the ground.

"His absence will really be a great loss to us," Karim said. "He's not only a great fighter, but his skills are unparalleled."

Delacroix remained tightlipped about how he could ... well, do what he did. Whenever anyone asked him, he changed the subject. However, having experienced it herself, she had a suspicion. But it wasn't her business, especially if the man didn't want to tell anyone.

"Jacob will probably follow him home too." The two had become great friends, after all. "I know he's probably missing his family and New York a lot. But surely you can wait until after breakfast to tell them?" The last few days had been hectic and she just needed one morning of peace.

"I'll break the news this afternoon. I will be sorry to see them go. But that is life, is it not?" Karim gestured to the breakfast table, where Amaya was already seated. "Come, *habibti*. Let's sit and enjoy the morning before we go about our day."

Karim ate his breakfast with Amaya, and they continued to watch the three men spar. When they finished, the combatants sat down and joined them. Deedee couldn't help but feel a pang of sadness, knowing that her two guards—no, they were more than that; they were her friends—would be leaving soon. But she knew why they had to go, and really, there was a bigger world out there.

When they finished, Ramin took Amaya back into the palace, while Jacob and Delacroix excused themselves.

"You have a long day ahead—"

"Wait," Karim touched her arm as she stood up. "I'm not ready to leave you and my son yet." He took Caspar into his arms and gestured for her to follow him to the edge of the balcony.

"What are you doing?"

"I think it's time I tell my son a story."

"A story?" She wrinkled her nose. "What story?"

Karim lifted up Caspar. "Once upon a time—"

"Oh Lord." She rolled her eyes. "Are you going to tell him a fairy tale? You know I don't believe in them."

He looked at Caspar with an exasperated sigh. "She still doesn't believe in fairy tales? What am I to do? Tsk, tsk. Well, if she doesn't enjoy my tale, maybe you will." He caressed the infant's cheeks. "Anyway. Once upon a time, there was a prince. This prince had everything he could want in the world. Wealth. Command. A land he ruled. He even had the power to turn into a mighty dragon that could smite his enemies."

She chortled, and when he smirked at her, she flashed him an innocent look.

"Despite all this, the prince was sad. He was lonely, and desperate to fill in something in him that was missing. One day, he met a beautiful woman."

"*Ahem.*" She raised a brow at him.

"Excuse me," he chuckled. "A beautiful and *smart* woman. She was also very special because she was like him. Only she turned into a gorgeous and magnificent wolf."

At that sentence, her inner she-wolf preened. *Ugh, ever since Karim started paying attention to you, your head's blown up a hundred sizes.*

It answered her with a smug yip.

"But that was not the only thing special about her."

"It wasn't?"

Karim's smile lit up his face. "No. Because when he looked into her eyes, he saw it. His dragon saw it, too, maybe even before he did."

She held her breath. "What did he see?"

His blue eyes burned like brilliant sapphires. "He finally

saw that which was missing in him." He paused for two heartbeats. "*His soul.*"

Her mouth opened, but nothing came out. But maybe no words were needed. Karim kissed his son's forehead, moved him to one arm, and then wrapped his other arm around her to pull her close.

Yes, she'd never believed in fairy tales. However, as she felt the heat of the glorious desert sun on her face, and basked in the love of not one, but *two* Prince Charmings, she could, just now, believe in happy ever afters.

———

Thanks for coming on this journey with me.

It's been a long one, coming to this point with Karim and Deedee.

If you want to read more, turn the page for a special bonus scene and my author's note.

I have some extra HOT bonus scenes for you - just join my newsletter here to get access:

http://aliciamontgomeryauthor.com/mailing-list/

You'll get access to ALL the bonus materials from all my books and my **FREE** novella **The Last Blackstone Dragon.**

AUTHOR'S NOTE

WRITTEN ON NOV 28, 2019

I really can't quite believe that this book is done. I feel like I've had Karim and Deedee living in my head for so long that I almost feel like I have empty nest syndrome now that they have their book written down.

Before you think I'm crazy, let me start from the beginning. When I first wrote Taming the Beast (Sebastian and Jade's story), I had meant to explain how Sebastian was turned into a dragon. However, I just couldn't find a place for it, and no one at the time really questioned it so I thought I would save the story for later.

Well, not quite anyone. My good friend L asked me after doing a beta read, "But how did Sebastian turn into a dragon?" And I immediately said, "You'll find out in their kid's book" (I hadn't named Deedee yet).

Little did I know it would take me more than two years to get to this point. I wrote another series I had in my head (The

Blackstone Mountain Series) as I needed a break from the True Mates world.

But now it's done! I'm still feeling a little sad (I had a cry when I typed "The End") but also so happy. This story turned out so much better than I had thought and I hope you loved it as much I did and thought it was an epic ending to this trilogy of the True Mates Generations Series.

If you noticed, Witch in Time, Highland Wolf, and this book all happened outside New York, but as I draw the series to a close with the last trilogy, I'm bringing us home.

Thanks for sticking with me on this journey.

Love,

Alicia

P.S. Go to the next page for a special bonus scene that explains a few things in the book!

SPECIAL BONUS SCENE

Sometime after I finished True Mates, I was challenged by my readers to write extra bonus scenes and snippets for their favorite character.

One reader asked me to write something about Daric seeing the future of one of the kids, so I thought since I'd been dying to get something down on paper about Deedee, I would do this.

Enjoy!

———

Written on June 2017

Happens about 30 years before the events of Daughter of the Dragon, a few hours after the epilogue of Taming the Beast

"C'mon, baby, it'll be good practice, for when we have the baby," Meredith whined. "Please?"

Daric sighed and looked at the pink bundle in his wife's arms. "Fine, give her here."

Meredith squealed and handed the baby to Daric. Jade and Sebastian's daughter was only a few hours old, but the couple couldn't wait to show her off to their friends. Everyone had a turn holding the newborn, except Daric. He knew he eventually had to hold the child, but he had been putting it off. He had seen some of the child's future when he touched Jade, and if he were honest, he had been reluctant to see any more. Knowing the future was a burden, one that he was hoping he wouldn't have to bear, especially now that he had Meredith.

As he took the bundle from Meredith, he held his breath and waited for the vision.

The vision was much like he had seen, but now he actually held the child, it was much more vivid. A beautiful, tall woman with long brown hair and light green eyes, standing on a balcony, dressed regally. A sea of people below her, chanting her name. And then above her, a large creature blocked out the sun, casting a shadow over the entire area. The sunlight hit its silver scales, creating a dazzling show for the people below and they cheered even harder.

"Daric? Are you okay?"

Meredith's voice shook him out of his vision. He looked down at the tiny bundle in his arms. Had he been anyone else, he wouldn't have guessed a destiny for such a small creature. The daughter of the dragon.

"I'm good," he said, handing the child back to his wife

with a smile. "Have you thought of a name?" he asked Jade and Sebastian.

"Well, I was thinking Desiree for my grandmother," Sebastian said. "It's my momma's middle name, too."

"And Mary for my grandmother," Jade answered. "Her name was Mary Desmond and she was a suffragette from here in New York, you know."

"Sounds like a good name," Daric said thoughtfully. "Desiree Desmond."

"Hmmm..." Jade's eyes narrowed. "I was thinking Mary Desiree, but I like it."

"You can call her DeeDee for short!" Meredith said. The baby girl in her arms let out a gurgle. "Oh, I think she likes it! Don't you, Dee?"

"All right then," Sebastian said. "Desiree Desmond Creed. Sounds like a strong name."